PRAISE FOR HEAT~~HER~~

I Like You Like This

"Hannah's story is primo, and the surprise twist of the epilogue will have readers stoked with anticipation for a sequel. Overall, a tubular story for readers looking for their next great melodramatic love story."

—*Kirkus Reviews*

"The two teens' unpredictable melting pot of emotions and attempts to find their place resonates."

—*Publishers Weekly*

"A poignant coming-of-age read full of heart-pounding drama and a swoon-worthy romance, *I Like You Like This* is guaranteed to captivate readers from beginning to end. Think *Riverdale*, but set in the 80s."

—BuzzFeed

"For fans of *13 Reasons Why*, Heather Cumiskey's new novel takes a spin on a classic."

—PopSugar

"This teen narrative will pull at your heartstrings. *I Like You Like This* is a book you'll definitely like!"

—*RT Book Reviews*

"The romance between Hannah and Deacon, the unexpected ending, and Hannah's transformation make this book a compelling read."

—*Readers' Favorite*, Five Star Review

ALSO BY HEATHER CUMISKEY

I Like You Like This

I
love
you
like
that

A NOVEL

by

HEATHER CUMISKEY

SHE WRITES PRESS

Published August 2019
Printed in the United States of America
Print ISBN: 978-1-63152-616-9
E-ISBN: 978-1-63152-617-6
Library of Congress Control Number: 2019933687

For information, address:
She Writes Press
1569 Solano Ave #546
Berkeley, CA 94707

She Writes Press is a division of SparkPoint Studio, LLC.

Book design by Stacey Aaronson

To all of the Hannahs and Deacons out there,
may you find your tribe . . . and thrive.

DARIEN, CONNECTICUT

June 1985

(six months after that night)

CHAPTER 1

A SIREN PIERCED THROUGH HANNAH'S BRAIN, CATAPULTING her straight up in bed. Her cheeks were wet. *No, no, I want to go back.* The jarring noise came from outside her window then stopped. She pulled on both sides of her scalp and squinted at the shadows sitting around her room. She jumped when the noise cut through the air again, vibrating from the floor. *Shoot.* She fumbled for the phone. She reeled it up by its cord and grabbed the receiver.

"H-hello?" she croaked, clearing her throat at the same time.

A shiver slid down her back into her damp sheets. This one felt more real than the others. His phantom scent of spicy vanilla and leather hung in the air. Her head whipped around. *Wait, he was just here.*

In her dream she'd bolted out the front of her house when she saw Deacon's car from her bedroom window, not giving a flip if she got caught.

Standing before her, he'd gently moved her hair off her eyes. His deepening gaze had summoned her heart to crack open . . . for him and only him.

He'd tugged her shoulders toward him. "You look incredible. *God,* let me *kiss* you."

She'd almost forgotten the sweeping angles of his face, how beautiful he was, dressed in his clothes from that night, the bloodstain from where the bullet entered his shoulder somehow gone.

She'd searched those soft chocolate brown eyes of his, the ones that spoke more to her than his words ever had. She'd known what she wanted, what she'd always wanted. "Will you *stay* this time?"

He'd swooped down as if to kiss her, stopping inches from her lips, and whispered, "Forever, Hannah."

Then he was gone.

"Hello?"

She cut off her breath, straining to hear anything at all as she pressed the receiver tighter to her ear.

"Hello . . . ? Peter?"

A sharp click, and the phone went dead.

It was always the same. *Stupid kids*, she thought. She changed her clammy tank top and dove back into bed with her eyes still closed.

CHAPTER 2

december 21, 1989

"IS HE GOING TO BE OKAY?" JADE ASKED, WISHING SHE were still high, her body already jonesing for another hit.

"The bullet went through the right side of your brother's chest and out the back of his shoulder. Luckily, though, it didn't pierce any vital organs. It appears he hit the back of his head pretty hard and bit his tongue . . . see here?" explained the bobble-headed guy with the pencil neck and oversized white coat who kept pulling Deacon's mouth open for her to see. Deacon didn't wake—he didn't even flinch.

It hadn't been hard to convince this alarmingly young doctor, who seemed incapable of knowing much about medicine aside from maybe having earned a merit badge in first aid, that she was family and not Deacon's drug-dealing associate.

Jade rolled her eyes, watching how he held the clipboard annoyingly close to his shiny face, squinting over the information as he spoke. If it weren't for the smell of antiseptic keeping her awake, she'd have blown out of here hours ago. *Just tell me when he can get out of here.*

"From the trauma to the head and chest, his body went

into shock and lapsed into a coma. Was he coherent for long after he got shot?"

"No idea, I wasn't there when it happened . . . two others were, in addition to his, I mean, *our* half-brother . . . th-the shooter. I heard that his girlfriend applied pressure to his chest, trying to stop the bleeding. Then he passed out. I got there when those two cops were loading him into the back of their car. I followed them here."

The young doctor swiveled his head to either side while poking the bottom of Deacon's feet with one of his shiny instruments. "He's not responding to any of my tests. It may be a few days before he comes out of it. Well, best case, that is. Then we'll know if any oxygen was cut off to the brain."

"Geez. So he may be a vegetable?"

"Hmm," he answered, jotting something down on Deacon's chart.

"Doc, do you know why those cops put him in that body bag? He's clearly alive."

"Giroux . . . Giroux?" a woman's voice bellowed from down the corridor.

"Fifth door on the left," someone called out from the nurses' station.

Jade shrank back into the room and away from the lights streaming over Deacon's bed. *Shit, shit*. She shouldn't be here.

Her chance to escape vanished at the appearance of a woman's shapely silhouette in the doorway, her hands resting elegantly on either side of the frame. Babette Giroux sauntered in wearing a red fitted suit and gobs of pearls circling her neck, her head held high like a lioness. The young doctor's jaw scraped the floor.

Babette took a couple of small steps toward her son, her brow hardening in a severe line as she fiddled with her wedding ring like it was a rosary, her lips mouthing something no one could hear.

"Is he . . . ?"

"*Lucky* . . . yes, very lucky," the young doctor beamed as if he'd singlehandedly saved Deacon from having the bedsheet pulled over his head.

"*Oh* . . ." Babette replied, the corners of her mouth dipping slightly.

Jade had seen his mother before, but never this intimately. Her eyes began watering from her heavy Giorgio perfume. She knew some stories about Babette Giroux, but was unprepared for the prickly sensation running through the center of her back from being in the woman's presence.

Babette smiled sweetly. "Doctor . . . ?"

He quickly cleared his throat and plastered on a horsey smile that Jade hadn't seen until then. "Klondike, Dr. Adam Klondike, madame."

"Doctor . . . *Adam*, I'd appreciate if you let *me* tell his father about our son's medical state. He's not in town at the moment. And there's already some reporter skulking around outside. We need to keep this incident quiet, if we can, so the family can have some privacy before the tabloids get ahold of this . . . you understand, don't you?"

Babette leaned over the bed, pushing her breasts forward in her suit jacket, her bejeweled, red-manicured fingers forming pop tents next to Deacon's body. Her violet eyes lured in the young doctor while her backside wiggled ever so slightly, as if she were purring.

"O-of course," he stammered, his face blooming pink blotches while the rest of him jittered like a pubescent sixth grader. He was clearly enjoying the show.

"Thank you, *Adam*," Babette said tenderly, straightening herself up, her boobs leading the way. She kept her gaze on the doctor's widening eyes and her back arched as she skimmed her hands along her hips, ensuring nothing was missed.

Wow. Jade tried to stifle a cough from the post-nasal drip she was experiencing, which was now part coke, part Babette's perfume.

"Now . . . *Adam*, can you give me a moment with *my son?*"

"Of course," the doctor replied, his lips gleaming with saliva. He bowed his head awkwardly, sending his glasses down his nose, before ducking out the door.

Jade backed away to exit behind the doctor. She sensed a plan percolating inside the older woman's head and wished Deacon would wake up already. She'd have to come back later—maybe then, she hoped, he'd be talking.

"Young lady?" Babette's voice lost its sugarcoating and sounded more like a car's tires on gravel.

Jade froze. She reluctantly faced her, folding her arms tight across her chest, her shoulders up around her ears. She hadn't realized how chilled she was until now.

"You're not to speak of this. As far as you know, *he's dead* . . . can you remember that?"

Jade's eyes fell to the ground.

"Do you understand *English*? He's *dead*."

"B-but . . ."

"I'll take this pillow and smother him right here," Babette snarled, exposing her side canine and twisting the bed pillow in front of her.

Jade flinched. "G-g-got it . . . he's dead. Totally." *Oh my god, oh my god.*

"Now leave us."

As she backed away, Jade's foot caught a chair leg near the corner of the room, sending her stumbling toward the door. Ignoring the screams inside her head, she looked back. Seconds strung together, holding her afloat, as she took in the sight of his mother still gripping the pillow. Finally, she fled.

CHAPTER 3

christmas eve day, 1989

DEACON'S EYELIDS STIRRED. IT FELT LIKE TWO SMALL weights were pressed upon them. Brenda's humming of "Silent Night" tickled his ear, as it had long ago when he was a small boy sitting on his father's campaign secretary's lap, watching her type like a maestra pianist.

He sensed her sweet breath on his neck. He fought to push his eyelids open, longing for the comfort of seeing her round, fleshy face again. When he succeeded, the humming ceased, and his dream was replaced by a young woman in teal-colored scrubs and a stethoscope who was standing next to his bed and busily scribbling something on his chart.

He batted his eyes a couple of times, unsure of his surroundings and the stranger before him. He watched her flit around the room with quick, short movements befitting her closely shorn, jet-black Sheena Easton hair and the pink Chiclet gum squares stuck to her ears.

He attempted to speak. His tongue floated like a large, misshapen rock in the center of his mouth. His head, chest, and right shoulder ached like hell. He tried to swallow, but the arid layers lining the inside of his mouth and throat restricted him. He managed a grunt and the young woman's head snapped to attention.

"Han-nah . . . w-where . . . is she *here?*" he garbled in hoarse, drawn-out syllables.

"Shhh, no visitors until you're stable. I just turned away your sister, again." The woman smiled swiftly, tucking short strands behind her ears as she spoke. "Good to see you've come back to us." Her eyes darted nervously from his face to the monitor next to him.

"My sis . . . ?" *Had to be Jade*, he reasoned. She would be the only one to track him here—mostly in hopes of finding clues to where the drugs were stashed. He never shared his hiding spots with anyone, especially her.

"Have my parents . . ."

"Not that I've seen."

"Are you my doctor?"

"Surgical nurse. I assisted Dr. Klondike in your procedure."

He winced. "I can't lift my arm . . . my shoulder . . . kills."

Her demeanor cooled as she changed his IV bag. She adjusted something on the monitor next to him and then rechecked the spot where the IV was inserted in the top of his hand.

His eyes wandered the room. "Where am I? . . . I need to call someone."

He didn't notice the needle with the brownish fluid in her hand until she began injecting it into his new IV.

"Wait, what's that?"

"Shhh . . . this will help you rest," she said steadily.

He could see her eyes fully now, a whitish gray, the color

of fog. His head began to spin, along with the rest of him. "I think I'm going to get sick . . . I need something . . ."

"It'll be easier if you just cooperate," she whispered woodenly.

"W-what . . . what did you . . ." The corners of the room began curling in as the beeping on his monitor quickened. He saw her pick up the phone next to his bed just before his eyelids crashed again.

He was dead. That's what they'd told him.

For two and a half days, the world outside, besides Jade, had believed him to be gone. The thought made him feel strangely at peace. He could hit the reset button on his life. His days and nights would finally stop running together. Things could be made right for once. For now, he needed to disappear. Before those two cops returned.

Jade *had* to come through.

They'd spoken on the phone, but he never really knew with her.

Deacon swung his legs off the side of the bed and gingerly pushed himself up with his good arm. Accompanying his sudden head rush came the curdling smell wafting from the meal delivery cart rolling down the hall, its pungency unwavering regardless of its menu.

He barely nodded at the redheaded aide when she dropped off his lunch tray. The small movement ignited a stabbing pain to run through his shoulder. She was the only person, besides his demon-eyed nurse and that Dr. Dork

Klondike, he'd seen since coming out of a coma. She was definitely working overtime.

She quietly closed the door behind her and Deacon's pulse fired off into a gallop. He focused on the folded clothes in the plastic bag next to his bed. He filled his lungs, holding the air inside, and carefully rose to his feet. He closed his eyes, trying not to give into the wretched pain. *Don't wimp out, asshole.*

He laid out the flannel shirt he'd worn the night of the shooting. The bloodstain draped over the shoulder was a deep brown and the size of a baseball mitt. He stared at it for several seconds, remembering everything that had gone down. *Remembering her.* The way she had applied pressure to his chest even though the sight and smell of blood made her queasy. Remembering how she'd cried for him to wake up . . . and how he'd tried.

After the evil nurse had zonked him out, Deacon had woken again—in more pain than before, and this time flanked by the same two federal agents who'd been following him for months. They'd stared down at him, their faces evolving from pensive to the excited expressions of kids on Christmas morning. He'd closed his eyes, hoping they'd go away. *If I act dead . . .*

It hadn't worked. The scarier of the two, a guy with red, protruding jowls and a bulbous nose who called himself Kodak, had proceeded to kick the side of his bed, jostling his injured chest and shoulder to the point that he'd wanted to hurl. He'd automatically lifted his right arm to stop him— and the pain had pierced through his shoulder turning the whole room white. The tears running down the sides of his face had set the two officers into a fit of menacing laughter. The skinnier agent, a man by the name of Eastman who sucked his cigarettes like he was trying to move berries through a straw, had doubled over and actually belly laughed. *We'll be back,* they'd told him.

I have to disappear. I can't do what they're asking.

He scanned the pile for his jeans. Pulling those on seemed like an easier task than getting his shirt around him. He used his good arm to guide his feet through, dismissing the second head rush that hit between his eyes when he leaned over. He pulled his bad arm through the shirtsleeve and draped the shirt over his bandaged shoulder. He then repeated the sequence with the jacket. When he reached around his back, pain shot like a knife through his chest and shoulder, making everything take ten times longer. *Hurry up, fuckhead.*

A sudden heaviness came over him. He stopped. Hannah's perfume still lingered on his clothes from that night. He sank down on the bed, wishing he weren't in this nightmare. Everything had gotten so screwed up, so fast. He was back to running again, just like when he was a kid living with his grandfather—running from him, running from the bullies in the park. He'd stopped running when he met Hannah. Now nothing would be the same.

He edged himself around the door. Upon exiting his room, he stuck his back to the corridor wall—and his jacket rubbed against it and knocked a cardboard cutout of a Yule log to the floor. *Too conspicuous*, he scolded himself, and he forced his body into a relaxed stride. He needed to pass as a visitor.

The facility was decked out for Christmas, with tacky decorations on either side of the hallway that were so distracting, he nearly ran into a woman coming out of the next room.

"Oh, excuse me!" she said, sounding embarrassed.

"No problem," he muttered without turning his head and walked quickly away.

He passed a set of couches where a guy lay reading, his head propped up on one of the armrests. A tower of board games teetered next to him. *What kind of hospital is this?* There were no hospital gowns anywhere, just a handful of people meandering in tracksuits and sweats.

He focused his gaze straight ahead of him, blinking back the bright lights above, and weaved himself through the busy hallway and meal carts in search of the nearest exit. He inhaled through his mouth to avoid the stench of hospital food and disinfectant. He caught sight of the redheaded aide coming around the nurses' station and quickly ducked around a corner.

He welcomed the dimness of the cool stairwell but not the way each downward step aggravated his shoulder more. He shifted over to the left railing, leaning his weight on his good side, and carried on, gaining speed and confidence until he was taking the metal steps two at a time. He became dizzy within seconds; it was the most activity he'd experienced in days. He staggered on the landing, feeling a fever rise up the sides of his face. He collapsed back onto the stairs to catch his breath. His good hand flew up to his bad shoulder. A warm stickiness seeped through the bandage and covered his hand, making him shudder.

His body wasn't ready to leave, but he couldn't wait for it to heal. The longer he stayed, the greater the chance others would learn he was alive. He was too vulnerable in that hospital room.

He pulled himself up. His heart raged even louder inside his chest. He continued moving, but more tentatively, and his lightheadedness and nausea subsided somewhat. He finally reached the exit door. He leaned his full weight into it and staggered out to the parking garage.

She's here. He almost collapsed with relief.

"Where to, boss . . . hungry?" Jade grinned.

"Hardly." He blanched at the mere thought of food. His body melted onto the backseat. He sucked in some air and reclined on his good side, bracing himself against the seat in front of him. "Where's the pickup spot?"

"I have the car keys, clothes, and our new IDs in here," she said, motioning to the backpack next to him, allowing her hand to softly brush his.

"You're not coming with me."

"Just thought you could use some company. You know, a travel buddy." She ran her hand through her hair, watching him in the rearview mirror.

He didn't move.

"Shit, we could be so good together. All the fun you want, right here baby . . ." Her hand skimmed the length of her body like she was a model on *The Price Is Right*.

"For all the drugs that *you* want, right?"

"Why not? A girl can party *and* play."

Deacon shook his head. "You never learn, Jade."

CHAPTER 4

christmas eve night

BABETTE CLOSED HER EYES IN THE HALLWAY OUTSIDE of Deacon's hospital room and took a few breaths. She fished around in her purse for the syringe and tapped its case with her fingernail when she located it. She must have appeared to be praying, judging by the sympathetic face she received from a passerby.

Mind your own business.

She'd been flooded with sweet relief the night she learned Deacon had been shot: one less problem to endure in her intolerable life, along with a title she never wanted—*mother.*

Her euphoria hadn't lasted, though. Seeing him still alive and possibly brain-dead, she'd felt robbed. *I didn't sign up to take care of a vegetable.* She'd spent the past two days convincing herself of what she had to do before Kingsley returned to town and heard the news. Both of their lives would be better for it.

Her hand trembled over the door handle, unsure if she possessed the guts. She ground her teeth into a snarl and squeezed her wrist to steady it. *One-two-three-four-five. No, again! One-two-three-four-five.*

A powerful chemical smell assaulted her senses inside the room, stopping her breath short, along with the rest of her. The bed lay empty. Not just empty—stripped, cleaned, and ready for the next sorry soul. All evidence of Deacon's existence had been eradicated.

She marched out to the hallway to recheck the room number. Her nostrils flared. She strolled back into the room and rested a hand on her hip.

Dr. Klondike would have called her if he had died.

No, she thought, *he walked out of here and he's not coming back.*

Finally, that kid grew some balls.

CHAPTER 5

christmas day

GRAY, DIRTY SNOW LINED THE CURBS LEADING THE WAY to her house. The roads and sidewalks lay dark and wet. The trampled white lawns with sled tracks and a one-eyed, leaning snowman stretched into one long, forgotten playground.

When did it snow? Hannah wondered. The days since Deacon's death had blurred together, similar to the neighbors' property lines, under a blanket of frost.

A couple of the neighbors stood outside greeting the holiday company that was coming up their walkway, balancing wrapped gifts and trays of food with cordial smiles. They stopped to stare as the Zandanas' station wagon passed. Others, she noticed, preferred to watch the show from their windows.

"Don't these people have a life?" Hannah muttered, mostly to herself. Her eyes shot briefly over to her father behind the wheel.

He pressed his lips together in response.

It was their first exchange, if you could call it that, since their visit with her mother and little sister in rehab that morning.

What exactly do they expect to see? She narrowed her eyes at the unapologetically gawking welcoming committee, then sank lower in her seat. Her life was more of a freak show than ever, thanks to her having witnessed the only murder to ever take place in their small town. The fact that both her mother and Kerry had been whisked away via ambulance a couple of weeks earlier for nearly succumbing to a Valium overdose, her little sister swallowing her mother's happy pills to be just like her, hadn't exactly helped either.

She caught sight of Gillian standing with the other members of her mean-girl coven, Leeza and Taylor, in her driveway. True to form they all turned in unison toward the Zandanas' car.

Leeza's sneer and fake mean-girl laugh (complete with hair toss) and Taylor's pitying headshake were the same as always. Gillian's face struck her as odd, though. The redhead's eyes were wide and bug-eyed.

What's her deal?

The awkward silence between Hannah and her father only grew louder when they arrived home, the air as foreign as it was fragile. She watched him rotate around the kitchen, opening the fridge and cabinets and coming up empty. A couple of times he looked like he wanted to call out to her mother but stopped himself.

He appeared lost in his own home.

Hannah closed her bedroom door at the sound of her father's heavy footsteps retreating upstairs to his room. *I guess that's it, then. Merry Christmas to you too, Dad.*

Inside the quiet of her four walls, Hannah's pain and loneliness flooded forward as if from a fractured dam. Her eyes jetted around the room, unsure how to contain the emotions. She dug her nails into her forearms, trying to make it stop. She flung herself on the bed and rolled onto her back. She couldn't stay still. She threw her legs off the side and edged herself off the bed until her butt reached the floor. She grabbed her diary from underneath her mattress.

I have nothing now with you gone, nothing to look forward to, just a cold, drowning emptiness. It hurts so much, Deacon. Even after we broke up, I thought of you every day, knowing I still loved you. My life came alive with you in it, from black and white to Technicolor. Good and bad. We could have gotten through the bad. Hearing you and Toby argue in the park, now I know what it was like for you to live in that house, feeling like I do here, dismissed and ignored. We were so alike in that way. Imagine that, you and me sharing the same secrets. I don't want to wake up and relive all over again that you're not here. That your breath no longer touches your lips. I'll never look into your eyes again or have your hands on me, your arms holding me, making everything better as long as I was with you. Why did this have to happen? Please. Why did you leave me here all alone with no one, no one *who can possibly understand?*

Hannah swept the tears from her cheeks. Her eyes drifted from the page and stared off to the side.

I wish we both died that night.

If only.

She began to rewrite the night of his shooting in her head. As she did, the two of them came into focus, lying in one another's arms like they were playing out the final scene in *Romeo and Juliet.*

She clutched her pen tighter.

My father finds me in the park. He regrets how he treated me, berating me for my acne, and calling me names like "harlot" and "whore" when he didn't like the clothes I wore. He realizes it all, but it's too late. Isn't it, Dad?

Mom is crying for me, wishing she had been a better mother and not pushed me away all those times when I begged her to hold me. She regrets never coming to my defense during one of Dad's tirades and telling me I brought my father's ugly words on myself.

Gillian, the evil one who set everything in motion, getting Toby to bring his father's gun to the park that night—supposedly to scare me into keeping her secret from everyone—sending Jade to tell me that I have to go to Gossamer Park because Deacon is in trouble and is trying to make things right between us . . . she doesn't cry.

I get Deacon's note warning me it's a trap and still I go . . . for him, always for him.

Those wicked girls and the kids who were mean to me all these years feel guilty now. They whisper, "We never really knew her. He must have really loved her. Heard they died in one another's arms. Deacon Giroux and Hannah Zandana are famous now. We never knew it was like that between them. Now they'll be together forever."

Hannah wiped the snot streaming from her nose. *God, I'm pathetic.*

- 20 -

Who's going to help me escape this house of pain? I want the nothingness inside of me to burn again. I don't want to go back to the old me, before there was you. I want to feel wanted, feel loved. Who's going to love me now?

Hannah pulled her legs to her chest and buried her nose in her knees. How had everything gotten so screwed up?

Merry f-ing Christmas, family.

CHAPTER 6

"Merry fucking Christmas," Deacon breathed into his coat collar. He drove faster down the highway. The frosted road lay riddled with swerving tire tracks. He didn't care. He rechecked the rearview. His injury would not interfere with his vigilance. He'd make sure of it. This was still his life. They weren't going to hijack it.

He gripped the steering wheel firmly, trying not to over-correct. He clenched his jaw against the headache looming between his eyes. This jalopy Jade had gotten him would have to do—if it didn't fall apart first. It was disposable anyway, with fake plates and registration. One of their dirtbag drug clients had owed her a favor. Deacon hadn't asked. With Jade, it was best not to know.

He rubbed the side of his face. The skin there was still raw and chapped from the night in the park—the night his asshole, half-wit half-brother had shot him and he'd basically been kidnapped. *Was that just four days ago?* Seemed impossible.

He glanced in his rearview and side mirrors again and released a sigh. So far he hadn't been followed.

What the hell am I going to do? God, she thinks I'm dead!

He needed time to think, and a place to hide and plan

his next move. More importantly, he needed cash. He'd left everything in Darien. What Jade had given him would only last a week, maybe two.

Think. Think. Who could help me on Christmas?

A mile down the highway, he passed a sign for Massachusetts. His head jerked back, and he nearly skidded off the road.

Thomas . . . of course, Christmas break.

If not much had changed, his old boarding school classmate would be the only one in the dorm over the holiday break. Next truck stop, he'd call. It was worth a try. Those cops would never know to look for him there. Plus, Thomas was loaded. His father owned a big commercial transport business.

Deacon's eyes spread wider. *My half of the cooler.*

He drove faster.

He'd find some way to get a message to Hannah to let her know he was alive.

Give me time.

This was still *his* life.

CHAPTER 7

———

"Why did you *hate* the boy so much?" Kingsley said in a low voice, looking forlornly into his tumbler. He leaned against the large ivory credenza across from Babette, swirling the contents of his glass in circles so the brown liquid left a caramel-colored mountain range along its edges. His white tongue jutted out like a cat's to lick the inside clean, his teeth clamping down on the rim.

Babette's nostrils flared as she waited for her husband's disgusting ritual to end. She turned from him and filled her glass generously at the bar. She replaced the phallus-shaped crystal stopper precariously atop the carafe, challenging it to fall to the hardwood below and shatter into a million beautiful pieces. Her mouth watered as she envisioned the blood that would course out if she ran a piece of the jagged glass across her beloved husband's neck. The thought aroused her. She took a rough swig; she was far from quenched.

Her fingertips flew up to her choker. *One-two-three-four-five.* She felt giddy from her fantasy. Her fingers hungered to touch each pearl in order. She repeated the sequence, careful not to miss a single bead, before continuing up the rest of the strand.

Behind her shoulder she sensed her husband's idiotic sadness sucking the oxygen from the room. She knew those pitiful eyes of his, crushed over the loss of their only son. She held back from laughing while he waited for her answer.

"Well?" he demanded. "Answer me. You're acting happier than I've ever seen you. Not like a mother who just lost her only child."

Babette buzzed the air in the back of her throat. "Christ, not this again, Kingsley." She laughed tightly and began playing with the hair on the back of her neck. "Oh, my aching neck . . ." *One-two-three-four-five.*

"Quit it, Babette."

"*What?*"

"I can see what you're doing. That obsessive *counting* of yours, always *fucking* counting." He said this last part under his breath.

She spun around, baring her teeth. Her manicured talons coiled around her shapely hip. "I'll tell you why! From the moment he was born, the way that kid looked at me—always needing this or that. Needing something all the time. Things I didn't have to give. Not like *you* were ever around. He'd talk your ear off until he got what he wanted. Talked me into the ground. *God*, the tantrums he'd have just to embarrass me. I'd walk away and act like he wasn't *mine*. Like the time I left him at Bergdorf's . . . *on purpose*." She peered back at her husband, watching his eyes swivel around the room. *Why the hell does he keep licking his lips?*

"I didn't give a damn, King. Store security called me and I sent the chauffeur. I didn't grow up with a mother. I never *needed* one, survived fine . . . though people talked. 'Poor Babette . . . poor little baby.' Such bullshit. I'm glad my mother jumped and ended her life. She was weak, just like *him*."

Kingsley moistened his lips again. "I wish I could have seen him before he was . . . you know . . . *gone*."

Babette sauntered back to the bar to top off her highball. "Kingsley, he died the night he was shot, I told you that. There was nothing you could have done."

"I would have come home earlier. Did you have to wait until Christmas morning to tell me?"

"Why spoil your trip?" she deadpanned, her back still turned.

"There's something else," he said. "I want Brenda's son to live with us. He's pretty shaken up after . . . *the accident* . . . and could use a stable home. He can have Deacon's old room."

Her shoulders dropped away from her ears as she released a long sigh. *Old room.* She suppressed a smile and walked over to her husband, one high heel in front of the other, like a catwalk model. She couldn't contain her delight. *I'm finally free.*

With a smug grin, she clinked her glass against her husband's, though his hand never moved.

"As long as he doesn't start calling me *Mom*, we've got a deal."

CHAPTER 8

milton, massachusetts

"SO, WHO ARE THEY AND WHAT DO THEY WANT FROM you?" Thomas asked, tipping back his third beer and trying to grasp that he wasn't still dreaming.

Four years had passed since his former boarding school buddy had moved back into his parents' Connecticut house. No longer boys, they were now young men, months from graduating from their separate schools, and the air between them had colored; an unspoken wariness existed now that hadn't been there before.

Thomas heard about the shooting days before, along with everyone at school, and had planned to properly mourn his friend's death the rest of winter break with a couple of close friends: vodka and cocaine. But when the phone had rung a few hours earlier, his bender had come to a screeching halt.

The extra lines of blow he had done that evening had made his temples pound when he pulled the phone up to his face, still half asleep. He'd tasted the sourness of the coke dripping from his nose into his throat. He'd reached over for the plastic cup next to his bed, taken a mouthful, and spewed warm vodka everywhere, his tongue and throat burning worse than before.

"Shit," he'd whispered angrily, and flung the receiver away from him.

"Thomas!" a voice admonished from the floor. "This is fucking serious."

It can't be, can it?

He slammed the phone to his ear again. It took a few head scratches to register that old "Teflon D" was ordering him around like they were back in seventh grade. His nickname had emerged from his ability to come away unscathed from every form of trouble. Apparently, he'd done it again.

"Okay, okay. Got it."

The reality that Deacon was alive had sobered him to his feet. He stepped into his jeans and the room rotated like a carnival Tilt-A-Whirl. He sat back down until it stopped. His throat blazed from the vodka and coke, making him drum up some nasty phlegm that he launched into the trashcan.

He thought he'd been partying to forget. The pit in his stomach, however, revealed something else: he'd been relieved by the news of Deacon's death.

No matter his efforts, Deacon remained the one person he could never beat. From surpassing him on the school swim team to the countless classmates who revered him and the swarm of hot girls who longed to be in his bed, the guy aced at life.

Thomas stared at him now, sitting on his roommate's bed. He'd been struck, when Deacon walked through the door, by how tall he now was, how broad his shoulders were, and how his mug had grown more handsome than ever. *Fucking shit.*

In between unrolling and rerolling his shirtsleeves,

Thomas pushed out his chest and raised himself up on his knuckles to make the two of them closer to eye level. He couldn't stand how Deacon had shot up and left him behind, making his commanding presence larger than ever.

"There're these guys that have been following me for a while . . . you wouldn't believe it if I told you." Deacon side-eyed him and lowered his brows.

Thomas stopped fidgeting. "Wait, the same ones who jumped you?"

"Nah, these losers have wanted my scalp longer than that."

"More like your territory." Thomas smirked. He could feel his crooked smile dragging at the corner of his mouth. It got more pronounced when he drank.

"No." Deacon's lips contorted slightly.

Thomas's eyes stretched wide; was he about to see his ever-so-tough friend lose it for the first time?

Deacon's head sank between his shoulders. "They're cops. Federal agents, actually." He exhaled somberly. "They want me to work for them."

"Sounds sort of kinky." Thomas laughed dryly, trying to lighten the mood, which was far too intense for his beer buzz.

"No, it's some scary shit they want me to do." Deacon carefully rubbed his shoulder. "Pretty bogus."

Thomas lost his smirk. He could see that Deacon wasn't playing. "What now?"

"Chill here until I can shake them . . . and I need my half of the cooler, too."

"It's secure." Thomas nodded. He'd buried the cooler near the lake and hadn't touched it since. Frankly, he hadn't needed it.

"I want to find a way to get Hannah back. With everyone, well almost everyone, thinking I'm dead, it shouldn't be too difficult to get a message to her and get her out of there."

"Your parents think you're dead too?"

Deacon flipped his beer cap toward the trashcan in the corner. It hit the inside edge and dropped in. "Yeah, even got a gravestone in the family plot right next to my lunatic grandmother, the same old bat who jumped to her death way before I was born."

"Sheesh, you saw your tombstone, dude?"

"Nah, Jade told me."

"That bodacious babe who works for you? How the hell is she still in the picture?"

"Uh-huh, the same. She's going to check on Hannah for me."

"Wait, what exactly did your family bury?"

"Dunno, but I have a feeling that the Feds managed something."

"Dude, you can't go back there."

Deacon nodded like he'd heard it all before.

"So, what's the plan?"

"At the moment, drink a few more of these." Deacon drained the last of his beer, then tipped his chin up toward Thomas. "May I have another, sir?"

Thomas sat transfixed, watching him propel bottle caps into the can. Deacon clenched his jaw harder after each successful bucket. Finally, he stopped and rubbed his brows with both hands. He jammed the edge of his palms into his forehead, turning his skin white. Whatever was going on inside of him, there wasn't enough alcohol in the world to numb it.

"So what's it like to be . . . you know, *dead*?"

Deacon sighed sharply though his nose. He examined the ground between his feet and scooped up another bottle cap. His pinched face didn't match his words. "Good, actually . . . freeing . . . except for the complications."

"Hannah—"

"And the Feds on my tail."

"What about that dipstick half-brother of yours . . . what's-his-face?"

Deacon guffawed. "Hopefully Toby's locked up for shooting me—but more than likely, he's gotten away with it thanks to our dear ole dad. Probably living in my house as we speak . . . *the fucker*."

"Pretty lame."

Deacon shrugged. "Everybody's happy now that I'm gone . . . except . . ."

"*Her*."

Thomas could see his old friend struggling and tried to lift his mood. "Come on, D, it's like getting a redo. Remember those when we were kids? Our swim team days? Every time one of us messed up, we'd call redo! Belly flop off the diving board, redo!"

"Yeah, I remember," Deacon said wistfully. "I wish this felt like that." He took a long sip of beer. "So . . . interested in doing a little business while I'm here? Big Bad Buddy still driving?"

"He sure is." Thomas grinned, then swung his arm around and caught Deacon's bad shoulder.

"Ass-*hole*!"

CHAPTER 9

darien, connecticut

———

"WE WERE JUST THERE A COUPLE OF DAYS AGO. WHY DO we have to go back?" Hannah stared out the window at the passing cars. She knew she was whining and didn't care. Her mother hadn't been so kind to her during their last visit to rehab. Why return for more?

Her father shot her a look. "Because she's your *mother* . . . think of your sister, what it must be like for them." He gritted his teeth. "These doctors will fix things and help put this family back together."

"Fix things? Mom's a pill-popping addict and most likely an alcoholic, Dad."

"Don't call her that," he snapped.

"She'll always be drawn to that stuff because she never learned to cope with losing her first child," Hannah persisted.

"I don't want to talk about it."

"And that's part of the problem."

He exhaled and tightened his jaw. "I'll drop you off with the donuts. Sign in and I'll park."

"Yeah, okay. Wait, are these considered contraband?" Hannah said, lifting up the Dunkin Donuts box.

He motioned his head toward the entrance, her signal to get out of the car already.

She stepped through the double doors and the attendant promptly confiscated the donuts. "All incoming food must be sealed," he announced robotically, eyeing the box. She noticed how he helped himself to a big bite of one of the donuts before she even made it halfway down the hall.

Hannah heard the arguing before the elevator doors opened on her mother's floor. She stepped out into the corridor and spotted two men in suits. The larger man had a red face and was angrily poking his sausage finger into the other man's chest.

Beyond them, a pair of patients in matching sweats headed her way. They awkwardly made eye contact with Hannah as they steered around the two arguing men. Hannah's shoulder skimmed the wall, knocking a cardboard Yule log decoration to the floor. She bent to pick it up, and heard the suits' conversation as they passed.

"They were supposed to watch him!"

"He couldn't have gotten far, boss," the other one said, puffing hard on a cigarette.

Hannah reattached the decoration back to the wall and took a deep breath before entering her mother's room.

"I forgot to tell you I saw one of your friends here," her mother said as Hannah walked in, foregoing a simple hello.

A friend? "Who was it?" Hannah asked, screwing up her face. A couple of minutes into their visit, and so far her mother was playing nice.

"A tall, striking boy. I think he was visiting someone down the hall."

"I have no idea, Mom."

Her mother frowned and smoothed out the front of her

tracksuit. She sat down next to the window across from Hannah. A 1,000-piece jigsaw puzzle (according to the colorful box top) featuring a partially completed pair of angora cats was spread out on the table next to her.

"My head's been foggy lately," she said gazing down and wrinkling her forehead. "I think I saw him once in the neighborhood?"

"Oh, you mean Peter. I'm not sure why he'd be here. Guess I'll have to ask him." Hannah smiled politely. She hadn't spoken to Peter—to anyone but family—since the night Deacon died, less than a week ago. She didn't want her fears confirmed that she could have done more to save Deacon.

"Where's Kerry?"

"Therapy."

"And you? How are—" Hannah began.

"What *about* me?" her mom said sharply.

Hannah's face flushed. She picked up one of the puzzle pieces, shaking her head. *Nice. Still acting all superior, Mother.*

She sensed an onslaught coming in the way her mother's eyes burned into her.

"I wish you'd brush your hair more, Hannah."

"It's curly. If I do that, it'll just be frizzy."

"It looks better when you straighten it. Didn't your father buy you a curling iron to smooth out your hair?"

"Yep." Her father had arrived home after work Christmas Eve with a bag of drugstore gifts from the Pathmark near their house for her to wrap: for her mother, perfume and a quilted toiletry bag; for Kerry, a couple of knock-off Care Bears; and for Hannah, a curling iron and makeup from the bargain bin to cover her acne—another aspect of her appearance that caused her parents, especially her father, displeasure. She should have known that her mother had briefed him on what to get.

"Well?"

"I didn't know I was supposed to come here all dolled up," she retorted, her ears growing hot. She scowled turning back toward the door, wondering when her dad would make it upstairs and yell about the donuts. She'd welcome that over waiting for another dart to fly out of her mother's mouth.

Part of her longed to tell this woman everything that had happened over the last three months—about dating Deacon, finding the pictures that led to their breakup, and the horrific night that had permanently ended it all. But how could she confide in her about the dark and dangerous boy she'd fallen in love with when something as basic as her naturally curly hair was such a constant source of disappointment?

"How you look is a reflection on *me*," her mother suddenly said, raising her chin.

Hannah swallowed hard; her eyes stung like she'd been punched. If only she could look the way her mother wanted her to and stop disappointing her all of the time. Maybe then she wouldn't have needed those pills. If she'd worked harder, maybe she would have been enough to help her mother forget her pain over losing baby Michael.

She knew it wasn't rational. It sure felt real, though.

Hannah riffled through the remaining puzzle pieces in the box. She moved aside the ones with pink on them for the triangle noses and ears, those for the white whiskers and green eyes, and so many others with fur that it was hard to tell which way was up—until she found the one befitting the moment.

"That's funny, Mom," she said, "considering *you're* the one in rehab." She snapped the puzzle piece with the cat's claws into its rightful place.

CHAPTER 10

milton, massachusetts

SLEEPING IN HIS FORMER DORM WAS GETTING OLD FAST and it only had been a few days. Deacon relied on Thomas for everything: food, extra clothes, company, etc. He couldn't afford anyone seeing him walking around campus or going into town and discovering that he was still breathing. In some ways, it felt like old times.

When Deacon attended boarding school in seventh and eighth grade, he and Thomas were the only ones who stayed on campus over winter break. He told everyone he was in between homes, which was basically true. Thomas's family, meanwhile, didn't celebrate Christmas, and his parents liked to take separate vacations. Whether Thomas was invited to join one of them, Deacon never asked. The two of them didn't elaborate when it came to family. Their mutual hatred for most things parental was enough of a bond.

Deacon was already dealing on campus when Thomas suggested a joint partnership. They could expand his territory by working locally for Thomas's father's commercial transport business in the mailroom, distributing packages to each of the buildings via a golf cart.

At first the freight drivers they approached, like Big Bad

Buddy, were skeptical, sizing up the young teens and wondering if they could manage such an operation and have the constant cash flow to make it worth the risk. Turned out, their cover was perfect; their age and general awkwardness let them move about without suspicion.

The drugs came in from the harbor. The boys met the drivers at one of their designated spots and loaded up an ice cooler. They transported it in the golf cart and later stored it in one of their dorm rooms. The route was so rich that they pulled in around five pounds of coke a month.

Thomas still used the route and a willing driver or two these days, but not to the same degree as when they worked together. The bulk of the profits was hidden in a secondary cooler on campus. Deacon's share of it was his ticket to a new life.

"Dude, I'm going to go crazy if I have to spend another minute cooped up in this room," he growled upon their third morning together. He'd forgotten how uncomfortable the dorm beds were. His feet hung off the end now.

Thomas was already up, madly opening and closing bureau drawers.

Deacon's sleepy lids barely lifted; his voice was still rough from another restless night. He woke up to the sound of his father's gun firing, sweating, his heart caroming inside his chest at seeing Toby and Hannah's faces and the shiny metal pistol between them, so vividly. Jumbled images haunted his night, twisting up his bed sheets and tying him down.

In his dream, he saw Hannah pressing the tip of the gun to his head. In another, it was his father smugly grinning behind the trigger.

A dark gloom enveloped him when he realized where he was that morning. *Another day without you.* Seven days since the shooting, and there never seemed to be enough air.

"You're beginning to reek, dude," announced Thomas, already dressed and grabbing his wallet from the jeans on the floor.

"Fuck you."

"Yeah, you too. Going out for food, dick. What's today's bag-O-barf?"

"Filet mignon."

"Be back."

"Not with my wallet, douche."

Thomas slammed the door behind him, and the sound of his footsteps faded down the hall.

Deacon rubbed his eyes, contemplating taking a shower. He knew it wouldn't be enough to clear his head, help him shake off the ghosts from the night.

"Screw it. One trip outside isn't going to kill anyone."

Deacon rounded the corner, choosing the shortcut between the dorms. He knew where he wanted to go, but the path looked different than he remembered—the trees taller, the grounds and spaces between the buildings tighter. He buried his head further into his collar and ran hunched over. He'd stolen one of Thomas's knit hats and it already itched.

He cut through one of the alleys and stopped where the path split off. *Where the hell am I?* He spun back, facing the direction he'd come from, and heard a car door slam. He dropped behind a stairway. He was too far from the dorm entrance. He pressed his lips together and waited.

Several minutes passed. The morning wasn't getting any warmer. He didn't have much time before Thomas returned. He told himself it was probably some family touring the campus. He listened again and didn't hear anything. He crept slowly along the side of the building, repeatedly checking over his shoulder to see if anyone was coming. A few steps in, his foot went into a hole. He struck something hard and fell to the ground.

He gazed up, shielding his eyes from the sun. A large, roundish man in a tan overcoat towered over him, smiling like a kid on Christmas.

CHAPTER 11

darien, connecticut

THE AFTERNOON SKY BEGAN TO DARKEN WITH THE NEW snow falling all around her. *It's going to be a beautiful night,* Hannah thought sadly, making deliberate crunching sounds with her boots along her driveway, just as she had as a child, when her world was far less complicated.

Over her ripped jeans she'd pulled on the same fisherman sweater she'd worn with Deacon, pretending it still carried his scent. During those sweet days when everything was new, he'd always managed to slip it off her, her skin tickling at his touch.

She lifted her face to the sky, wrapping her arms around her waist. Frozen wet flakes flew to the hair tied loosely atop her head, some sticking to her lashes and cheeks.

What would we be doing tonight?

She kept finding herself fantasizing about these what-ifs in between wallowing in her room and staring at the TV with the sound off. She was sick of her house, especially its pounding silence, and finally ventured outside.

She remembered her conversation with Deacon about New Year's Eve. It had seemed so far away then. They were going to spend it together, her first one with a boy—well, other than Dick Clark on TV, but he didn't count.

She slid down her driveway, taking long strides toward the street. In the middle of her daydream, a car slowed in front of the house. The driver appeared to be lost. The car passed by, then turned around at the end of the block, pulled back up, and stopped before Hannah. The window lowered.

"I want to talk to you," a voice called out.

Gillian. To Hannah's surprise, she was alone.

Hannah spun back toward the porch. She had no desire to be anywhere near her—the catalyst that had led to Deacon's last breath.

"The cops ruled his death as accidental," Gillian shouted after her. "The charges against Toby were dropped. He's not coming back to school."

Hannah pivoted around and stomped toward the car, glaring. "Sounds like it worked out perfectly for you. Deacon's gone. Your secret's safe." She resisted the urge to reach through the window and hit her.

"There's no way you can prove I had anything to do with it," Gillian said. "If you go to the cops with some story, I'm just going to deny everything."

Hannah blinked a few times. The girl just didn't get it. "You're going to have to live with that, you know. Whatever you did to get that nutcase, Toby, to bring his father's gun to the park that night, that's on your conscience and yours alone. He may have pulled the trigger but you paid for the bullet, bitch."

"You threatened to *out* me!"

"I don't understand," Hannah said. Her forehead creased with confusion.

"Tell everyone I prefer girls, *idiot.*"

"I only did that to get you to stop being so mean, to stop bullying me. I'd had enough, okay? I would never have told anyone."

Gillian lunged from her seat, nearly climbing through the window in Hannah's direction. "How could *I* know that!? You know what that would do to me? I couldn't live here. I couldn't go to school. My parents would disown me. My friends. All of it. *Over.*"

Hannah's eyes widened at witnessing her nemesis so rattled. "I had no idea," she said softly. "I wouldn't. I swear. I still won't."

Gillian hung her head like it had become too heavy to hold up.

"But the gun, Gillian. Why the hell?"

"Toby was supposed to only *scare* you . . ." she said, rolling her eyes like he was incapable of following directions, or simply just stupid.

"Why didn't you just tell me the deal sooner?"

"Why would *you* keep *my* secret?"

"Because I know what it's like to not fit in . . . to be different than everybody else. The constant insecurity. The difference between us is that your freak flag is hidden, but mine's out for everyone to see."

"If you hadn't threatened me, your boyfriend would still be alive. Enjoy living with that!" Gillian snarled.

"You! You caused all of this to happen, you put Toby up to it. It was easy for you, just another one of your puppets." Hannah's heart was beating inside her throat. She turned away trying to calm down. The snow, she realized, had stopped falling. "Like I told Jade . . ."

Gillian's head whipped around. "You spoke to *Jade*?"

Hannah chopped a patch of ice with the heel of her boot a few times before answering. Jade had come to her house a couple of days earlier, all jittery and unable to sit still. Whether she was high or jonesing for another hit, it irked Hannah that Deacon's former associate could barely look at her. What was she hiding? Had she played a bigger role in that night than she'd led her to believe?

She cleared her throat. "She apologized for what happened and for conning me into going to the park that night. She said you were freaking out . . ."

Gillian stared over the steering wheel, her thoughts somewhere far away.

"You've been torturing me most of my life . . . but I never would have told anybody about you guys. I don't care. It's none of my business who you like. I didn't know how else to stop your taunting . . ."

"You're such a loser, Hannah." Gillian started the car's engine.

"Are you *even* listening? What you do to people hurts! You hit first before they can, cause you're so afraid of them finding out. It's got to be exhausting to be you." She sighed stiffly. "I can't believe I used to want to be your friend. That what you thought of me once mattered."

"Fuck *you*," Gillian mumbled, putting it in gear.

Hannah's feet froze watching her disappear down the street into a small, distant dot. She stood there for several moments, until the snow began to fall again.

Alone in her room later that night, Hannah's head ached from replaying her conversation with Gillian a million times over, wishing she'd said more, so much more.

She closed her diary and slipped it under her mattress. She was too beat to write. She poked her head outside her door, testing for signs of life. Her father's television boomed from upstairs, its volume level coinciding with how much reality needed to be drowned out.

She toyed with going upstairs to check on him; maybe they could play some cards or something, like they used to when she was little. That felt too weird, though. She also knew what his answer would be.

She flopped onto the gold corduroy couch in the living room. Minutes from the strike of midnight, her thoughts drifted to her mother and sister being in that cold, antiseptic place. She hated how she and her mother had spoken to one another just days before. Why did she let her mother get to her?

She was especially sad and lonely without Kerry around. Did her little sister even understand why she was there? They'd be coming home soon, and then what?

Happy New Year's, family.

She walked across the room and pulled out the plastic power knob on the dark oak television set, the one Kerry liked to unscrew all the time and hide among her toys. The TV was a Gamma Mimi hand-me-down with grooved, swirling designs and faux drawers with brass handles. It usually took a minute or two for the tubes to warm up. Even once the picture appeared, it often looked like it was snowing along the edges of the screen.

She turned the volume low before she rocked back and sat cross-legged on the floor in the dark. The picture warmed up right in the middle of *Dick Clark's New Year's Rockin' Eve*, with Night Ranger singing: "When You Close Your Eyes."

Hannah smirked. The ball—which looked more like a neon apple—poked around and missed its intended midnight touchdown on Times Square; the 1985 sign, however, glowed on schedule. The cheering and the kissing couples commenced for the cameras as bad hair bands tried singing "Auld Lang Syne."

Somehow the whole thing is orchestrated to make you feel bad, Hannah thought. *Pretty people partying, while you, neither pretty nor partying, watch.* She slipped her lips inside the neck of her sweater and hugged her knees to her chest. Her warm breath felt good against her skin. "This will be my year," she said, and exhaled deeply.

A commercial for the movie *The Flamingo Kid* came on. The camera zoomed in on Matt Dillon's face. The actor reminded her so much of Deacon in the way his bushy eyebrows swept up his animated face that she yanked her chin back out of her sweater with a grimace.

"Hannah?" her father called down to her. She hadn't heard his TV go off.

She switched off the living room set without a word and slipped into her room, carefully closing the door behind her.

CHAPTER 12

milton, massachusetts

THEY HEADED INTO THE WOODS ONCE IT GOT DARK with Thomas holding their one light source, an old camping lantern stolen from another kid's room. The quarter moon swirling in the clouds did little to lead the way. Without Thomas's help, Deacon realized, he never would have found the route to the large lake north of campus.

The frozen ground crunched under their boots as they trekked in the negative temperatures, accompanied by a relentless wind. Deacon's black Dr. Martens were already soaked through from the clumps of snow he'd picked up along the trail. He couldn't feel his toes anymore. He blew into his cupped hands and jammed them back into his overcoat.

"Fucking freezing out here. My balls are about to fall off," he called out. The cold air stung his face, making his eyes water. The large clearing ahead told him that the lake was nearby. In a few minutes, it would be over. *Soon, I'll be coming home to you.*

"They've been calling this weather system the Big Freeze, asshole. Where've you been?" Thomas yelled over his shoulder.

The sound of Thomas's chattering teeth reminded him of their long swim practices as kids. Thomas's scrawny body used to shake like nobody else's—in *and* out of the pool.

The other kids teased him. But Deacon never left his side.

"Fuck it's cold," he said, dismissing the memory.

"Should have done more blow," Thomas said, laughing, and just like that they were thirteen again, embarking upon another caper together.

"Totally. Where's the cooler, asshole?" A chunk of the fast food he'd eaten earlier traveled up Deacon's throat. His nerves were steadily chipping away at whatever guts he thought he possessed. *Shit, this is hard.*

"Here, over here." Thomas led him off the trail and deeper into the forest. They stepped through the trees, slipping over the knotted roots simultaneously. They both caught themselves before they fell but bumped into one another as they did, jostling Deacon's bad shoulder. A sharp pain stabbed his lungs when he tried to breathe. The bone-cold Massachusetts air had never been his friend.

He was wondering how much more he could take when Thomas finally stopped inside a cluster of trees. Their trunks cocooned the boys from the wind, silencing the air and making the frigid temp almost bearable.

Thomas spun around, holding the lantern at arm's length in front of him. His lips moved like he was counting trees. His eyes expanded as they landed on a large tree ten yards away, and he sprang toward it. Deacon saw that the ground on one side of it had been dug out at some point.

Thomas passed Deacon the light and knelt down to remove the tree brush concealing the trunk's rotted opening. That accomplished, he stooped again to drag the large, cumbersome cooler from inside the tree.

Deacon lowered the lantern and the Coleman lettering

appeared. Thomas braced his gloved hands against the lid. They slid off; the cooler was slick with ice. He crammed the tip of his boot inside the lip of the cooler, pressing his weight on it, and pulled up hard. The plastic top swung open, revealing stacks of cash.

Thomas sank to the ground on his knees.

"'Bout how much?" Deacon asked.

"What? You know . . ." Thomas's eyes narrowed. "You think I've been skimming?"

Deacon didn't respond.

Thomas pulled his lips tighter and the skin between his brows knotted into a wishbone. "It's *all* here. The entire amount we made together before you left. What the *hell* is wrong with you?"

"Just tell me . . . how . . . how did we do this?" Deacon demanded, blinking rapidly and nodding.

Thomas's face stiffened. "Why the *fuck*—"

"Just do it!" Deacon screamed, sending Thomas tumbling off his knees.

"What's your problem, asshole?" Thomas glared, pushing his hair away from his eyes. He rose to his feet and smacked the snow from his jeans.

Deacon ignored Thomas's stare down. Finally, his friend threw up his hands in exasperation.

"It took us over a year . . . we used my father's transport business and paid off the drivers. The coke came from the harbor nearly every other week. We took turns with the transactions . . . and agreed to hide the cash here until you could come back for it. I never touched it, man. This was ours . . . our baby," he said, slapping the side of the cooler.

"Our baby," Deacon agreed solemnly.

"Ours." Thomas smiled.

"Our baby just got fucked," Deacon said, opening the top of his coat and yanking on his collar. Like a lightswitch, the bottoms of the trees illuminated. Two sets of headlights climbed the other side of the clearing, stopping just short of the lake. Car doors flew open. Dots of light bounced in the distance, growing bigger.

"Hurry, someone's coming!" Thomas grabbed Deacon's sleeve, pulling him along behind him.

"Just look, will you!" Deacon's voice caught. He ripped off the wire and opened his palm, revealing the recording device under the glow of the lantern. His eyes filled with tears.

The blood drained from Thomas's face. "W-what? No, no, no! You didn't just, you didn't . . . we're friends . . . we're friends . . . to the end, D, like you always said . . . just us!"

Deacon covered his ears, twisting his body away. Thomas's voice escalated. He was a shit and he knew it. *I had to; they didn't give me a choice.*

"We were in this together . . . since we were kids . . . how could you? You said you'd never work for them . . . fucking liar! I hid you in my room, fed your damn ass . . . and all this time . . . you were a narc? Why? Just tell me *why!*"

A high-pitched sound rang in Deacon's ears. He couldn't feel his feet; they were frozen to the ground. His brain screamed for him to run. His body only swayed. The beams of light disorientated him and concealed the only way out through the trees.

"Look at me, asshole!" Thomas insisted. "I'm through being invisible next to you. I won't be ignored, not *now!*"

He pivoted around just as Thomas flew at him. His hands clutched Deacon's throat, his thumbs pressing deeper.

Thomas's sudden strength knocked Deacon off balance. He gripped his friend's wrists, but couldn't break them. He could no longer see Thomas's features, just the light surrounding his head like a halo. Thomas wedged the air further down Deacon's windpipe. Darkness filled in the edges of Deacon's peripheral, then slowly, it started closing in . . . growing darker . . . and darker . . .

It's over . . . it's over.

"Nah you don't, we need him," barked Kodak. He and Eastman jerked Thomas back, sending Deacon onto the ground, gasping for air.

Thomas struggled against them, swearing, "You're never going to live this down . . . because you're never going to *live.* YOU. WILL. DIE. FOR. THIS!"

Deacon coughed uncontrollably. The front of his throat burned. All at once, his stomach unclenched and their last meal together resurfaced. Everything blurred around him. Half wheezing, half crying, he spat, trying not to choke on his vomit.

When his stomach was empty, he leaned back wearily against a tree, dazed, and rested his head on its bark. His lungs hurt. His heart hurt more.

"Yo kid, you okay?" asked Eastman, panning a flashlight over him and checking for damage the way you would with a small child.

"He'll be fine. Just got his ass kicked," Kodak said with a laugh.

Deacon exhaled heavily inches from the glass, fogging up his view. He moved his mouth onto another spot until the majority of his window in the backseat of the Feds' white Buick was covered. He didn't want to watch the crew of cops standing with Kodak and Eastman cuff his former friend. His fog screen failed, though; Thomas's unwavering glower cut through it easily.

The second cop car drove off with Thomas moments later. Deacon's head fell into his hands. Even without cuffs, he was their prisoner. He cried without making a sound, wondering if what he'd done to Thomas had been worth it. He didn't know Kodak and Eastman's plan for him. He did know that he didn't want any more memories from this night. *Screwed your only friend to save yourself. Coward.*

He could hear the two of them arguing next to the hood diagonal from where they'd put him, behind the driver's seat. He peered through the metal cage partition. They were hunkered over an Exxon map that Kodak was holding sprawled across the windshield on the passenger's side, using Eastman's flashlight to illuminate it. The map shielded him from their view. If he was going to escape, this might be his only chance.

He tugged gently on his door handle. *Locked. But wait . . .*

Eastman's mangled seatbelt caught his eye. It had fallen behind the driver's seat and was wedged in his door. He shoved harder against it, trying not to make a sound. *Just one good push.*

His heart thudded outside his chest as he threw his upper body into his door like a running back in football. It flew open, and he paused. Somehow the Feds' bickering had drowned out the sound of the door opening.

He'd have to find his way back in the dark. He couldn't lose another minute. More sourness crawled up his throat. *Go . . . go . . . go . . .*

He heard Eastman slap his partner's chest. *Faster now, run!*

"Oh nooooo, we're just getting started," growled Kodak, as he circled the back of the car, heading him off. Eastman came at Deacon's back. "This isn't over by a long shot."

Deacon stumbled back, away from Kodak, and Eastman grabbed him and pulled his arms behind his back, sending sharp pains through his sore chest and shoulder. He was trapped.

The fallen flashlight by Kodak's feet shone up at the agent, giving his sneering face and jagged, pointy teeth a ghostly presence. He resembled a triggerfish like the ones Deacon's grandfather kept in his home aquarium. *Nasty fish,* Deacon had always thought. The fish could rotate each of their eyeballs independently, which was sort of what Kodak was doing now.

Puffing hard and somehow sweating in the frigid air, Kodak pulled a set of cuffs from his belt. "Now look what you're making us do. We're going to have to cuff and shackle you for the trip."

"Probably better anyways," Eastman snorted past the cigarette still in his mouth.

"Yep kid, you're going someplace warm—very warm—this winter," Kodak said.

"You can thank us later," Eastman quipped, blowing smoke into Deacon's face. The fast-smoking agent held his cigarette between his first two fingers like a cue stick.

"Jail?" Deacon blanched. "You said if I wore the wire and got Thomas to confess, I wouldn't do any time. That was the deal we made."

"That was just a test to see if you had the balls," Eastman said. "Now the *real* game begins. You're going on a little vacation . . ."

Deacon envisioned them shooting him in some alley and dumping his body until Kodak added, "Want the good news? We're going with ya, kid."

January 1985

CHAPTER 13

THE FEDS OBTAINED A VAN THE NIGHT DEACON SET
Thomas up. True to their word, they cuffed and shackled him
for most of the trip. He spent two days bouncing around the
back of the vehicle, thanks to Eastman's shitty driving, without a clue as to where they were taking him.

The second morning, he woke up to palm trees outside
the small back windows and Kodak banging on the van's
metal partition.

"Wake up, kid, time to unload."

Eastman swung open the back doors. Deacon stumbled
out, lowering his eyes to avoid the sudden brightness.

"I need to shower, eat something," he mumbled to Eastman.

"Yeah, yeah," answered Kodak, coming around the van.

They brought him to a bleak motel room, Bates Motel
style, where roaches and other creepers crawled freely. He
faceplanted on top of one of the beds and didn't move for
hours.

When he finally woke up, Deacon ate, showered, and slept
again while the Feds kept watch. They informed him they
were waiting for another agent to show up, and if he did anything stupid, they'd shoot him.

The next day, sitting in a diner outside of Miami, Deacon asked, "Why didn't you just grab me in Darien?"

"Didn't need to show people you were still ticking," said Kodak, gnawing on his bacon like a piece of rawhide. "We had a feeling where you'd end up. Plus, we wanted you to get us close to that kid, Thomas. See if you had the guts to go through with it."

Deacon pushed the food around on his plate. "He's small-time," he said with a wince, rubbing the side of his face.

"Maybe, but he bought from someone far bigger. Our boys up there will squeeze him and get some names."

Deacon wondered if his old acquaintance, Jack—the seventeen-year-old park kid who'd taken him under his wing when Deacon was just eight—was still alive. Jack had taught him everything he knew about dealing, exposing him to people no young boy should ever be around in the process. Deacon had grown up quickly in those four years, and he'd been grateful for Jack's protection and guidance at the time, believing they were friends. Now he understood that Jack had groomed and used him from the start.

Eastman made a clucking noise with the side of his tongue and passed a manila envelope across the table. It took a moment for Deacon to realize it was meant for him. The insignia on the upper left-hand corner resembled a yachting club crest, with red, white, and blue flags as well as black and gold ones, and three tiny ducks on either side of the coat of arms.

"Go ahead, kid . . . oh . . . and happy birthday," Kodak chortled, splattering his chin with bits of egg. He motioned to the waitress for the check while wiping his mouth and missing most of it.

"What's this?" Deacon unwound the string-and-button closure. Inside was the birth certificate of a guy born two years before him and some new IDs with his face and a name he'd never seen before on them. *Shit.*

"Who's Xavier Coyne?" Deacon scowled, locking his eyebrows together. "What a stupid name."

"A teenage kingpin who started to make a name for himself," Kodak said. "He's known for his insider connections to the Colombian cartels. He's provided some preliminary information, a few names here and there; we need to sell you as him. You're gonna be our informant."

"You're talking about him like he's still alive."

"He's currently being hidden in our witness protection program for reasons you don't need to know about. The FBI is resurrecting him as your cover so we can move things along with the Miami cartel."

"How's your high school Spanish, kid?" Eastman snickered.

"Wait, *what?*" Deacon could feel the heat rising up his neck. His appetite for breakfast stalled. "You want me to pretend to be *him?*"

"You already are," Kodak said. He passed Deacon several photos from inside his suit jacket.

"This is me in Connecticut. I recognize the street. It's blurry, but—"

"Connecticut, Colombia, it's all the same. Drugs, thugs, same everywhere. They don't discriminate."

Eastman glanced at the photos and snorted. "Yeah, yeah . . . could be anywhere."

"Why me? Why don't you just use *him* for the mission, have *him* be your informant?"

"He comes with a few complications," Kodak said, biting his bottom teeth into his upper lip and somehow focusing his right eye on Eastman while keeping his left one trained on Deacon.

One ugly trigger fish, Deacon thought again.

"There's some loose baggage we couldn't nail down. We needed to infiltrate Miami with a fresh set of eyes . . . a young, street-smart dealer who fits the part."

"This is never going to work." Deacon pushed the folder away. "As soon as I open my mouth, anyone from Colombia will know I'm not a native."

"The real Xavier Coyne is American, left Colombia before he could walk. You'll do fine. A local undercover FBI agent will be in constant contact with you, show you the deal in no time. And you, Xavier Coyne . . . you'll run the streets of Miami like you own them."

"Why the hell does it have to be in Miami?"

"Read the news much?" Kodak glared. He took a toothpick from the table dispenser and twirled it between his teeth. "I didn't think so. The U.S. government and the cartels are in the middle of a drug war down here."

"Dealers already know me in New York City and Connecticut. If they have connections in Miami or if my photo shows up, my cover is blown. *Please*. I'll do anything else but this."

Kodak slid the check to Eastman. "It's done," he said and stood, which was Deacon's signal to follow.

Eastman paid the bill and they escorted Deacon out of the diner, Kodak's meat hooks casually choking his upper arm. Deacon desperately searched the patrons' faces as they exited, hoping someone would realize he was being kidnapped, right there out in the open—and by the federal government, no less.

No one took any notice.

Eastman walked around the newly rented sedan and dropped down into the driver's seat. Kodak launched the toothpick from his mouth and onto a pile of broken glass on the sidewalk. He opened the passenger-side door and lowered himself into the seat, making the car dip on its chassis.

Deacon's pulse raced. "Wait, what's happening? Am I being left here?"

"If you think about running, we'll find you and charge your ass so fast, along with your girlfriend's tight you-know-what. You go missing, she goes missing. Don't test us." Kodak slammed the door.

Eastman revved the engine. He lowered his partner's window, leaned over, and yelled to Deacon, "Or get yourself killed like . . . what was that moron's name?"

"Wait, you've done this *before*?" Deacon slapped the roof with his good arm. Kodak didn't flinch. "What is happening to me now . . . where are you going? Tell me what happened to the last guy!" Thoughts of lifting the car and toppling it over on its side entered his mind. If only he were the Hulk. *This can't be happening.*

He knew the stories of Feds arresting dealers and then providing them with a more lenient sentence if they agreed to assist them in various drug stings. They dressed these young informants to blend in and allowed them to commit pre-authorized crimes to help sell their cover. Many of them didn't survive, though—partly due to their lack of training, partly due to the DEA's inadequate efforts to protect them.

"After our last couple of guys fell"—Kodak cleared his throat—"we decided that we needed a fresh face down here. You'll see, they'll like that you're new, not known yet. It'll help you fly under the radar for a while."

"Who, the cops or the buyers? Why would they trust someone they've never seen or done business with before? I sure as hell wouldn't."

"Miami likes them pretty."

Deacon shook his head. "That's not me. I'm not your guy."

"It's done."

"Wait, what happened to the last mole you used?"

Kodak shrugged like he'd just been asked about the weather. "Cartel got him. Cut up his body 'bout the time he was pushing through a half million pounds of weed and a shitload of rocks."

"The moron was mutilated," Eastman added, "body diced up with a chain saw. Then they lit him up like a marshmallow."

Deacon's mouth went dry. His head felt feverish; the street threatened to swallow him like quicksand. *This is never going to work.*

"Sounds like it went real well," he said tersely.

"Hey," Kodak said with a sneer, "if you're backing out now, we'll gladly put you away for what we found in your car back home . . . *pretty boy.*"

"You know that was bogus!" Deacon growled.

Kodak's jowls flushed a lobster red. Through tapered teeth, he hissed, "If you want a lesser rap, you'll buy from whoever we tell you to, and you'll wear a wire while you do it. You'll gain their trust so we can bring these assholes down!"

Eastman smirked. "This should be easy for you, pretty boy. Get close to these guys *and* in with their girlfriends, find out when the shipments are arriving. Simple."

"One more thing," said Kodak, his voice slippery like an eel. Deacon ignored the smile crawling around Eastman's face. "Your new boss just arrived."

Eastman stomped on the gas and sped out of the parking lot.

A white Ferrari with dark windows rolled up next to Deacon. Its passenger-side window descended, revealing its driver—a young woman in a snug pink tank dress, wide, arching eyebrows, and pretty, twinkling blue eyes. She arched her body across the seat and smiled broadly, flattening her top lip so that it nearly touched the tip of her teardrop nose. The fresh-faced California blonde reminded him of the girls in those Hawaiian Tropic ads—the ones who ran through the surf and never got their suits wet.

"Hello, cowboy. Agent Claudia Safire. Get in . . . Xavier."

CHAPTER 14

darien, connecticut

———

HANNAH'S STOMACH TWISTED LIKE SHE'D SWALLOWED A knife as she waited for Peter to arrive, unable to shake the guilt. *Can't cheat on a corpse*, she told the girl in her bedroom mirror. The girl didn't look convinced.

They hadn't seen each other since the shooting. For two weeks she'd let herself brood around the house, her days and nights running together as she hid from everyone. But after Taylor, the impossibly beautiful and airheaded boyfriend magnet—not to mention a member of Gillian's coven—had dropped by her house six months pregnant and unabashedly admitted that she'd led Toby to believe her baby was his, Hannah knew she'd had enough. She'd drummed up the courage to call Peter—and she was glad she had. His words had comforted her; he'd helped loosen her grip on the fantasy that she could have done more that night to help Deacon.

Peter, after all, knew what had happened; he'd been there to see it unfold. With him she never needed to explain.

She heard his car pull up outside and answered the door before he rang the bell; she didn't want her father to come downstairs.

He grinned when he saw her. "Hey."

"Hi," she said, a little nervous. "What movie did you bring?"

"Two, just in case," he said, slipping off his jacket. He wore a cornflower blue sweater that made his blue-hazel eyes pop. Hannah carried his jacket into the living room.

"Parents home?"

"My father. You'll hear his TV pretty soon."

Peter glanced around the room. "So how's your mom . . . and sister?"

"Recovering, I guess. I'm not sure what's going to happen . . . They're still meeting with shrinks, trying to figure things out."

She watched his eyes grow large as they perused the décor in the room, from the pumpkin and gold floral curtains to the ugly corduroy couches.

Does it look like the home of an addict? Do I look poor to you now? I wish you never came . . .

She pulled on the ends of her hair. Maybe this *was* a bad idea.

"And you?" His ocean eyes smiled into hers as if he knew something she didn't.

"W-what?"

"How are *you* holding up?"

"I-I don't know . . ." Tears sprang up, smacking her cool exterior to the ground without warning. Clearly she wasn't ready for company, even though she wanted to be. Hannah turned and hid her face. "Maybe you—"

"They're sort of comedies."

"W-what?"

"*Risky Business* or *Spring Break*?" He held them out to show her.

Hannah gently pressed her middle fingers under her eyes, wiping away the eyeliner that was surely spreading underneath them. She sniffled and smiled weakly.

"I like Tom Cruise."

"Done." He winked and headed toward the VCR on top of the TV console.

Hannah flopped on the couch by the window. She lifted an afghan blanket over her legs and curled them underneath it. Peter hesitated, watching her, then rubbed his hands down his thighs and lowered himself next to her.

She began twirling her hair around her finger. "I never asked you how you were doing since that night. You knew Deacon longer than I did. Is it weird that he's gone?"

"I only knew him in elementary school, before he and his mom moved away. We weren't *exactly* friends later. He became pretty full of himself."

"But you had warned me, saying he 'wasn't a good guy.'"

"Yeah, he was a drug dealer. Can't get lower than that," he said like it was a dumb question.

"So you look down on me for dating him?"

Peter shifted in his seat. "I didn't think he was good for you; I didn't want to see you mixed up in all of that and hanging around those types of people . . . what if you began using? I . . . I don't know. I just felt like I couldn't watch you go with a guy like that."

He opened his hand next to her, resting it between them. Their fingers nearly touched, but she didn't take it. She pulled her body up straighter, releasing the strands of hair she'd been playing with.

"But why . . ." she persisted.

A shy grin wrapped around Peter's face. He turned back to the movie, bumping his shoulder into hers. She didn't move away. It felt weird. It felt new.

"I love this part," she said, watching Cruise slide across the floor in his underwear to the first bars of "Old Time Rock and Roll."

"Me too." Peter sighed and folded his arms.

"Want a Coke or anything?"

"No, I'm good. Real good."

CHAPTER 15

south beach, miami

"EVER BEEN TO MIAMI?" CLAUDIA ASKED WITH A LINGERING sidelong glance. Deacon noticed that she tilted her chin up when she spoke.

He hesitated as they passed under the WELCOME TO MIAMI sign on the MacArthur Causeway. "Nope."

"You're in luck. It's currently going through a revival."

"Oh," he said coolly, not masking his disinterest.

"Here's a little history lesson that could come in handy. What you see on *Miami Vice* is not reality . . . though maybe one day it will be."

"I've never seen it."

"Kind of ironic, since you're going to be working undercover with the Miami police."

"It wasn't by choice."

"You *do* know why you're here, don't you?" Her voice went up a few octaves.

He shrugged and looked off to the side of the road. "To not get killed."

"To help us take down these drug cartels and monstrous criminals who have turned this place into a ghost town . . . one full of fear."

She waited a beat for his response. When he said nothing, she jerked the steering wheel, cutting across three lanes of traffic, and took the next exit at lighting speed, pinning Deacon's shoulder against his door. He was thankful her car hugged the turn—unlike his stomach. As soon as he could, he reached over and pulled his seatbelt across his body, wondering what other kinds of reckless things Agent Safire liked to do. *Seriously, she's the one in charge?*

"Ah, this is it. Your new home," she said with another chin tilt, practically singing, as she merged into the slow-moving traffic on 5th Street.

"It's nothing but old people," Deacon said, propping his elbow on his door. He rested his head against his fist as Claudia's Ferrari idled near the corner of Collins Avenue, waiting for an elderly woman and two men to cross. The man in the middle, dressed in a plaid leisure suit and cap, appeared to be steadying the other two—which wasn't reassuring, since he wobbled nearly as much. They all wore thick rubber-soled shoes and some sort of jacket, even though the temperature felt like a Connecticut summer.

Claudia nodded. "Yes, it wasn't always like this. It used to be vibrant, an exciting area with a booming nightlife.

"Uh-huh . . . *booming*."

"The drugs are making the streets deserted. The city just had a major bust a couple of weeks ago."

"My job is done then," Deacon scoffed, wiping his hands together like he was washing them.

She slammed her hands against the steering wheel. "That's not even the tip of it, kid!"

"*You* don't get to call *me* 'kid,'" he said, raising his voice. "Geez, we're about the same *age*."

Her top teeth dropped onto her boney jaw like a guillotine; her broad lips resembled the end of a lemon. She smacked the car lighter with her palm, drew a cigarette from the open pack in the center console, and started raising and lowering it between her lips like a tollgate. She tossed her wavy golden tresses behind her shoulders, then brought the lighter's glowing ring to the tip of her Virginia Slims and inhaled.

Through puffs of smoke, pointing with her cigarette hand, Claudia said, "Innocent people are dying every day because of these cartels. These guys don't *play* . . . and will kill *anyone* who gets in their way."

She took another long drag. This time the smoke streaming from her nose spread over the dash like rolling fog. She flexed her long, skinny fingers on top of the steering wheel, sending all ten hot-pink nails pointing skyward. Then she curled her left hand around the wheel like a cat's tail and swung the car up Collins Ave.

She sped down the avenue while Deacon peeked at her profile, gauging the kind of trouble coming his way. Except for the fact that the lipstick marks on her cigarette matched her nail color, she didn't appear to be someone who had it all together.

"You speak from experience?" he asked, anticipating another gruesome story.

She didn't reply at first. Then she shook her hair behind her shoulders again and said, "Yeah, I do . . . they took someone I loved very much. He meant everything to me."

"Who did?"

"The worst of the bunch, a drug lord named Chalfont."

"French dude?"

"It's just a cover."

Deacon shifted in his seat. "Is your name really Claudia Safire?"

"Not in a million years."

———

Deacon stood with Claudia in the alley between The Carlyle and his new home, the Leslie, a bright yellow and white hotel on Ocean Drive in the center of South Beach's famed Art Deco District. Its entrance faced Lummus Park, a palm-lined public stretch of grassy land with paved walkways, playgrounds, and volleyball courts that separated the strip of hotels from the beach.

Claudia was still rambling as Deacon chewed on his tongue, listening. He didn't feel like spending another moment with this chick. He wanted to run—far from her, and especially this place.

"Are you hearing what I'm saying, Xavier? *I'm* in charge of you now. I can help you become the mole we need to bring these guys down. One false move means a call to Kodak and Eastman—and then you're toast, remember that. Because they'll find you. Count on it."

She met his furrowed gaze head-on. He noted the navy-colored ring around her clear blue eyes that lit up when she was angry, like now.

The sooner I do this . . . He closed his eyes and gave her what she wanted. "When do we begin?"

Claudia practically squealed, bouncing around and nearly touching her forehead to his. "That's more like it! Come on, we have to go in through the back before people see you like this."

She looped her arm through his like she was Dorothy in the *Wizard of Oz* as they walked. She practically skipped in her pink high heels, pulling him along beside her. Her mane swung around as she talked.

"First stop, a private salon that I know. We'll start practicing your Spanish and teach you to pepper your sentences with some Spanglish, as they say. I've got tapes you can listen to. You'll need to know enough Spanish to get by, since the real Xavier Coyne has drug connections in Colombia. He was born there but he grew up in the States, so using English around the cartel will be fine. Later on, we'll go shopping. Show you how to act around these guys. *Comprendes?*"

"Great, so now you're my pimp and I'm Richard Gere from *American Gigolo?*"

"That would be your choice, but I wouldn't recommend sleeping with their *chicas.*"

"Their *who?*"

"Their girlfriends. Could get very messy." Claudia grinned wider, exposing a small gap between her front teeth. The flaw added to her bevy of eccentricities.

Deacon felt a lump grow in his throat. "Like what happened to the last mole?"

"Wasn't pretty, Xavier."

CHAPTER 16

THE FEDS BLAMED HIM FOR BRINGING THE CHILL OF Massachusetts with him. A few days after his arrival to Florida, the whole East Coast plunged into an arctic freeze. Florida was experiencing the coldest temperatures in its history, which meant Miami wasn't seeing anything outside of the mid thirties.

"Figures, you come down here and all hell freezes over," Kodak mocked, sending Eastman into a twittering fit of laughter. The agents scarfed down their hotdogs, stuffing them into their mouths like they hadn't eaten in days, while Deacon and Claudia stood shivering outside their car.

"We've heard rumblings that they're moving a large shipment in the next few weeks. Claud, we need Xavier's introduction to Chalfont to be pushed up so we can intercept the drop."

"Got it, we've already begun practicing," she said, lighting up a cigarette and nervously eyeing Deacon.

Deacon scratched his scalp, which was itchy from the bleach, and shifted his weight from one foot to the other. He averted his eyes to the ground so he wouldn't have to watch Kodak spit pieces of food as he spoke. He hated how they were discussing his fate like he wasn't even there.

"Are you even listening, kid?" Kodak barked.

"Yeah, I got it," he said.

"You better. And drop the victim act. You need to sell that you're Xavier Coyne, teen kingpin of Miami."

Claudia's private salon had ended up being the basement of some hairdresser's apartment that reeked of Giorgio—the same intense floral perfume his mother wore—and a mix of those nose-burning hair chemicals.

The yellow gingham curtains strung across the basement windows swayed when they stepped through the doorway. Deacon didn't know what Claudia's relationship with this guy was, and he found it interesting that she had her own key to the basement's exterior door.

The cramped space exploded with color: splattered neon paint colors covering its low tiled ceiling, cement walls, and floor. Styrofoam headstands topped with wigs lined one wall; rainbow racks of clothes and shoes filled the other.

A squat, burly man in his mid-fifties glanced up from his *Vogue*. He seemed uninterested at first, but his eyes sprang to life once he zeroed in on Deacon and he whistled softly, rising from the lone barber chair. He removed his long purple silk robe and hung it on the end of a rolling rack comprised of evening dresses swirling in vibrant colors. Rhinestones and sequins spilled out from the shoulders and sleeves, along with a few feathers, as if Cher had just stepped out of them.

Deacon was startled by the man's lack of eyebrows and hairless face, which contrasted with the black, curly hair poking out from his stretched white tank. His arms and legs were waxed and shiny. He wore striped boxers and black dress socks tucked inside pink slippers, and introduced himself as Vivian.

After hearing the word "transformation" roll off Claudia's lips several times, Vivian bleached the majority of Deacon's head a white-blond color, leaving only the roots dark. He trimmed several inches off the top and sides so it would easily stick up with the help of some gel, à la Billy Idol. He showed Deacon how to style it with a lilting, lisping voice. *I look like an ass*, he thought.

Next they headed to one of those claustrophobic tanning bed places a few blocks away, where he was given the same skimpy Speedo suit he used to wear as a competitive swimmer, along with some little eye goggles, and instructed to climb inside.

While he tanned, he overheard Claudia, on the other side of the door, scheduling appointments for him three times a week, confirming that bronzing would be a part of his new regime so he'd fit in with the rest of the perpetually suntanned locals of South Beach. The more his skin deepened, the more his teeth appeared to be glowing like he was in an Ultra Brite toothpaste commercial.

In between Spanish lessons, Claudia took him on private shopping appointments—early in the morning, before the stores opened and the streets filled. All sorts of elegantly dressed male and female storeowners pulled his outfits together, acting like they were sculpting him out of clay.

Each time he emerged from a dressing room in his newly tailored clothes, he didn't recognize the person staring back

at him. He looked like he was headed to a costume party—
except this was now his life.

In the last store, he paraded in front of Claudia in a pas-
tel-pink dress shirt with the top buttons unbuttoned, a loosely
knotted, squared-end knit tie, gray Versace cashmere pants,
and a matching jacket.

"Ooh, sexy. The Eurotrash look is perfect! You seem years
older, too," she crooned, flicking her cigarette ashes into the
black-and-white lacquer ashtray stand.

It made him uneasy the way her pretty eyes surveyed his
body.

"Here, try these on," she commanded, passing him a pair
of dark Gucci sunglasses. She frowned. "No, these." She
handed him a different pair and stepped back. "One more
thing . . . that's it, perfect," she said, wrapping a scarf around
his neck like he was Snoopy.

Deacon snorted. "I look like a joke."

"Let's test it out. See how people react to you when we
walk around South Beach. Especially the women."

CHAPTER 17

darien, connecticut

———

"You didn't come to see me much."

"I-I know. I-I'm sorry for that." Hannah gulped at the air. Her stomach contracted with nerves. Not wanting to be her mother's human pincushion hadn't been her only reason for not visiting her again in rehab. She'd also worried that she was interfering with her recovery by being there. She'd kept her feelings from her father and managed to avoid additional visits by claiming she was unwell, one time even using the "bad cramps" excuse on him.

"It's good to have you home, Mom."

Her father held her mother's elbow and guided her up the driveway and into the house, though it didn't appear she needed the assistance. He steered her to one of the living room couches until she gestured to him that she was fine. Still, he hovered.

Her mom looked as if she'd come back from vacation: well rested, and with some color back in her cheeks.

"Where's Kerry?"

"Gamma Mimi's. Your father brought her there yesterday."

"Why? . . . I didn't know . . ." Hannah's stomach plunged. She didn't want to be alone with just the two of them. She'd been looking forward to hanging out with Kerry and starting to be a more attentive big sister. She couldn't wait to squeeze her into a hug and play with her hair like they used to when Kerry was a preschooler. She'd missed her little sister so much it hurt.

"The doctors thought it'd be best. She comes home Friday. Gives me time to get settled here," her mother said, watching Hannah's father's face as she spoke.

"Are you hungry?" Hannah asked. "The fridge is stocked and—"

"That's all I seem to do is eat these days. I'm sure I've put on a few pounds over the last month and a half." Her mother laughed tightly.

"You look great, Mom, really."

"Hannah, I think your mother would like to rest now," her father said in the same tone he used with neighborhood solicitors. He tilted his head, motioning for her to go to her room.

Hannah flushed. "W-why? I haven't seen her . . . I just want to—"

"Go," he ordered, giving her one of those *leave her alone, haven't you done enough?* looks.

Hannah stared at him slack-jawed for a couple of seconds while her mother ignored them and was busily inspecting her hands like she needed a manicure. She'd been furious with her mom the last couple of times she visited her in rehab—but the fury had later turned into guilt, gnawing at her. Now that her mother was finally home, Hannah didn't want to leave her side. She longed to make it up to her and be that caring daughter, if she'd let her.

A sudden sadness draped over her, witnessing her father's demeanor. It was hopeless when the two of them joined forces. She stomped to her room, kicked her door closed, and dove into bed, sweeping up her pillow into her face so they wouldn't hear her. It didn't matter, though. She could hear *them*.

"Can I fix you something?" her father asked.

"That would be lovely," her mother said sweetly.

CHAPTER 18

south beach, miami

IN THE PICTURES CLAUDIA SHOWED HIM, CHALFONT reminded Deacon of exercise fanatic Richard Simmons. In them, the drug lord wore loose-fitting pastel tanks with dolphin shorts, as if he'd come from the beach. He was a diminutive man, barely clearing five foot two, with unusually long, hairy arms that seemed disproportionate to his body. His black, wiry hair sprang from his head in an irregular afro, framing his tanned, pockmarked skin and obsidian-black eyes. *Eyes of a psycho*, Deacon thought.

Beads of sweat poured from the back of his neck the closer he got to Chalfont's secret location. Two and a half long weeks of learning his lines, practicing his backstory, and adopting basic Spanish words and phrases into his speech to help him sound authentically Colombian-American under Claudia's tutelage, and he was nowhere ready to face the most wanted drug lord in Miami.

What the hell did I get myself into? If the Feds couldn't catch Chalfont, how in the world was Deacon supposed to without getting killed?

He gripped the crumpled paper wrapped around the steering wheel of Claudia's white Ferrari, smearing Chalfont's address more. It reminded him of the Blow Pop box

Jack had used to scribble down the address of his first drug errand. Second time in a month he'd thought about those days of being separated from his family, utterly scared, and powerless over his own life. He was going through it all over again, trying to survive in a world where he didn't belong. *Same shit, different day.*

He'd have to use whatever he'd learned over the past ten years to stay alive on the streets of Miami, where they took selling to a whole new level. He was no longer dealing with teens, kids around his age. In this world, whole crime families and underground organizations ruled the trade. And the Feds had assigned him to infiltrate the worst in Miami's history.

Deacon clasped the back of his neck, where moisture spewed from around his collar. The cold snap he'd brought with him had disappeared. He wiped the sweat, grumbling to himself how it could be this warm in January.

Claudia had dressed him in one of his new Miami street ensembles: a tan, lightweight suit and loosely knotted pastel tie. He looked like he was headed to a nightclub, not a business meeting. *That's how they do it in Miami*, she'd told him. She approved of the way his appearance was changing. The more he became Xavier Coyne, the more Deacon Giroux faded away.

Putting on the costume helped him become the ever-cocky teen kingpin. Adding the feigned bravado and debonair charm had also come easily around the women Claudia had introduced him to at the various nightclubs where they'd practiced his new persona. But the clothes still felt like a straitjacket.

If the Feds' intelligence was incorrect and Chalfont knew

the real Xavier Coyne, Deacon would succumb to the same fate as the previous informants. At least they'd agreed he shouldn't wear the wire during his initial meeting. Only once he'd gained Chalfont's trust would the mission to collect enough evidence to trap him commence.

The safe house that Chalfont occupied had initially been used to hide illegal immigrants from Cuba. Chalfont had started sharing the space with them under the pretense that he could provide the families protection. Eventually, he forced all of the undocumented immigrants out and his operation swelled inside.

The single-story ranch appeared modest and unremarkable from the street. The exterior had probably been white at one time. Now shadows of age stretched across its eaves and broken pickets lined the front of the yard. The vanilla house sat amongst other faded exteriors in a neighborhood that Deacon guessed few visited at night. The average Joe could have lived there, which was probably the point.

Deacon knocked—three short knocks, as instructed—and the door cracked open. After a beat, a man poked his head through. He was a striking twentysomething with chiseled male-model features whose wandering eyes traveled from Deacon's face down to the area between his legs. As his gaze dropped, the corners of his mouth rose.

He ushered him through the sweet coconut fog of suntan lotion and into a larger room whose flamingo pink walls were lined with a horde of South American men in tank tops and snug-fitting dolphin shorts. Their scant clothing set off alarms inside Deacon's head; was he was walking onto the set of a porno?

The guards' faces locked on Deacon. Whispers started. One man called him *una estrella de cine*. Deacon puffed out his chest and lifted his chin, forcing himself to not make eye contact. At first glance, one would have thought Chalfont's men were gigolos; the black machine guns and assorted armaments strapped to their well-built, tanned bodies, however, endorsed the notion that this was one serious protection detail. Chalfont definitely dabbled in paranoia—and had a penchant for beautiful men.

In the corner, static sizzled from a shortwave radio, broken by bursts of decipherable words. A well-dressed blonde sat next to the radio, copiously taking notes. *Encrypted radio network*. Dealers down here communicated in code, Claudia had told him.

The man from the pictures suddenly appeared. "Ahh, Xavier, *mi paisano*. I've heard much about you. Carlos speaks so highly, says you're going to be a *gran adición* to our team. Colombian but raised in America, he say. Miss the homeland?"

Deacon shrugged. "I left when I was a *bebé*."

"Ahh, yes, well. This is *mi compadre*, Luis," Chalfont motioned to the guy next to him. Luis towered over Chalfont. He wore his slicked hair in a low ponytail over the collar of his baby-blue suit and white tank. His eyes tightened on Deacon and he slipped one hand inside his pants pocket, as if covering a weapon. Sounds of a camera shutter went off several times. Deacon's head snapped around to either side, but he was unable to detect its origin.

"You come with *información*?" Chalfont smiled like a cheetah, revealing a few gold teeth and distracting Deacon from remembering his next line.

He feigned a cough and quickly got back on script. "*Sí,* my suppliers in Colombia show great interest in your *operación.*" Deacon hoped his newly acquired accent—which he and Claudia had worked tirelessly to perfect—and false charm weren't slipping under the weight of his faltering nerve.

"From the pockets of the Melendi cartel?"

"*Sí,* the same."

A slow grin spread across Chalfont's face. He glanced at Luis, who nodded his approval. Chalfont rotated his body to the side and stomped his foot like a matador. A large wall behind the drug lord moved aside on a track in the floor. Mountains upon mountains of white appeared before him. Deacon's eyes grew tall. He blinked rapidly at the bags of cocaine stacked like pancakes, higher than his head. He laid a hand on his heart, which was cantering inside his shirt. It was by far the biggest supply he'd ever seen. Its snowfall of worth re-lubricated the inside of his mouth.

"*My, God,*" Deacon sputtered under his breath. Chalfont's safe house also doubled as a stash house.

Without warning, Chalfont whipped one of his hairy limbs up to Deacon's head and pressed a pistol hard against his temple. The drug lord's eyes pulsed with menace. Seconds ticked into minutes without a word passing between them. Sweat surged down Deacon's face. His eyes ricocheted from the drug lord's face to Luis's, then to the stacks of cocaine before him.

Everything comes with a price, Little D, he heard Jack say in his ear. He bit down into his lip, tasting the salty iron of his own blood. His knees started caving around a torrent of nausea that was circling his body like a cyclone. Game over. *This is it. He knows.* Deacon cringed, staring into the ugliest face on the planet.

With the flourish of a marksman, Chalfont seized Deacon's hand and lay the gun in his palm, covering it with his top hand as if it were a bible. The drug lord's black-marble eyes bored into Deacon's. The moment felt intimate and sexual. The relief of no longer having a gun cocked to his head blinded him with euphoria.

Chalfont lifted his chest and inched his body uncomfortably close, his tequila breath nearly setting Deacon's lashes on fire.

"I am your *capitán*, no, Xavier?"

"*Sí*," Deacon said, swallowing the remaining retch in his throat.

June 1985

CHAPTER 19

darien, connecticut

"WHY CAN'T YOU JUST FORGET ABOUT HIM? GEEZ, IT'S been months. He's gone, you know?" Peter said, squeezing the padded armrest of the gold couch in her living room. His other arm draped across the back of the sofa, emitting an undeniable heat that Hannah found hard to ignore. It didn't help that he had arrived from his lifeguarding job all fit and tan. The cold drink she offered him he'd drained in seconds. Then he'd tried to kiss her.

Hannah stole a sidelong glance while gathering her thoughts and trying to dismiss the way his muscular thighs poked out from his shorts.

He waited for her to answer.

"I can't . . . he was my first—God, never mind." She sighed, pulling the ends of her hair across her lips, and tried again: "Not a day goes by when I don't wonder what we'd be doing if he were still here. Deacon opened up parts of me I never knew existed. With him, for the first time in my life . . . it was where I belonged. We just fit."

She released her hair and absently clawed her thighs like a rake.

She turned to him and his jaw softened, his liquid blue eyes watching her intently.

"I can't shake him. I know he's gone." Her throat tightened. "But he's still lodged in my brain, and in my dreams." She tugged her elbows into her stomach and swung her body back toward the coffee table. "It's pathetic, I know . . . I actually get excited thinking I'm going to see him out somewhere. I can't help it. I find myself searching for his face wherever I go—at the mall, in town. I can still *feel* him."

"Is that why you took that job at The Candy House?"

"W-what? No . . . I don't know. I needed something to occupy my time, distract myself from thinking about him."

Peter gripped the armrest harder while his other hand tentatively touched her bare shoulder. She fidgeted with the neckline of her tank, not looking at him.

"It's like there's this ghost between us," he murmured. He raised his arm from her shoulder and palmed the top of her head like it was a basketball, turning her toward him. "Hannah, if you let me, you'd see that I'm way better for you. Just let *us* happen. Don't stop it. You know you have me as a friend. That's not going to change. I would never put you through what he did."

He dropped his hand to her shoulder again, and his fingers traced mini circles on the upper part of her arm. After a moment, he covered his lap with a pillow and leaned back, closing his eyes.

"What?"

Peter sighed. "He was only going *through* you, like he did with everybody. Hannah, he almost *killed* you."

"*I* approached *him*."

"And he exposed you to some f-ed up situations."

"They were *my* decisions. No one made me."

He slapped the end of the couch and she flinched.

"Sorry." He took a deep breath and relaxed back into the seat. "Hannah, let me in and you'll see . . . fall for me the way I've . . . fallen for you," he said lifting her chin with his fingertips.

"I know it would make things easier . . . but this hole I feel," she said, rubbing the boney part of her chest, "it's always there, it never subsides."

"Come here," he said, folding his arms around her. After a moment, he kissed her cheek like he'd been doing for months. This time, she turned her face to him and he didn't hold back.

She closed her eyes, tasting him on her lips, willing herself to just *try*. It wasn't exactly what she wanted. *Why can't you be him?*

"That felt nice, do it again," she said almost to herself, wondering what it would be like to have Peter's hands on her.

"Let me love you, Hannah." Peter kissed her harder.

CHAPTER 20

south beach, miami

DEACON STEPPED INSIDE THE PHONE BOOTH NEAR THE dock. He left the door open and cradled the clammy handset between his ear and shoulder, shifting his weight to either side, waiting for Kodak to pick up. He grimaced as he swatted away the ever-present mosquitoes from around his face. Every streetlamp sported a halo of them, and he'd already inhaled too many to count. Between the heat and the bugs, he'd learned quickly that Miami in the summer was no joke —even in the wee hours, which was when most of his work for Chalfont took place.

He wiped the sweat trickling toward the collar of his white button-down polo. He rerolled his right sleeve and pulled the shirt from his chest to circulate some air.

He would have never been caught dead wearing this ensemble back in Connecticut. He looked like the Good Humor Ice Cream man.

"Come on, pick up, pick up," he steamed under his breath.

He rechecked around him, both for random cops and for henchmen from competing cartels who might be lurking in the shadows. The silence of the streets that time of night made him jumpy; every random car loomed, full of potential trouble.

Working for the Feds hardly guaranteed his safety. Other officers could easily pick him up—or worse, shoot him—for his connection to the cartel, not knowing his undercover status. Would Kodak and Eastman even bail him out? He'd be an easy write-off for them. He thought about what he would do if he got arrested. Revealing to an unsuspecting cop that he was an informant could put his life in jeopardy. Good guys or bad guys, he was a sinking brick in either ocean.

Sweat dripped from the sides of his neck and down his shirt. His patience waned. *A couple more rings*, he told himself. He couldn't wait any longer than that.

He was about to hang up when Kodak answered.

"Finally," he growled into the phone. "We're meeting in an hour, parking garage on 7th. Yeah, I'm riding along. Wait, though, so your guys don't get there before I have a chance to leave. I'm coming back with Luis. Claudia is picking me up outside the safe house."

All at once, the truck's lights lit up the other side of the loading dock.

"I gotta go. They're ready for transport."

Deacon climbed inside the truck where Luis waited. The air rippled with tension between them. Six months of being around Chalfont's second-in-command had done little to soften the guy. The ponytailed wonder was never one for idle talk.

"Who were you calling?"

Deacon flinched at the sound of Luis's steely voice. He needed to be more careful around the guy.

"*Mi novia*," he said evenly, without looking at him. He crossed his arms over the pit growing in his stomach. "She's picking me up later."

"Chalfont doesn't like outsiders knowing his business. You should have her meet him."

"She's shy . . . probably not."

"Rambo arrived, free and clear," he announced to Chalfont, who was busily leaning over some files scattered on the long table in the dining room that doubled as his office.

The drug lord smiled slightly, creasing the pocked skin along his face.

Deacon's brief moment of confidence in amusing Chalfont with his new Sylvester Stallone code word was instantly squelched by Luis's presence stalking him from behind. Deacon could feel the henchman's disdain crawling up the back of his head.

"Good work, Xavier. I haven't worried about these drops with you on board," Chalfont said without glancing up from his desk.

Luis cleared this throat.

"Ahh, Luis, I didn't see you there. Good work, *mi compadre*."

Luis shifted his stance behind Deacon.

Chalfont spread his gold-capped grin wide. "We should celebrate . . . *conocer* a few of my *chicas* tonight, no?"

"*No puedo* tonight, *mi novia me está esperando*," Deacon said, motioning like they could see Claudia's Ferrari through the walls.

Chalfont's coal eyes narrowed along with the corners of

his mouth. "The blonde in the white car? I'd like to meet her."

"She's a bit *tímida* when it comes to this life."

Luis walked around to Chalfont's side so he was facing Deacon. He clasped his hands behind his back like one of the guards, shifting the energy in the room.

"*Si tú eres de la familia, ella también. Preséntamela.*"

Deacon's stomach dropped. "Of course."

"She takes good care of you, *mi hijo?*"

"*Sí,*" he nodded wondering what sparked Chalfont's sudden interest in Claudia after all this time. His eyes flitted to Luis. His smirk said it all; this had been his idea.

"Can you trust her?" Chalfont said, his eyes shining wildly.

Deacon nodded, trying to read him. "What is it?" he said, but the drug lord's silence told him they were done.

———

Deacon cut across the driveway to Claudia's car, wishing he were headed back to the hotel. His stomach churned, chewing itself up inside. Chalfont had a way of doing that to him, along with making his arm hair jump to attention.

Claudia's long, balletic fingers tapped the side of the car, her lit cigarette threaded through them. She took a long drag and a Puff the Magic Dragon-size ring of pink smoke floated out. Her eyes widened when she saw the worry on his face.

"He wants me to introduce you."

"After six months, *now* he wants to know who the hell I am? No way, I'm not going in there. That's why we have *you*. I'm just decoration so you don't turn into one of Chalfont's *playthings.*"

"Change of plans, *girlfriend*. Try acting like an agent for once."

"Shit."

He walked Claudia into the safe house, half pulling her along, wanting to get the introduction over with. She wasn't in her usual heels and could keep up with his stride. Deacon knew that as much as she hated Chalfont, she was more embarrassed for him to see her in her T-shirt and jean shorts.

The second they walked through the entrance, everything was chaos. Guards yelling in rapid Spanish streamed from every hallway, buzzing between the rooms, packing up guns, and sealing the house down. Chalfont's voice rose in the next room. Deacon rushed ahead and Claudia followed, sticking close to him. He sensed her fear and grabbed her hand tighter. He thought she'd be a better actress than this.

"*Rápido, rápido,* get out of there!" Chalfont yelled before slamming down the phone.

"What is it, *capitán?*" Deacon said, skidding into the room.

"*Hay una complicación.* Go," Chalfont ordered, throwing one of his hairy brown arms at them like a baseball pitcher. His brow pressed low over his twitchy eyes at the sight of Claudia. His perspiring upper lip curled as he scanned her from her frosted tips down to her scuffed Keds.

Her pretty face froze like she was a child caught for misbehaving; her reddening cheeks betrayed her. She couldn't tear her eyes from the diminutive drug lord.

"Come on, Claud, move it." Deacon pulled her to him and took the car keys from her. They rushed to her car.

Deacon didn't know if the drug lord's "complication"

meant more federal agents or a competing cartel. He had no idea where Chalfont went when he needed to disappear. *Familia* or not, the drug lord hadn't invited them to join him.

"Why weren't we warned about the raid?" Claudia said when they were blocks away from the safe house. "That's not how it's supposed to go." She gripped her seat and pitched her body forward. "I feel sick . . . seeing that monster up close. Did you see the way he treated me? I'm a goddamn FBI agent, you bastard!"

"Yeah, you missed your chance to take him out, Claud," Deacon sneered. "What the hell was that all about back there? You couldn't even deal. I thought you were a *trained* agent."

They didn't speak all the way back to the Leslie. Deacon parked behind the hotel and glanced at Claudia. Her fists were bunched in her lap. She exhaled and leaned her head against the window.

"I haven't been an agent for long. I asked for this assignment . . . I thought I could handle it."

"Who was this person you knew, the one Chalfont killed? A boyfriend?"

Her face began to pucker. She punched the glass with the side of her hand. "No . . . my baby boy. He was playing in Lummus Park. My mom took him there on Sundays. A group of teenagers was working out on the beach. Chalfont pulled a gun on one of them. A stray bullet . . . got him."

"Kodak and Eastman know?"

"No," she said, wiping her face. "I had a different name back then. A different life. I lived with my uncle Vivian, the drag queen who helped with your transformation."

Deacon sighed. He didn't know what to say. "We can't fuck this up. I've got to get out of here. And you . . . we, I guess . . . need to put this bastard away."

"Or bury him in the ground."

CHAPTER 21

darien, connecticut

———

THE SOUND OF THE PHONE JARRED HANNAH AWAKE.
"H-hello . . . who's there?" *Damn it, how many times are they going to keep calling and hanging up?*

She collapsed onto her bed, too annoyed to go back to sleep. The frequency of the prank calls was increasing. *Summertime and the neighborhood kids have nothing better to do.*

The calls were becoming a problem. If she forgot to drag the phone into her room before bed and her father answered one, he'd yell at her like she had instigated it. Her mother, it seemed, had stopped hearing the phone altogether.

The last two phone bills she'd pulled from the mail did little to shed light. Outside of Peter's and the doctor's numbers from the rehabilitation center, an unlisted number periodically came up as "unknown caller." That was it.

She doubted it was Gillian, Taylor, or Leeza. Prank phone calls were pretty childish, even for them.

Besides, the coven had met its demise. That had been the best part of the second half of sophomore year.

The events began when Taylor, the former It Girl, gave birth in April, two months before school was out. No one at school saw her or her matching headbands after that.

Weeks later, overachieving Leeza with her frosted hair

and ice-pink lips—the one of the three most desperate to be popular—suffered the ultimate public humiliation.

Hannah was among the crowd of kids meandering off the school bus that spring afternoon when conversations rippled into snickers and kids elbowed one another toward the show down the street.

"Whoa, someone's getting towed!" exclaimed one of the boys.

"Whose house?" bubbled the girl next to him.

"Leeza's . . . I think."

"Yeah, definitely hers," another one chirped.

"Hey look, it's Repo Man!" the boy called out, sounding like Emilio Estevez from the movie of the same name. "Don't look in the trunk!"

They all started laughing and pulling away from Leeza one by one. Her so-called best friend, Gillian, followed the crowd.

"I know, right! Mr. Bradley in social studies doesn't have a clue. My dad, you know, who's a trader on Wall Street—" Leeza started breaking into one of her see-how-great-I-am stories, pretending not to notice. It was obvious to Hannah, though, that she already had.

The skinny, ferret-faced driver fueled her public humiliation more by busily repositioning his manhood several times in his grimy coveralls as he stood next to his truck, oblivious to his audience. He drove Leeza's father's BMW onto the car ramp and Leeza started to blubber, "Oh, that's right . . . I knew that was happening . . . we're getting a new car this week . . . a better one." She fumbled with the contents of her purse, searching for something she never found.

Jeers erupted around her like Fourth of July poppers, sending her fleeing into her house. Gillian sidled up to one of the boys, both of them snickering.

How fast they turn, Hannah observed. For the first time, she felt bad for the girl who seemed to have it all. Leeza was beyond popular, and pretty and smart to boot, but those things couldn't save her from the social embarrassment of her parents' money problems. Hannah, too, had learned what it felt like to be the center of neighborhood gossip after witnessing her mother and sister being carried away via ambulance last December—and how lonely it could be.

"When's it going to end, Gillian?" Hannah yelled back over her shoulder after the crowd had drifted down the street and her nemesis was walking alone up the driveway to her house. "Does acting like that make you feel better about yourself?"

The redheaded terror's shoulders tensed as she hurled one of her icy stares at her.

Just as Hannah turned back toward home, Gillian called out, "It's better than being a *loser* like you!"

Hannah's lips formed a steely smile. "I'd take that any day."

A few weeks later, the kids at the bus stop were chattering about how Leeza's family had gone to live in an apartment somewhere in Norwalk. Hearing this, Hannah had made up her mind to reach out to her and let her know that in time, those snarky kids would forget and move on to their next victim. The humiliation didn't last. Even mean girls like Gillian lost their sting eventually.

She approached Leeza by her locker the next time she saw her. "Hi, how's it going?"

Leeza continued to gather her books, ignoring her.

Hannah wasn't buying her snooty popular-girl charade. She knew she'd become a social outcast. None of Leeza's so-called friends talked to her now.

"Leeza, I just wanted to say that I am sorry to see your family move—"

The girl slammed her locker shut and turned on her heel.

"Really, you're just going to blow me off? I'm trying to be nice to you. I know what it's like to have a family that lets you down. I'm still living it. And you're going to ignore me? You don't deserve my empathy. Wow."

"Why would I stoop so low and talk to *you?*" Leeza rolled her eyes.

Blood rushed to Hannah's face. "Because you're at the bottom, too, bitch."

"You're the reason everything got so screwed up that night. Deacon would be alive if it weren't for *you.*"

The mention of his name, along with the accusation, smacked Hannah in the face. "Like you were even there." Her lower lip quivered. She sucked in her breath to hold herself together.

"All I know is what Gillian said."

Hannah knew Gillian had started that rumor around school to save face in case anyone tried to connect her to Deacon's murder. It still hurt like hell to hear it.

"You mean your former best friend? She wasn't there that night. She laughs along with the neighborhood kids as your parents' cars get repossessed, and you still believe what *she* says?"

"I don't need your pity. You're the last one—"

The busy hallway cooled around them, their classmates transfixed. Hannah rummaged for whatever crumb of courage she had left.

"It wasn't *pity*. I was trying to be a friend. But you wouldn't know because you've never *been one*." Hannah turned, staring ahead down the hall and ignoring the rubber-neckers as they split to either side, creating a path. Her body trembled all the way to class.

She hadn't seen much of Leeza after that. Before the end of the school year, Gillian had managed to attract a new crew of hungry posers—more wannabes clamoring to scale the popularity ladder for some adoration and attention. This new coven eclipsed the last one in size.

Thinking about sophomore year always brought Hannah back to Deacon.

Six months without you. Now it's summer.

She rolled onto her back and stared up at the moonlight poking in around her curtains. Sweet memories of him climbing in her window the first night they kissed flooded her mind.

The hole he'd left behind strummed inside her chest—as if she could forget it was there. Letting the tears spill out the corners of her eyes, she placed her hands over it and looked up at the ceiling, summoning his ghost from above.

I'm more alone than ever. Come back to me . . . in my dreams . . . come back to me.

CHAPTER 22

south beach, miami

DEACON WAITED OUTSIDE THE BANK ON THE CORNER OF Collins Ave and 5th, tapping the steering wheel and moving his uninjured hand from the one and three position and back again as if it were a clock. The day was already a scorcher, the heat transforming the sidewalks and streets into hot skillets. While walking through the Leslie's parking lot to his car, he'd felt its intensity through his shoes.

Claudia was inside, opening up another account for the cartel under a phony entity. She had recently joined the ranks of a few of the other females in Chalfont's operation in charge of setting up his accounts and performing most of the money laundering. No one suspected the fresh-faced California blonde was pushing money through for a dangerous drug lord, when the only thing she looked capable of pushing was Florida orange juice in a TV commercial. If the banks knew who her employer was, they didn't show it. The margin of profit was so high on these miscellaneous accounts that most welcomed her like family.

Claudia had become Chalfont's recruit after several members of his *familia* were arrested the night of the raid. No longer behind the scenes, she now dealt with the cartel's top henchmen regularly.

Deacon knew she worried that Chalfont would see through her and sense her hatred for him. Being in continuous proximity to the man who had caused her young boy's death, however, had only escalated her resolve to exact revenge.

Deacon wiped his brow and cupped his forehead in his hand as he leaned against the car door. He didn't bother with the radio. Another Madonna song wasn't going to alleviate his loneliness. He blinked the moisture from his eyes and spotted a group of utility workers fixing the streetlamp across the street.

One hardhat rode the cherry picker while the other two stayed below, monitoring his ascent. They reminded Deacon of the janitors that kept him company in those early-morning hours in Darien High's cafeteria. He remembered how they'd greeted one another with slaps on the back and animated exchanges as they moved about their jobs.

A familiar ache punctured Deacon's chest, solidifying his crappy mood. He'd dreamt of Hannah last night. During those fleeting hours of sleep, her face, lips, and curly, wild hair had flashed through his mind like a never-ending movie reel. He'd woken with his sheets twisted around him.

He shook off the image and pulled his baseball cap down over his sunglasses. Since the night of the raid, he and Claudia seldom went anywhere alone anymore, and spent much of their energy trying not to garner any attention. The charade was exhausting.

Last night's deal had been especially rough. Deacon had been with Chalfont's henchmen in the multi-tiered parking garage by Lincoln Road Mall when three police cars barreled in behind them, blocking the entrance. Deacon had been standing in front of the truck as it was being unloaded; at the sight of the cop cars, he'd quickly ducked and scrambled into the shadows. Behind him, Chalfont's men had yelled, "*Es Xavier Coyne! Arréstenlo . . . hijo de un señor de la droga* is here!*"*

When Chalfont began calling Deacon "*mijo*," jealousy among the other men had spread nearly as fast as Xavier Coyne's growing reputation throughout Miami. Being Chalfont's pet came at a price.

To his relief, the cops hadn't acted on the men's unsolicited tip. Deacon crawled around and under cars and eventually got out, and no additional cops came after him. Whether they knew about his informant status or simply didn't believe Chalfont's henchmen, he wasn't sure—but either way, he knew that he was one lucky son-of-a-bitch to have made it out of that parking garage.

The officers had sealed off the area, sending Deacon to hide for hours behind a storefront while more cop cars patrolled the surrounding blocks. It was 3:00 a.m. before he was finally able to make the trek back to the Leslie. Along the way, he underestimated the Miami streets, ignoring a homeless man in the shadows muttering something about spare change, just seconds before the shiny blade of a kitchen knife met with his hand and forearm.

Sitting outside the bank with his wrapped hand, he stared at the utility workers numbly. The skin around his ears bristled at their simple life, where broken things were fixed easily and left in a better state than they were found. It was the flip side of his world, treading water among broken people living broken lives and situations swiftly fixed by bullets and decrees of loyalty to the *familia*. It was Chalfont's way or your last day breathing.

Deacon shuddered. He'd do anything to change places with one of the men across the street.

"Xavier, is that you?" a warm, gravelly voice called from the sidewalk behind him.

The interruption roused Deacon from his thoughts—and just in time, before they spiraled off and darkened further under the sky's unrelenting heat lamp. In his side mirror, he spied one of the neighborhood regulars waddling toward his driver side window. He shifted his baseball cap off his forehead and rallied his energy for conversation.

"Paul." He nodded. "Headed out for some *leche*?"

The old man was somewhere in his sixties and dressed in a striped polyester shirt and coordinating pants that favored that burnt squash color everyone had seemed to love in the '70s. He wore his trousers pulled up over his half-melon belly, wrapped in a wide whale belt. His concave chest sprouted a few gray stragglers; they poked out from his shirt, glistening below the gold pendant around his neck.

He pulled a face at Deacon like he was an imbecile. "Where else would I be going, stupid?"

"Where's the missus?" Deacon asked. "Her wheels getting oiled?"

"I left her for dead, dick," he said flipping off Deacon with one of his gnarled, arthritic fingers.

Deacon couldn't help but laugh. The ache in his chest loosened some. Paul always managed to get him out of his head and spinning thoughts. Their short exchanges left him feeling closer to human. For a few minutes, he'd forget how far he was from home . . . *and from her.*

Out of the throngs of senior citizens living in South

Beach, Paul was the only one who had approached him. It had all started over his car, a black Chevrolet Camaro—the first type of car that had come to mind when Claudia asked what he wanted to drive in Miami. *Better than Toby's stupid red one*, he thought.

Paul had approached him the first day he drove it, asking him the car's year, how it ran, and its city and highway miles per gallon. Deacon hadn't had a clue about the last part, and that had instantly summed up his intelligence in the eyes of the old man.

"What kind of twit doesn't know that?" Paul had demanded.

Deacon was speechless. He hadn't owned the car long and this information was off script.

"Are you some rich kid from New York or something?" Paul sniffed. The guy called it like he saw it.

"Nah, born in Colombia. Moved around a lot."

Paul's string of inquiries made him uncomfortable. He found it hard to keep up his pretense with the inquisitive old man. It was something about his kind eyes and the way the lines around them softly crinkled when he spoke, even with the putdowns and expletives streaming out of him. A colorful repartee had eventually developed.

"Well, see ya," Paul said abruptly.

"Give my regards to—"

The old man waved him off and headed across the street to the drug store. Deacon turned his attention back to the utility worker coming off the cherry picker.

He looked down at the cheesy Rolex Claudia had given him. He was sure that the Feds had pulled it off some dead body. He rechecked it twenty minutes later after several customers had left the store—none of which were Paul. Bored, Deacon decided to follow him inside.

The front cashier counter stood empty, as did the aisles. *Where is everybody?* The hairs on the back of Deacon's neck stiffened. His head swung around to the sound of a child's whimper. A sharp voice cut through the silence: "Give it to me, old man!"

Deacon swung his gaze to the back of the store. Two teens had Paul backed up against a wall near the pharmacy. Both youths wore matching bandanas and identical tattoos on the side of their arms.

The panic on Paul's face clutched something inside of Deacon. The boys were taunting the old man; the bigger one was demanding the gold around his neck, the smaller one holding up an Rx bag in Paul's face—the old man's prescription, Deacon assumed.

"Hey!" he shouted. "Knock it off!" Three heads swiveled toward him. The boys' mouths dropped open.

Deacon reached for the pistol Chalfont had given him during their first meeting. He briskly strode toward them, holding the gun next to his leg. It felt cold and awkward in his hand. He prayed the gang members weren't armed; he'd never fired it. Thankfully, they didn't waste a minute before running out of the store. The smaller one dropped Paul's pills in his haste to escape.

Deacon, exhaling with relief, placed the gun back inside his jacket—but not before Paul saw it. Deacon's face pinched with shame. He didn't want the old man to see him as a thug and no better than those street kids. For some reason, Paul's respect mattered.

He picked up Paul's prescription from the ground and handed it to him. The old man braced himself against the counter, grabbing his chest and coughing violently. Then he removed the carefully folded handkerchief from his pants pocket and dabbed his forehead with it. Minutes slipped by as Deacon waited beside him, unsure what to do next. Through wet eyes, Paul tried to thank him, but the words seemed to be getting stuck.

Deacon hesitated a bit before placing his hand on Paul's shoulder. He motioned toward the refrigerator case. "Come on, let's find you that *leche* before Ida starts thinking you left her."

CHAPTER 23

darien, connecticut

HANNAH STIRRED TO THE SOUND OF THE FRONT DOOR slamming—not once, but twice. *Good, he's gone.* Her father leaving for the office was her cue to get moving. She was on the early shift that morning, serving customers behind the confectionery bays at The Candy House, a freestanding shop in the center of the mall.

She was proud of herself for applying early for a summer job. She'd known she'd need something to do when school got out—and she especially needed the money. Lately, she'd been catching her father staring out of the living room window from his recliner with an opened doctor's bill or past due notice from the rehab facility in his lap. He'd meticulously refold it, squeezing his thumb and middle finger together along the creases, before slipping it inside the torn envelope. She'd find them later stuffed under the tray of kitchen utensils. Every week, the drawer became harder to close.

The Stamford Mall's corridors converged on The Candy House similar to a five-pointed star, making it the ultimate people-watching spot. It provided zero privacy; Hannah was on constant display. She often plastered a smile on her face when a cute guy or bunch of boys strolled by, hoping to get noticed. It wasn't working so far. After dating Deacon, she found herself craving the attention and ego boost of having a boyfriend more than ever. Even though she hung out with Peter, it wasn't the same.

In between daydreams, usually involving the last cute guy who had just walked by, her tasks were pretty monotonous, from filling candy trays to cleaning bay windows. The shop was slow until the afternoon, when weary shoppers began to crave a sugar fix. Hannah ate candy and little else throughout her shift, starting with the gummy bears, gummy worms, and Swedish fish, and then moving on to the chocolate-covered Oreos and caramel turtles. By the end of it, her stomach usually swirled in pain from the zoo she'd managed to consume.

She stretched her body long in the bed, flexed her feet a few times, and let out a sleepy sigh. She'd give anything to roll over for another five or ten minutes, but she knew she'd be late if she did. Still, her body didn't move.

She blinked the sleep from her eyes, focusing on the random cracks and peeling paint around her window's wooden frame. The steadfast sunlight projecting onto the bed left her feeling something between possibility and dread.

Another day without you.

She kicked off her sheets and let the sun's warmth sink into her body and tickle her skin. She watched the little hairs on her arm rise. Her hand traveled to her breast and her nipple rose easily. She closed her eyes, remembering the way Deacon had touched her that November day when they both were off from school. He had been so gentle and loving when they were alone together in his bedroom, without parents or beepers and with the house to themselves.

Why people called it "losing your virginity," she'd never understand. She hadn't lost anything, only gained it, from the darkly romantic, handsome boy who, during those fleeting hours, had unabashedly revealed his heart to her. She had been his everything as he caressed and dragged his lips over every inch of her, creating little fires wherever he went. *And he went everywhere.* Each time he'd left a spot, she'd felt her skin yearn for more. *How is this possible?* she'd wondered. It was obvious she'd been dead inside until he showed her what love could do. *It* was *love.* They had both known it. Now she was starving for him again.

She threw her legs over the side of the bed and begrudgingly sat up, rubbing her neck. Dreaming of Deacon would put her in a funk all day if she let it. She ran her hands into her hair and shook her scalp awake, yawning hard.

She listened for any movement above from her parents' or Kerry's bedroom. She'd check on her little sister before she left for work. Her mother still had trouble getting up in the morning, leaving Kerry to watch too much TV. Her family didn't join swim clubs; they hadn't enrolled Kerry in summer camps. She was probably bored to bits, and it was still only June.

The previous night, Hannah had gone with Peter to see *Rambo: First Blood Part II.* They were now in a comfortable routine of going to the movies or watching them at his house. Peter's was far cleaner than hers and typically smelled like lemon Pledge. His mom kept their fridge stocked with snacks Hannah liked and always asked her how she was. Hannah barely spoke to her parents, even on a good day.

The nights they stayed in, Peter would microwave the

popcorn while Hannah grabbed the sodas and a blanket for herself before turning off the lights in his den. His family's nightly entertainment centered on an extensive VHS movie collection, many recorded off the TV. The two of them still checked out the rentals at Blockbuster most nights.

Hannah had learned that Peter possessed some definite opinions when it came to his cinema. He knew every actor out there, especially when it came to gory horror and strange sci-fi flicks. The more spurting blood the better. Neither genre interested her, though anything was better than sitting through the freak show at her house.

Their friendship status had changed after their first kiss in the living room, fueled by Peter's persistence and enthusiasm for more between them. She'd given in. *Why not?* she thought. Maybe if she fell for Peter, she'd finally stop obsessing over Deacon.

They'd returned to his house last night after the movie. In the glow of the TV, Hannah had studied the way his honey-colored, muscular arms wrapped around her body. She felt safe with Peter, and, most of all, wanted. He was sexy and clean-cut like a catalog model. His dark blond, feathered hair —lightened from lifeguarding—made him appear more California surfer than New Waver. His concert T-shirts had now also been replaced by OP tees and black-and-white-checkered Vans, solidifying his new look.

She liked how his sea-colored eyes studied her face, the way he gently moved her hair away from her eyes and said silly things to get her to smile. But she didn't feel butterflies with him. *Why can't I fall for him? He's so nice and caring.*

His sweet affection charmed her when they were alone.

In public, though, she couldn't stand to hold his hand, and she didn't know why.

When they made out and he touched her—nothing major, mostly over her clothes—she liked it. She felt the power of being with someone who was more into her than she was him. It was so different from her relationship with Deacon. This one was free from worries, especially when it came to where it was going, mostly because she didn't care. So she let him kiss her, and caress her. *What's the harm in that?* she thought.

Stepping from the shower, Hannah watched the water droplets travel down from the hollow of her throat to her chest and in between her breasts before she patted her skin dry. With the same towel, she wiped the steam off the mirror, leaned over the sink, and began scrutinizing her face. Her fingernails flew to her nose, finding the blackheads first. It didn't matter how much she scrubbed, they sprouted like poppy seeds, leaving pinholes in her skin after she squeezed them. Before or after the extractions, it was hard to tell which looked better. Her pores were moon craters compared to the ones she saw in other girls' creamy complexions. The summer sun helped her acne, so she'd been going outside whenever she could, turning her pale Irish skin pink with blotches of sunburn.

She opened the bathroom door and heard the theme song of *She-Ra: Princess of Power*, Kerry's favorite cartoon, emanating from the living room. She plopped down next to her little sister, who was busily snuggling her ragged Droge bear. Her favorite stuffed animal was on its last life, missing an eye and most of its fur. From what Hannah could tell, old

Princess Adora on TV seemed pretty crabby that morning while fighting off evil in the world of Etheria.

"How ya doing, Kerry . . . can I watch with you?"

Kerry's eyes didn't stray from the screen.

"Where's Mom?"

"Still sleeping," she said quietly.

"Wish I didn't have to work today . . . maybe we can do something later."

The digital clock on top of the television ticked faster than normal. Hannah would have to get moving if she was going to make it to work on time. The mall wasn't far from her house, but walking in the heat and cutting through back-yards to get to the main road always took her longer than expected.

"Maybe we'll hang tonight? Watch that show you like?" *Punky Brewster*, about a colorful ragamuffin of a girl who's abandoned by her mother in a grocery store, was another of Kerry's favorites. Not exactly uplifting, but Kerry couldn't get enough of it.

Hannah squeezed her little sister's shoulder before heading off to her room.

Standing before her bedroom mirror in her white tank and underwear, Hannah slipped her red knit skirt over her hips and stepped into a pair of matching flats. She fastened her studded double-wrap belt below her hips, trying not to hear her father calling her a harlot for wearing a denim miniskirt to church as she did. Her mother, of course, had stayed silent, not coming to her defense despite having approved of the outfit before they'd left for mass.

He'd kicked her out of the car and made her walk home

that icy winter morning. To him, she was no better than trash on the street. That had been freshman year. She'd never even kissed a boy at that point.

When Dad's away . . .

Hannah smiled at the girl in the mirror. She wasn't going to let him or anyone else make her feel like trash—never again.

CHAPTER 24

south beach, miami

FROM THE BACK TABLE OF THE COLONY HOTEL'S TERRACE, Deacon peered over his Ray-Ban aviators at the young couple arguing diagonally from him near the curb. Both of them were dressed like they'd spent a night out clubbing—her makeup was smeared under her eyes, and so was his. *They have to be baking out in this sun*, he thought. He could barely stand Miami, especially its sweltering heat. Even under the awning, his pastel polo was already sticking to him, and his day had only just begun.

"No, *gracias*," he repeated to the waiter refilling his water when he asked him for the second time if he wanted an espresso. The server was new; given how nervous he was around Deacon, he must have gotten tipped off by the owner about who he was. All of the local merchants, restaurant owners, and their staff fussed over him, as if worried that the *hijo de un señor de la droga* could blow at any moment. All Deacon wanted was to be left alone. But one couldn't work for Chalfont and not have word spread.

He liked to clear his mind in the early mornings here, in the calmness of Ocean Drive before it filled with its usual crowds of bronzed locals and sunburned tourists. He enjoyed this time of day—the sidewalks newly hosed down, the glitzy Eurotrash posers of the night still lay asleep—neither Claudia nor Kodak chirping in his ear yet.

He flipped up his collar and bit off the end of his croissant. He wasn't hungry. His lack of appetite wasn't helping his growing ulcer. He held the morsel in his mouth as he continued to watch the couple. He felt himself getting drawn in by the way her eyes drilled into her boyfriend. Something about their body language made Deacon think they'd had this fight before.

The young woman started punching the guy in the arm. She walked away, made a semicircle, and then was right back in his face, ready to go again, like a boxer. She did it repeatedly until the guy's voice crescendoed into a few colorful expletives.

Deacon missed being a teenager like that, where your biggest worries were a fight with your girlfriend. Those simple days were now gone.

He discarded the rest of the pastry and turned away, blinking back the sting. *God, I miss you. I miss us.*

Seven months ago, Hannah had surprised him on his birthday with roses. No one had made an effort for him like that before. He couldn't remember the last birthday he'd celebrated. Then . . . she'd found the *Polaroids.* And with that, her once-blossoming affection had shriveled within minutes. The disgust in her eyes was a memory he still couldn't shake. Would he live long enough to prove himself, to show her that he was doing all of this for her and for them to be together? Or had she already moved on, forgetting him forever?

Someone grabbed his shoulder and he jumped.

"X-av-ier," Claudia sang, swinging her golden hair around.

He coughed up the croissant tip still sitting in his mouth. "Claud . . . so early, especially for you. Not even noon yet."

She plopped down across from him and hijacked the remainder of his roll. She raised two fingers to the waiter, who was already carrying a couple of espressos to another table. He turned on his heel and placed the demitasses on theirs instead. Claudia pushed one toward Deacon.

"We need to strategize. *Tonight* it goes down." She smiled, her blue eyes twinkling with excitement. She was getting addicted to the danger, even as Deacon was getting sicker from it. The pain growing in his stomach coincided with Chalfont's increasingly unpredictable and erratic behavior.

His attention drifted back to the couple on the street. They were now leaning their heads into one another. The girl nodded a few times before burying her face into her boyfriend's chest; their arms circled one another.

Claudia followed Deacon's gaze. She cupped his chin and roughly turned his face toward her. "Pay attention, we don't have much time," she said drawing in her lips like she'd just sucked on the end of a lemon.

"Don't!" he warned, swatting her hand away. It was too early for her petty behavior to commence. "I know where *I* have to be tonight. Don't you have another bank to rob?"

"Funny, cowboy." She ripped off another section of the croissant with the front of her teeth.

Watching her devour his food was making him ill.

"I'm out of here," he said, clutching his stomach.

"You gotta eat. Get some breakfast."

"You and the Feds took away my appetite . . . along with everything else."

Upstairs at the Leslie, Deacon flipped on the last cassette of *Speak Spanish: The Just Listen 'n Learn Method.* Though he'd listened to the tapes numerous times, for some reason hearing the robotic female voice on the tape alternate from English to Spanish comforted him like a lullaby. He unbuttoned his top buttons, pulled his polo over his head, and made his way to the bathroom sink.

From inside the bathroom, he heard Claudia's knock on the adjoining door between their rooms. She entered without waiting for an answer and opened the bathroom door—wearing, as per her reflection, only her wide, flattened smile.

She coyly stepped inside, holding on to one side of the doorframe with her hands overlapped, like they were tied at the wrists. She leaned her weight to the other side, jutting out her hips and filling the entry. "Thought we could use a fix to calm our nerves before tonight."

She moved her wavy tresses off her chest, fully exposing her brown, goblet-shaped breasts. Her erect nipples were the color of worn brown leather. She came up behind Deacon at the sink.

"I don't think that's wise," he said, keeping his back to her and drying his hands on a towel. He didn't want to give her the satisfaction of desiring her. She could never be anything to him. He hated that he was already aroused.

He glanced over his shoulder and caught her admiring herself with him in the mirror, like they were a couple. He saw all of her in the reflection. Her body was beautiful, with proportions like that of a comic book temptress, and she knew it. She flexed her back and touched her breasts to his body, followed by her pelvis. From the look on her face, she could get off right there.

Her fingertips slid up his spine, then veered toward his shoulder. Her hot pink nails curled around his upper arm.

"If we're going to survive this life, we need one another, Xavier . . . or we'll go crazy. I know you're lonely. So am I. You'll feel better, you'll see. Don't you deserve a little *release?*" Her talons pressed into his skin as she turned him toward her. She rose on her tiptoes, raising her chin, and kissed him. She tasted of Listerine and cigarettes.

———

Her handprint on the bathroom mirror taunted him when he stepped from the shower. He wiped away the steam, erasing the evidence of what had transpired. He didn't feel any cleaner.

He wrapped a towel around his waist and splashed his face with handfuls of cool water. Resting his fists on either side of the sink, he peered into the mirror, searching for traces of the kid from Darien. Underneath the white-blond hair and tan, was *he* still there? He couldn't tell. His eyes no longer looked the same. They were blacker now, with dark circles starting in the corner of his eyes. He looked haggard, too skinny. Deacon Giroux had been erased.

He staggered backward, slamming his back into the wall. He wanted out of his hotel room and Miami altogether, before he went crazy. He didn't know who he was or why he did anything anymore. He'd become as robotic as those Spanish tapes.

He yanked the door open and found Claudia still in his

room, sitting with her legs crossed at the end of his bed in one of the hotel's white terrycloth robes. Her hair was wrapped so tightly in a towel that her eyes were pulled up, like she was in a permanent state of surprise. Without makeup, her face teetered toward homely.

The growing pit in his stomach wall resurfaced. Earlier, in the bathroom, she'd mistaken his anger for ardor. Now he could barely look at her. The sex had been swift and all business, though she seemed positively content.

"Hi," she cooed, batting her eyelashes at him.

"Stop it," he said, retrieving his clothes from the closet. The hotel dry-cleaned everything, down to his socks and underwear.

She lit one of the skinny cigarettes from the half-crushed pack of Virginia Slims 120s next to her. She took a long, deliberate drag, sucking all of the oxygen in the room through her gapped teeth.

Everything reeked of smoke because of her: their rooms, his hair and clothes. He couldn't smell or taste his food anymore. No wonder he didn't have an appetite.

"I just heard from Kodak." White puffs billowed from her mouth as she spoke, like she was chewing on them.

"Must have been a short call."

"He wants you wired tonight."

Shit. "And you? When do *you* get wired?"

Her eyes narrowed. She bit her cigarette and flicked the ashes off the side of his bed. "Don't check me, cowboy." She clamped the cigarette between her lips and tightened the belt on her robe with flexed hands, using just the webbed area between her thumbs and index fingers to do it, as if her nails were wet. She sighed after a moment, and pressed her smile back together. "I've been making copies of all the bank statements."

"Don't we have enough to get him with that *alone?*"

"Chalfont is slippery. He'll disappear and go underground, like before. We need to weaken the cartel further. Eventually the arrests will lead to more confessions and we'll have all the intel we need—and an airtight case."

"You sound so sure."

Claudia didn't respond. She stood and snuffed out her half-smoked cigarette on the side of the desk in front of her.

Classy, Deacon thought.

She placed her pack of Virginia Slims and lighter in her robe pocket. "I'm going to lay out by the pool. Interested in joining me?"

He gestured no and fumbled with the buttons on his shirt. His fingers weren't working.

"Is it your bad hand?" She actually sounded concerned.

"No, it's nothing," he huffed, turning away. He yanked his slacks from their hanger so hard that the cardboard-wrapped wire bent down the middle. The walls in his room were folding in on him; her presence was making his ears ring.

"Where are you going?"

"Out."

"See that old man again?" she asked.

He didn't look up, but knew she was watching him. He ignored her. Her mentioning Paul pissed him off.

"I don't get it."

"You wouldn't." He examined the bottom front of his dress

shirt, realizing he'd buttoned it wrong. *I've got to get out of here.*

Claudia walked past him, running a hand up his back as she did. Deacon flinched. She strolled over to the mini fridge, pulled out a can of Tab, and handed it to him. "Help a girl out, will ya?" she asked, indicating her pristine nails.

Deacon rolled his eyes, opened the soda, and passed it back to her.

"Tonight . . ." she said, motioning the pink can toward him as if it were a scepter.

"I know, I know. Chalfont told me about meeting with Thompson."

"Kodak says this dealer, Thompson, is one of the biggest suppliers down here. He used to only work with the Melendi family. Chalfont has been courting this guy for a while. Access to his routes will make the entire cartel a fortune. Get this guy on tape and he'll definitely blab in order to protect his family . . . they live here in the States. He will help end this for us."

"What happened with the Melendi cartel?"

"Rumors spread of a mole, someone working both sides."

"Like me. *Jesus.*" If things didn't go well tonight, "Xavier Coyne" and "Claudia Safire" would become fish food.

"Kodak thinks your cover is still airtight. It's going to be fine. You've met other suppliers before. But just know . . . this guy is smart. He'll smell you a mile away if you're not confident. This deal has to be perfect. You need to practice what you're going to say around him, X."

"Now I'm a one-letter target," Deacon grumbled.

"Thompson knows some English, enough to get by. He's straight from Colombia."

"Why have I not met him before?"

"Chalfont trusts you now. *Mijo*, you're his golden child." Claudia smirked as her brow shot up.

Trust. Deacon had fallen short of that word far too often to count: pretending the drugs he sold his clients were the best in town; promising Hannah he'd never hurt her; leading Thomas to believe he was his friend to the end. And now trust was aiming its sharp arrow in his direction by him toying with Chalfont all these months.

She sauntered to the door that joined their rooms. Before she walked through it, she stopped and glanced over her shoulder at him. "Watch yourself around Chalfont. I see him with his people. His crazy eyes don't match his mouth. Down here, things are not as they seem."

"Like you not being a real blonde."

"Funny, X, real funny."

CHAPTER 25

darien, connecticut

"MOM? DAD? ANYBODY HOME?" HANNAH CALLED OUT, entering the house through the garage door. Her clothes stuck to her body from the humidity outside. The space above her eyes throbbed. Between that and the lightheadedness she always experienced after her long shift and daily candy intake, she felt like she might pass out.

She stuck the same cloudy glass she'd used that morning under the kitchen faucet and chugged the cold water without taking a breath.

The ugly, burnt-orange starburst clock in the kitchen ticked loudly. The echoing silence in the house crept up the walls and across the ceiling.

Where are they? she wondered. Evidence of her family was strewn about like they'd left to escape a fire. Her father's suit jacket hung haphazardly over one of the kitchen table chairs, its cuff skimming the linoleum. His worn briefcase had vomited papers across the table, just missing the dirty breakfast dishes. Several of her mother's coffee cups and Kerry's toys littered the table and countertops, and probably would for days.

That's a lot of coffee, Hannah thought, *even for Mom*. She brought one of the mugs up to her nose, then another. They both contained the same coffee aroma, giving her some comfort. She pivoted around and looked for others in the sink.

Her hand hesitated for a millisecond over the dishwasher before tugging on the handle.

The plates were smeared in Chef Boyardee and some sort of Manwich variety, the juice glasses pink from Kerry's Kool-Aid. Behind them more coffee cups were lined up, lip to lip, on the top rack. Her father didn't drink coffee.

Hannah sniffed the inside of one, then another. The vapors from these smelled like the rubbing alcohol she'd once used to sterilize her first pair of pierced earrings.

The emptiness spread through her just like the cold water had. She was that little girl again, running through the house in her white First Holy Communion dress with bloodied knees, looking for someone to hold her.

It's only vodka. Not the pills. Her thoughts rambled. *It's okay, parents can have an occasional drink. Occasional, or every day? What if it's every hour?*

She squeezed her eyes shut to stop her brain from spiraling into ugly thoughts about what her mother did when no one was paying attention. That was the problem. No one in her family paid attention to anything. She wasn't even sure if either of her parents knew where she worked at the mall. Then again, maybe they didn't care. Now she knew why.

Since the summer began, Hannah had equated her family's home life to four spinning tops whose paths never crossed. Her dad left early most days; her mother didn't get up at all in the morning, leaving Kerry and Hannah to fend for themselves. And by the time Hannah got home from The Candy House, everyone else would be out somewhere. She couldn't recall the last conversation she'd had with her mother. *It's like I don't exist.*

Hannah yanked on the freezer door handle and started shuffling through the piles of Swanson and Banquet frozen dinners Kerry and her father dined on most nights when her hand landed on something cylinder-shaped. She pushed the boxes out of the way to see what it was. Behind the boxes, in one of the storage trays where extra ice was kept, a large jar of Jif Extra Crunchy lay on its side. *Weird.* Hannah brought it up to her face, wiping off the stars of freezer burn.

Her heart sank inside her chest.

The jar, meticulously cleaned, was filled halfway to the top with little pills: yellow ones with tiny fives imprinted on them, and blue ones imprinted with tens. The yellows far outnumbered the others, like someone was purposefully leaving her least favorite M&M color in the bottom of the candy dish. That same person had screwed the peanut butter jar's lid on crooked, as if she had done so in haste—sort of like how the kitchen had been left.

Hannah bit down on her lip, toying with the satisfying idea of dumping the whole container down the toilet. She looked around the kitchen, guessing where the other jars might be.

Will flushing them finally end this, or will she only get more? How can I stop her?

She flung open the door again, placed the jar in front of the boxes for the next person who opened the freezer to see, and slammed the door shut. A wave of control flooded her; she was finally doing something.

She grabbed a Diet Coke out of the fridge and let the fizz singe her throat. She winced, feeling the tears rise. She stared at the freezer door thinking of little Kerry, who loved peanut butter and jelly sandwiches on Wonder Bread with the crust cut off. Hannah couldn't just leave that bottle in plain sight.

A long sigh escaped her lips.

She placed the peanut butter jar back in the storage tray behind the boxes.

She crossed her arms over her chest, her fingertips searching for the little bumps on the back of her triceps. She dug and scratched. Her anxiety still rose.

Those damn doctors didn't fix a freaking thing.

———

"Hi there! So, where are we headed?" Peter grinned up at Hannah from inside his car.

"Anywhere but here," Hannah said dully as she slid into the passenger seat.

"Hungry?"

"No, I just wanted to get out of there." She flicked a hand toward her house.

"Okay," Peter said. "Let's hang indoors somewhere. It's still boiling out."

Hannah gave him a small smile as he put his green Chevy in gear.

The restaurant arcade in Norwalk had been a popular place for kids' birthday parties when she was in elementary school. Though she'd never been invited to any, the place had always appeared to contain a small circus.

Her expectations of a glittery spectacle quickly plummeted at the sight of the arcade's dark, wet-looking carpet and the locker room smell that assaulted her senses the moment she and Peter stepped inside. The stench followed them everywhere, especially into the darkest corners of the arcade. The midnight-colored carpeting covered in bright neon swirls had clearly been selected to mask more than just dirt.

Families began filtering out by the time Hannah and Peter arrived and were quickly replaced by roaming teens. Packs of clone-like, dressed-to-impress girls, from ribbon barrette-wearing pre-teens to older girls with crimped hair (à la Demi Moore in the new *St. Elmo's Fire* movie), circled groups of boys, laughing and nudging one another and trying to steal their crushes away from their games.

A few came paired and meandered around holding hands or with a hand in one another's back pockets, leaning over games that lit up their faces as they engaged in long, R-rated kisses. *Summer romances in full bloom*, Hannah thought. It was obviously a huge pickup spot.

Beside her, Peter acted like one of the kids she used to babysit, pulling her from game to game and trying to get her to join him. Her head pulsed.

"Wanna get out of here?" Peter finally said, as if realizing how little Hannah was enjoying the experience.

"Please."

They drove toward the lights in Gossamer Park. Hannah's stomach dropped at the memory of what had gone down there six months earlier. She pushed away those thoughts.

There were a few cars out that night. Peter drove to a different parking lot, near a freestanding picnic shelter that was deserted.

He took her hand and led her into the structure. The full

moon lit up the varying levels of concrete walls inside. He sat on a low wall that enclosed the fire pit within the structure, while Hannah, on a whim, chose to walk on top of a narrower wall that led up to the shelter and around the backside. All at once, she felt daring and alive, pretending she was atop a balance beam.

"Come sit by me," he urged.

"I'm showing off my gymnast skills . . . tonight, I have great balance," she announced, her arms extended wide.

"You always say how clumsy you are . . . look at you now." Peter chuckled, watching her.

"I know, right? Must have been my need to get out of the house. The night air feels great."

"What was going on with your family, anyway?"

"Nothing, just more of the same. They weren't home when I left."

"Come here will you? I want to kiss you." Peter patted the concrete next to him.

"I've never been able to do this before . . . look, one foot!" She stretched her arms in front of her like Superman and raised her leg behind her, imitating those little gauzy-ballet-skirt girls she'd always envied. She smiled, steadying herself. Her eyes flicked over to Peter to see if he was still watching—and Hannah lost her balance.

She cartwheeled to the ground and landed on her side. She went from shock to relief that nothing was broken or bleeding. Then a gush of laughter expelled from her lips, turning quickly into unstoppable tears.

Please, Mom . . .

I'm so tired of it all.

I can't keep pretending.

Peter jumped to his feet. "Oh my God, are you okay?" He stood over her. "Guess you are since you're laughing. Here, let me help you up."

"Thanks," she said, twisting her face away from him to blot her lower lashes with the side of her finger before reaching for his hand.

Peter dusted her off, and together they walked back to the concrete wall where he'd been sitting. He pulled her into his lap and circled his arms around her. She rested her head on his shoulder.

"You're sure you're okay?"

She nodded. "Just uncoordinated . . . as always." She grimaced. She knew she'd feel the fall in the morning.

"It was pretty impressive—"

"Until I spazzed out," she said, making them both laugh.

He tugged gently on the back of her hair, pulling her head back like a marionette, and kissed the front of her neck.

His hands released her hair and slid down her back. He shifted to the side so he could look her in the face, and his handsome features grew serious.

"Your eyes are sparkling in this light."

Hannah's eyes drifted off to the side. She didn't want to talk about it.

He lifted her chin and began kissing her. He turned her to face him and pulled her left leg into a straddle around his waist. Her hands traveled up his strong arms and gripped his biceps. She could feel the warmth in his lap, sense his excitement growing. It excited her to be so wanted. She closed her eyes and inched her pelvis onto him. With both hands, he positioned her butt in closer and let out a low sigh.

"Oh, Hannah, I want you so much," he whispered into her hair.

"Hmm," she murmured, hoping that was enough of an answer.

He lightly sucked on her top lip. "Do you want me . . . too?" he breathed.

She didn't know what she wanted, but she didn't want his attention and affection to stop. She enjoyed the high it gave her. Wanting to get lost and desperate to escape, she tightened her legs and arms around him.

Her actions made him crazier. Every part of him was aroused, and it made her feel powerful and in control.

Maybe I can fall for you.

He kissed her harder, and it felt good to get lost in his arms. To. Just. Not. Think. He was completely into her, and she wanted to turn him on more.

Hannah leaned back—dizzy with desire, from the heat between their bodies. Her hands cupped the back of his neck, while his found her breasts. He laid her back on the cool concrete, his fingertips outlining the curves of her body. His light touch gave her chills. She wanted this boy to do things to her; she wanted the sensations he sent through her to lessen the drowning feelings she couldn't escape.

She sucked in air between every kiss, stopping her lonely secret from surfacing. She shut her eyes, forcing the images of those coffee cups and the jar in the freezer to fade.

His hands traveled faster over her body, like he couldn't get enough. "Oh, Hannah." He dragged his lips over her face. "Let me love you . . . *I'll* never leave you."

Her eyelids flipped open. *What the hell?*

"Peter, you can't say that."

"Why? It's how I feel. I've been into you for so long. I know what I want. It's you—"

She pulled back. "It's me, *what?*"

"It's you . . . who needs to . . . to get over a *ghost.*"

"I . . . I . . ." Him bringing up Deacon at the height of them making out made her head spin. *Where did that come from?*

"Your body tells me *yes* . . . it's just that pretty head of yours," Peter said, tapping the side of her temple, "that likes to tease, and give me mixed signals all the time."

The warm smile on his face clashed with his words, which held an underlying tone of—what was it? Anger? Was she wrong to be with him like this when his feelings were more intense? She thought her feelings could grow in time. But what if she was merely using him for the attention . . . or, worse, as a distraction?

"I'm sorry, I'm being selfish," she said slowly. "If this doesn't feel right, I don't want to hurt you."

"You're not *hurting me,*" he said with a bleak chuckle. His eyes tightened, and he looked away.

"I didn't mean—"

"I'm not some *weak* guy."

"I know you're not."

Peter clicked his teeth together. "I want more, Hannah. I want to do *everything* with you because *you* want me to. Because you can't imagine being with anyone else."

"I know."

He kissed the tip of her nose and her face softened. His

smooth fingers strummed the top of her shorts like raindrops before he found the metal button fastening them . . .

Hannah jerked back and his hand dropped. She closed her eyes and leaned her forehead against his. "I can't."

"Be with me," he whispered.

"Is that a request or a command?"

"Both." He smiled, looking more like himself again. "It's okay . . . I'm not going anywhere."

"Peter, I like being with you . . . *obviously* I do," she said pulling her hair off her sweaty neck. "I'm just not sure I'm where *you are* . . . yet."

"Is that a question or a promise?" He smirked. "Never mind, don't answer that."

"You make everything sound so sexy." She laughed, hoping to lighten the air between them.

Peter cocked his right eyebrow. "Be with me and you'll realize . . . just how crazy you *are* for me."

CHAPTER 26

south beach, miami

DEACON UNFOLDED HIS HEAVY LEGS FROM HIS BLACK Camaro and emerged onto the dark, palm-lined street that connected some of the largest houses in Miami Beach. He swallowed back the acid rising into his throat and stood gingerly, holding his abdomen. He most certainly had an ulcer.

He hesitated, staring at the car keys in his hand, flirting with the notion of running away, driving far out of town, and never being seen again. He could run for the rest of his life from the cartel and Feds. Who was waiting for him back home? A loving family? Friends? *What a joke*, he thought.

But then there it was. Hope.

Hope that she still cared.

It was all he had left.

"Damn hope," he grumbled, and dropped the keys inside his coat.

His weighted legs moved like he was walking in a swimming pool. His brain switched to autopilot as he crossed through the tall hedges and into the gated driveway.

He was walking toward his own suicide.

The cartel's new safe house—a pink, four-bedroom mansion on the Biscayne Bay—was a benign enigma to its well-to-do neighbors on either side, all of whom would surely move if they knew of its occupants.

The house's street-side entrance opened to a large circular driveway with tall palms planted in a wreath formation at its center. The full moon reflected off the lush leaves like a spotlight.

Deacon stopped at the sound of voices streaming out into the night air from inside. It didn't matter how many there were; everyone would be armed. And in a few short hours, sunlight and the Feds would crack this place open.

This could be it.

He paced a few times in front of the ring of palms like they were his jury. He cupped both sides of his neck to calm his nerves and replay his spin on the story before Chalfont drilled him. *How did you let this happen . . . so many of my men gone . . . and yet you get away . . . how did you manage to escape?*

He climbed the stone steps with a hand over his exploding heart and the wire that was taped to his skin, underneath his shirt. He was reaching out to knock when the double doors sprang open and Pedro, one of Chalfont's henchmen, lunged at him. Without a word, he took hold of Deacon's collar and dragged him into the house.

Oh, shit.

They were equal in height and had never officially met. Deacon didn't interact with most of Chalfont's henchmen—mostly out of fear and his inability to keep up with their Spanish. Tonight, Pedro's round face appeared two shades darker than Deacon remembered it being, and his eyes were blood-red, like every vessel in them had burst. His hair and face were wet with dirty sweat. His strength and rage took Deacon by surprise.

"*Tú, puto!*" Pedro spat, pulling him down the hall and into the kitchen.

"W-where's Chalfont?" Deacon sputtered. "There was a problem. Thompson never showed. The cops—"

"You *cobarde* . . . you abandoned them! *Mi hermano* was with you tonight, and you just ran off!" Pedro screamed through spit and tears. He pulled Deacon's face closer to his and a drop of his saliva flew into Deacon's eye.

"I didn't, I swear," Deacon said, cringing away. "I got lucky. I thought one of the cops was Thompson. I didn't know until he started shooting at us!"

"You abandoned your *hermanos*, my blood, you are *un traidor*, disloyal to *la familia!*" Pedro cried, bringing a knife to Deacon's throat.

Deacon cursed himself for not seeing this coming—the day that one, if not all, of them would turn on him.

He fumbled, trying to get the gun from inside his coat.

Pedro grabbed him tighter and pressed the blade deeper into his skin. Deacon's knees caved; the blood from his upper body rushed to his feet.

People ran through the house like thunder, speaking feverishly in Spanish. *What is happening?*

A round of shots peppered the wall behind them, causing them both to jump.

"*You*, Pedro, you're the *traidor*. Leave *mi hijo* alone!" proclaimed Chalfont before firing into Pedro's chest. The knife and Pedro dropped to the floor, his blood decorating the wall above the stove.

The room spun. Deacon grabbed onto the nearest counter. When the shouting ceased, Deacon looked toward the sound of a woman crying and saw only Chalfont with Luis at his side, both of them statues of composure.

Deacon coughed like mad. Neither of them said a word. *He's going to kill me next.*

"C-Chalfont, listen, we had a problem with the transport," he blurted, trying to catch his breath. "Thompson never showed. The police ambushed us. They intercepted the drop at the docks. We lost a shitload, *capitán!*"

Chalfont's beady pupils shrank into pinpoints. "Luis, have one of the men clean this up," he ordered in a low, razor-sharp tone. He slung his gun over his shoulder, his eyes never leaving Deacon's. Luis's look of amusement confused Deacon even more.

The drug lord's face stiffened. His cold, demonic eyes told Deacon to follow him.

They entered a side room that had been converted into his office. Facing him, Chalfont tilted his chin up toward the door. Deacon closed it behind him, afraid to say another word.

He didn't have much time to take in the small room before the drug lord stomped toward him and slapped him across the face.

"Do not speak to me in that manner, Xavier! I'm not some lowlife drug dealer. I'm the Lord of Miami. You will respect me!"

Stunned, Deacon took a moment to realize his mistake. Chalfont's eyes blazed wild and glassy, like a crazy person's. Fear rose up Deacon's scalp, sending every follicle to attention. This man may have saved his life, but he was no ally.

He bowed his head to the drug lord. "*Si, perdóname, mi capitán*—I'm sorry, *lo siento*."

Chalfont grabbed Deacon's hip and yanked him closer.

The wire.

The drug lord's fingers were inches from the part that traveled down his stomach and around his back. Deacon steadied his face, trying to conceal his panic.

"Show me," Chalfont ordered. "Show me you're sorry, *mijo. Show me.*"

"*No comprendo, capitán.*"

The drug lord's eyes surveyed his face, resting on his lips.

Deacon's eyes widened as he realized what he was asking.

Yelling on the other side of the door made them both flinch. Luis barged in, announcing, "Men in boats are coming in. Xavier may have been followed."

"Come!" Chalfont commanded both of them. He ran his fingers down Deacon's back before striding past him and out of the room.

CHAPTER 27

darien, connecticut

"I THINK I'M GOING TO STAY IN TONIGHT," HANNAH SAID, twirling the phone cord between her fingers.

"I can come over," Peter pressed.

"I'm tired from work. We'll hang out tomorrow night . . . okay?"

She hung up and felt her shoulders relax for the first time that day. She turned up her cassette player just as the Violent Femmes struck the chorus of "Kiss Off." Her body melted into the floor, and she rested against the side of the bed. She closed her eyes and let the pulsing music become her heartbeat. She didn't want to think about where things were going with Peter or whether she was being unfair to him.

I like being with you. I like fooling around, too. Just don't try to be my boyfriend, okay?

Guys do this all the time, make out with girls who are more into them. Is it wrong to stay in a lopsided relationship? If I end things with him, am I throwing away someone who is good for me? Do I just need more time?

Hannah called BS on herself. Truth was, she couldn't stand the thought of being alone for the summer.

She knew she was a terrible person for feeling that way. But Peter understood how she felt and he'd chosen to stick around, she reasoned. And she liked going out with him. They usually had fun together. But just how much longer could she hold him off?

"Hannah!"

She scrambled to her feet and yanked open her door. "Yeah, Dad?" she said, leaning out of her bedroom. She heard the jangle of keys near the front door.

"I'm taking your mother and Kerry to Dr. Shapiro." He was the family counselor the rehab facility had recommended. After their last appointment, Hannah had found out from Kerry that the three of them had gone to Carvel.

"Dad, I need to talk to you about that."

"It'll have to wait. They're in the car and we're running late." Without hesitation, he slammed the front door, sending the transom windows on either side shaking.

Hannah watched them pull out of the driveway, wondering why *she* never went to the counseling sessions. Wasn't *she* part of the family?

She sank to the floor again, pulled her knees to her chest, and let the sadness slice into her. *It's not getting any better. This pain inside won't go away. Everything's so screwed up.*

She pulled her diary out from underneath her mattress and scrawled the words onto the page until the tears came.

STOP IGNORING ME! Peter wants me too much. You and Mom want nothing to do with me. I want loving parents to exist and for the love of my life to still be here. Deacon understood what this feels like. Feeling

*insignificant, being ignored. I need to hear your voice
again. I felt whole with you. Now I'm using someone else
to ease the pain. I HATE MYSELF. I don't care enough
to walk away, give up the little power that I finally
have . . .*

Hannah's head whipped around in the direction of her
cassette player. *That damn song again.* Her heart dropped like
an elevator every time she heard it. She closed her eyes and
let its haunting lyrics have their way with her. *Who will pick
me up when I fall?*

She threw her diary to the floor and clutched her knees
tighter. If she heard that mesmerizing Cars song, "Drive,"
one more time, she was going to lose it. All of the questions
in the lyrics seemed aimed at her, as if Deacon were singing
it. Figured, it was about a girl on drugs, spiraling out of control. He had been her drug.

She'd dreamt of him the previous night, and all day her
insides had felt wrung out. The more she thought about how
she'd been with Peter the other evening in the park, the more
guilt plagued her. *You don't belong with him,* the nagging voice
in her head insisted.

She shoved her diary back under the mattress and froze.
I know how I can hear your voice.

She grabbed the phone off her bedroom floor and
flopped down on her bed. She remembered the first time
she'd called Deacon's private line, thinking how rich he must
be to have his own number. He'd brushed it off, acting neither proud nor embarrassed by his parents' privileged life, just
suffocated by it.

Maybe there's an answering machine or something, she thought. She dialed and pinned the handset between her neck and shoulder. The first few rings made her heart sing a little. Hope, even. But as the ringing continued, she started to feel like an idiot.

"Hello?" a male voice answered.

Hannah's heart flipped out of her bra. *Holy shit.* Her body snapped straight up in the bed. The receiver wobbled next to her face. She'd contacted a ghost.

"Who's this?" the guy demanded.

"Who's *this*?" Her mind raced, trying to recognize the voice. It sounded too young to be Deacon's father. *Could the number have been reassigned that quickly?*

"Toby Giroux."

She gasped and hung up. *Oh my God, oh my God. One son dies, the other one moves in? And your son's killer, no less—what the hell?*

She sprang from the bed and began pacing around her room. She crossed her arms, clenching her elbows, and soon her fingers found the small bumps on the back of her arms, readied to scratch, pick . . . soothe.

His voice transported her back to that awful night. Deacon's half brother had given her the creeps the first time she'd met him, and now, after everything that had happened, she understood why.

She leaned over her dresser, holding its sides as if it would carry her over the rapids. The cruel memories pummeled her forehead like bullets from a semiautomatic. She clamped her eyes shut to stave them off. She could see Toby in Gossamer Park on that dark December night, his knees sunken into the frozen ground, the end of the gun slipping from his temple after realizing he'd shot his brother.

No, no, no!

She'd tried to get to Deacon before it was too late. But Toby had turned the gun on her. "*No witnesses,*" he said. *Bang.*

"Stop it!" she commanded, the base of her palms crushing the sides of her head. *Stop it.*

Photographs in her mind of Deacon's last breath . . . the way the shiny gun wobbled in Toby's hands . . . the blood spilling from underneath the knit hat she'd used to apply pressure to his chest . . . each image shifted like ghostly patterns in a kaleidoscope, tearing slowly away and leaving a cold, blank page.

Her eyes fluttered open. Still holding on to her dresser, she peered at the sweaty face in the mirror. *It's over; it's over; you're okay now.*

She collapsed onto her bed like a ragdoll, her emotions spent. She lay like that for several minutes. She didn't want to dwell on the events that had taken Deacon away, she wanted to relive those days of calling him whenever she wished.

She picked up the phone and dialed his pager this time. At the tone, she entered her family's number and waited for it to ring back. She held her finger down on the receiver like she used to, not wanting to waste a minute of talking to him. She felt stupid, but she didn't care. She wanted to taste those sweet, fleeting days again when everything was new, when they'd steal moments together without her parents knowing. When he'd meet her at the library, where she was supposed to be studying, and they'd wind up back at his house and in his bed.

The phone in her hand rang. *Holy . . .*

"What?" an annoyed voice bellowed.

Hannah's tongue stuck to the roof of her mouth, choking her words. "H-hello?" she croaked.

"What?" the voice grew louder and more impatient.

"Jade?"

"Who's this?"

"Hi, it's . . . H-Hannah." She popped off her bed and couldn't stand still.

"What do you need?"

"Ahh, nothing . . . I just—"

"Listen, don't call my pager unless you want to buy."

"N-no, I didn't realize you took over Deacon's business."

"Yeah, well. I'm slammed right now."

"I guess I just miss him, wanted to hear his—"

"Yeah, not me. I'm fine without him."

"But—"

"He's fine where he is, Hannah. Drop it!" Jade shrieked before she hung up on her.

The dial tone buzzed in Hannah's ear. *He's fine where he is? Like buried, underground?* "What a bitch." She stared at the handset cradled in her palm. Her head felt severed from her body. *What the hell?*

In a matter of minutes, she'd managed to speak to two of the people from that ill-fated day.

"Oh my God, get a grip!"

CHAPTER 28

south beach, miami

———

"WHY DO YOU CARRY A GUN, YOU A COP OR SOMETHING?" Paul asked, motioning to one of Deacon's pockets.

Deacon glanced at him, then back to the Mini Mart on the corner, watching its clientele closely. Though they were in Paul and Ida's neighborhood, his vigilance never faltered. "No," he said, wishing Paul would drop it. He wanted to keep these somewhat normal moments with him separate from the chaotic ones he lived in Chalfont's world.

"You're not mixed up with one of those street gangs, are you?"

Deacon lowered his baseball cap over his aviators. "Paul, I can't go there, and you don't want to know. You hungry, old man?"

Paul snorted. "I could eat."

Deacon walked with him to the Nathan's hot dog cart on the corner, matching the old man's slower, bowlegged stride. Deacon thought for a split second what a hot dog would do to his ulcer and shrugged it off. He liked being around Paul and found himself looking forward to their time together more every day.

Deacon raised two fingers to the vendor.

Paul tipped up his wraparound sunglass covers and squinted at something across the street. "See that building over there? My grandmother used to own it and a few others in this town. She was one tough lady. Shrewd as hell. It was rare for a woman to own real estate back in those days. She was from Colombia, like you. Came here with nothing. Worked hard and created a life here. One tough Latina. A real looker, too."

"What? I thought you were Jewish. How do you have a Colombian grandmother?"

"Imbecile," Paul scolded. "This is America, your ancestors can come from anywhere. My mother was Jewish, God rest her soul. Not that 'Jewish' is a nationality. You think they don't have Jews in Colombia?" He chuckled. "Anyway, where's your family, boy? You an orphan?" Paul asked these questions loudly—a tendency of his from when his hearing was damaged after a bomb detonated near him during World War II.

Deacon eyed the man behind the food cart, who was obviously listening. "Paul . . . stop."

The vendor handed Deacon his order and practically saluted him. "On the house . . . sir!"

"What in the world?" said Paul, wheeling his body around toward Deacon. "They think you're the mayor now?"

Deacon rolled his eyes. It didn't matter what part of town he was in, they all feared him and his connection to Chalfont.

They walked back to Deacon's Camaro, then leaned against the car to eat their hotdogs. The conversation flowed easily, and Deacon's shoulders began to relax. A part of him wanted to come clean and tell Paul everything.

"This car's filthy," the old man said.

"Yeah, it is." Deacon agreed with him, for once. His father's face flashed in his mind. He frowned, thinking of how pristine Kingsley kept his fleet of sports cars, like they were the most important things in the world to him, apart from his gun collection. They probably were.

"A man should take care of his things, have some self-respect, especially when he owns a fancy car. You don't even lock it, dingbat."

Deacon laughed. "It's not high on my list. If they want it, they can have it."

Paul scowled. "You didn't earn it, then. Do you know what it means to work hard and deserve such nice things?"

"*I* work, okay?" Deacon retorted. "Every day."

"Is it illegal?"

"Are you a cop, Paul? What's with the third degree today?"

"My gut. Plus, you keep looking over your shoulder. You in trouble?"

"That's another question."

"Whatever kind of people you're mixed up with, you need to drop them and start living a decent life. You're not doing right. You need to change your ways before they change you . . . for good. These new Colombians that come here now are nothing like my grandmother. These crooks give my ancestors a bad name. Low-life criminals are single-handedly destroying Miami and this country. Vets like me who protected this country's freedoms are getting robbed and shot up every other day. There's no respect anymore. These streets have changed. It's heartbreaking."

"So you say," Deacon said dismissively, waiting for his rant to end.

"I've seen it. Men who surround themselves with bad people, it just leads to more bad choices and bad things happening, until one day you can't go back, even when you try."

"You wouldn't understand, Paul—"

"There's always a way out. Figure it out, dickhead."

"Why do you call me these names, old man?"

"Cause you're a knucklehead. But you're all right . . . mostly."

Deacon sighed. "You're mostly okay, too, Paul."

Paul finished the last of his hot dog, leaving remnants of mustard in the folds around his mouth. When Deacon pointed to his own face to show him, the old man wiped it away and grinned, sticking out his picket-fence dentures like a snapping turtle.

Deacon couldn't help but smile. For some reason, he just liked the guy. He wished he'd gotten to know him under different circumstances.

"Where's that blonde of yours . . . Fraud, is it?"

Deacon snickered. "You mean Claud? Claudia's at the bank."

Paul whistled through his teeth. "She's there a lot," he said, eyeing him askance. "Got a figure on her, that girl, like a pinup. You like her?"

Deacon didn't answer. He bunched up his wrapper and threw it in the garbage.

"What? Blondie's not keeping your bed warm?"

"It's a long story . . . not one I'm going to share, either."

"Fraud's always smiling when she's not saying much. Her eyes, though . . . hard as glass. Probably her heart, too."

Deacon smirked.

"She doesn't like me much. I can tell she's not too keen on you having friends of your own."

"You're probably right."

"Xavier, you're young, smart, and not bad looking. I can tell you're not happy. What are you doing with your life?"

"Trying to get home, Paul, trying to get home."

CHAPTER 29

darien, connecticut

_I wish I had a mother. This one wants nothing to do
with me. And never has. She's a stranger. One that
swallows little yellow and blue pills and sips her vodka
out of coffee cups all day. Dad walks around the house
calling So-Called Mom's name while she spends the day
holed up in her room. He's stressed about her and the bills
that are piling up. He at least talked to me once in a
while when she was gone, away in that facility. Now I'm
invisible again. So-Called Mom doesn't even hear little
Kerry yelling for her. We're both back to walking on
eggshells, trying to stay hidden and away from
everything. Dad keeps trying to get through to her. It's
because So-Called Mom lost her first baby and has no
more room in her heart for the rest of us. I wish I had a
mother. I could use one now more than ever._

Hannah shoved her diary aside. Her eyes stung from her
eyeliner dripping into them. She bet she looked a mess. She
blew her nose and glanced down at the letter next to her.

Last year Mrs. Myers, her English teacher, had tried to
help her deal with the kids at school, the same ones who used

to snicker when she passed by and call out her name, teasing her. She'd always felt like an outsider. She never fit in or had friends. Strangely enough, Deacon had been her first friend —and he'd quickly become so much more.

Hannah had committed her teacher's words to memory:

You are better than them. Smarter. Braver. Stop getting in your own way. Believe in yourself. You, Hannah Zandana, can be and do anything. They're afraid of you. Now act like it. Go.

She had started to stick up for herself after that and ignore the teasing, which eventually died down. Mrs. Myers had also encouraged Hannah to write. She'd helped her apply back in January for Bard College's three-week Young Writers Workshop at Simon's Rock in Massachusetts for "gifted and promising students." Her acceptance had arrived today. Hannah crumpled up the paper, along with the rest of her dreams. There was no way, not with their money issues. She knew not to ask.

She felt ugly for being so selfish. How could she think about herself now, when her family was writhing in utter turmoil? Especially Kerry. She was so young. What was our messed up family going to do to *her*?

"Oh, Kerry," she whispered, covering her nose and mouth with her hands. "Little girls need a mother. I know . . . because I need one, too."

- 154 -

July 1985

CHAPTER 30

darien, connecticut

HANNAH LEANED HER BUTT AGAINST THE DISPLAY CASE with her back to the mall traffic. It had been especially slow that day; she knew she wasn't snubbing anyone. Her manager, Howie, always wanted them to stay busy refilling candy trays and making sure the bays were cleaned and straightened. He still hadn't forgiven her for using Fantastik on the glass. Seriously, who knew there was a difference between glass versus all-purpose cleaner?

The morning droned on as she restocked shelves and adjusted the temperature in the refrigerated case. The warmer the day, the more the chocolate formed little ladybug-sized water droplets. She eyed the torn cuticle she desperately wanted to rip off and noticed a residual of her morning's work under her left middle finger. She sighed.

She was licking the last bit of chocolate off her nail when a deep, melodic voice interrupted her: "Excuse me?"

Hannah's head swung around, her hair falling into her eyes. With her finger embarrassingly still in her mouth, she froze at seeing the striking boy with the deep-set eyes standing before her. He looked about the same age as her. She'd never seen him before. His pretty face unsteadied her right away. His smooth cheekbones melted into chiseled hollows as if he was sucking them in, down to his *GQ* chin. She forgot to breathe.

"Hi, can I help you?" she sputtered and reached for a piece of tissue paper, ready to retrieve his request. Her day had finally gotten interesting.

"Are you guys hiring?"

"Sure, let me get an application." Hannah smiled, dropping the tissue, and walked around the bay to find the form. She passed him the paperwork, along with a pen from the register. "We'll need your driver's license."

She pretended to refill the same tray of chocolate caramel turtles that she had an hour ago. Its location provided the best angle from which to study the boy further.

He wore a slightly wrinkled white button-down shirt and khaki pants with a denim jacket tucked under his arm. *Preppy, but not over the top.* Something about his attire told her he was filling out applications all over the mall.

Rarely did a cute boy approach the candy counter. Most of her customers were harried parents with whiny kids or teenage girls traveling in packs. She dreaded the latter more. The stuck-up ones she recognized from school pretended not to know her, even the girls she'd met through Deacon. For fun, she liked to address one by name, which seemed to make everyone in the pack uncomfortable. *Wait, you're friends with her?* they'd whisper loudly, if they were especially obnoxious. On cue, the girl would shake her head vehemently and rearrange her face to convey: *Like that could be possible.*

Hannah saw it all: queen bees arm in arm with their fawning sidekicks, usually trailed by the weaker members of the clique. Each worked harder than the next to stay in the pack and avoid expulsion from the group. It amused her how they dressed alike in their Limited Express clothes—boxy, colorful cut-out T-shirts over a matching tank, paired with jean shorts or a miniskirt with white Keds and slouchy socks. They styled their hair the same, too—feathered away from their face, and usually in full imitation of the queen bee, who always wore it best.

Last summer it would have bothered Hannah how they treated her. How they couldn't stand up to their friends and acknowledge a fellow classmate, regardless of her social standing. All she saw now was a "girl prison," one she no longer envied. *Pa-the-tic,* Hannah thought.

The cute boy looked over his application for a moment. Then he came around to the other side of the shop to find her. He *was* handsome.

Hannah grinned. "All done?"

He handed her the application and his driver's license. She wrote his license number on the form and handed back his ID. *Bryan Summers, nice name.*

Howie, her manager, appeared out of nowhere just then, clearing his throat behind her. He was a cranky, hungry-looking man with a slight build and a long, thin nose that held up chunky glasses. His breath and body odor smelled of pickles. It was so pronounced that Hannah and the rest of the staff kept conversations with him to a minimum to avoid the rancid cloud that followed him.

Howie coughed again and she didn't bother to turn around.

She glanced at the application. "Oh, you go to Trinity. I'm at Darien."

Bryan flashed a polite smile, and Hannah immediately felt herself get swallowed up by the whiteness of his teeth and the deep dimple that creased his chin. The moment lasted only a millisecond, to her dismay; then he averted his eyes and turned away, taking his radiant smile with him.

She watched him walk away, wishing she could think of something else to ask him. Then his application got ripped from her hand—and a strong dill odor invaded her space.

She turned to see Howie ripping the paper in half.

"Why are you doing that? she demanded. "He seemed nice."

"We don't hire that type," Howie said, wrinkling his nose.

"Why, because he's black?" Hannah asked, already knowing his answer.

"Get back to work."

At the end of her shift, Hannah spotted Bryan walking down one of the mall corridors. She grabbed her LeSportsac from under the candy counter and walked quickly after him. She began fumbling with the zipper on her purse as she passed him, hoping he'd notice her going by and say something, but when she looked up, he was studying something in a store window.

"Any luck today?" she asked, making sure he heard her.

"What?" he turned, a blank look on his face.

"You know, with getting hired?"

He looked perplexed. Then his face lit up. His wide smile reached his eyes and made them brighter. His *GQ* dimple also returned. "I must have applied at a zillion places," he said, raising his brows. His animated face immediately put her at ease.

"It's kind of late in the season. They usually hire in the spring for summer jobs."

"Yeah, figures."

"Where else are you looking?"

"Bennigan's."

"Ever been a waiter before?"

"Nope," he said with an exaggerated, robotic nod "yes."

The corners of Hannah's mouth curled up. She liked his attitude.

"They said that the best I could get without experience was seating host. Meaning no tips. I'm Bryan, by the way," he said extending his hand. His fingers felt cooler to the touch than hers, and smoother, too.

"Hannah."

"Want to get something to eat?"

———

They sat across from one another at a booth in the food court. He got a McDonald's meal with a Big Mac and large fries. Hannah's stomach was still churning from the zoo of gummies she'd eaten that day. She decided on a strawberry shake when he offered to pay for her. The additional sugar didn't help, but at least it was cold.

"So," Bryan said, "you go to Darien. Do you know Steve McGuiness?"

"No," she said quietly. She hated questions that started with "do you know," because she usually never did. It made her seem like a loser; how could she possibly not know the person they were talking about? *Everybody knows so-and-so, he's the funniest, best guy ever. What? Don't you have a pulse?* "It's a big place," she added.

"He just graduated," Bryan said.

"Oh . . . I'm a junior." *See, not even in the same grade.*

"Me too." He smiled. "Got to start earning some cash if I'm going to drive to school this year."

"At least you have a car. So, where do you live?"

Their conversation flowed effortlessly. She couldn't believe they'd just met. He was funny, too, in a self-deprecating way, which she hadn't expected. *Someone as good-looking as him could definitely be stuck up*, she said to herself. Then she realized she was doing what she found annoying in other people—making quick judgments before getting to know someone.

Just when she thought they'd run out of things to say, he came up with more questions for her. "So, what kind of movies do you like?"

"Comedies mostly . . . romantic ones too." She laughed and pulled at the ends of her hair. She tucked her clammy palms under her legs to stop her urge to twirl it. "Guess that sounds pretty lame."

"Not at all. Those are good." He smiled, watching her face, and took a sip of his soda. She wondered what he was thinking. "So no slasher or action movies for you?" he said.

"Only if Freddy Kreuger wasn't so ugly and Arnold Schwarzenegger wasn't as annoying."

"Who would win in a battle, Freddy or Arnold?"

"Let's see . . . both are pretty cranky . . . The Terminator does dress better . . . though Freddy does like his hats and horizontal stripes."

"That he does," he nodded, chuckling.

"Freddy can walk through walls and perform supernatural things on people in their sleep. Arnold just blows everyone away. He does have a great accent, though."

"Hmm . . . true, all true."

Hannah shrugged. "It's a tie. Unless . . . Freddy is invisible and his powers work on machines. Then it's all Freddy."

Bryan laughed. Hannah liked being able to make him do that. How funny it was that someone as handsome and as nice as he was could find her interesting when most of her male classmates ignored her. *Why is that?* she wondered. *Once a loser, always a loser in their eyes.* She wished some of those kids could see her now.

"What do you like to do after work?" Bryan asked. "Let me guess . . . *shop?*"

Hannah smirked, lifting one side of her mouth, "Yeah, especially at Chess King. Wish I had *that* employee discount."

"Hey, hey . . . not fair . . . I just applied there." He laughed, raising his palms in defense.

They were both smiling when Hannah noticed someone approaching her booth out of her peripheral vision.

"Hey," Peter said stiffly, unloading his attitude full-throttle in her direction.

"H-hi," she replied. Her eyes bounced between the two boys. "Ah, Peter, this is Bryan . . ."

Without acknowledging him, Peter blurted out, "I was waiting outside for you."

"Oh, I didn't know. I usually walk home."

"Yeah, well," he said, looking away and shifting his weight from side to side.

She felt caught, like she was doing something bad. But was she? She rose out of her seat and then remembered her shake. She turned to grab it—and that's when she saw him, staring at her from several booths away. *Oh. My. God. No way.*

Hannah glanced back at the table, feeling dizzy. "Nice meeting you, Bryan. And good luck with the job search."

"Thanks." He nodded in the same polite manner he'd used applying at The Candy House.

———

Hannah stopped Peter as he was opening his car door. "What was *that* all about?"

He looked off to the side. "Are you *dating him?*"

"*What?* No! I just met him. He applied for a job at my work."

"Now you're working together?"

"What in the *world?* I've never seen you *act* like this."

"It's nothing. Forget it. Here, get in."

CHAPTER 31

HANNAH DECIDED TO IGNORE PETER'S LITTLE OUTBURST when she got home. She'd come clean about how she felt about him. She didn't need to explain herself. Now it was up to him to get over it. She dropped her purse in her room and was heading for the fridge when the phone rang. She already knew who it was.

"It's okay," she said interrupting his stream of rationale.

"It's not like you can't talk to another guy . . . I'm not saying that. I know that we're on sort of a break. I was moving too fast. Man, I just can't let you go right now. I'm trying, Hannah, I am. When I saw you with that guy, it just looked like you had already moved on—"

"It wasn't like that—"

"It's just that when you didn't come outside after work, I got worried and went looking for you."

"I didn't ask you to pick me up."

She heard him clear his throat and slip a smile into his voice. "I wanted to surprise you."

"Thanks, but—"

"That okay? We're still friends, right?"

"Sure, but . . . you can't act like that if I talk to a guy."

"You were smiling . . ."

"Yeah . . . what, I can't make friends at work?" *Where is he going with this?*

"You're friends now?"

Yeah, Hannah Zandana has made a friend, stop the presses!

"I thought you just met."

"We did . . . we were just talking, Peter. It doesn't mean we're going out." She twirled the phone cord around her wrist, cutting off its circulation. A headache was already forming from her overdose of sugar at work. The McDonald's shake definitely didn't help.

"Listen," she said, "forget it. It's over. I'm beat, though. We'll talk later?"

"Hold on. The reason why I wanted to surprise you was because I got your birthday present already."

"Peter, you don't—"

"I know, but you're going to be so psyched."

"What?"

"I got Cure tickets. They're playing at the Palace in New Haven. We can go before I have to leave for school."

"Oh, cool," she said, ignoring the sinking feeling inside her chest. She pulled on the ends of her hair and wondered if she wished she were going with Deacon, or if something else was gnawing at her. "Yeah, that sounds great. Thanks. You're right. I'm psyched."

"Awesome!" Peter said, back to his old self.

"Okay, bye."

She could hear how happy he was and it made her feel guilty for agreeing to go. This was not going to help cool things between them. Then again, it was The Cure; how could she say no?

She wandered into the living room and stopped short at the sight of Kerry sitting in front of the TV. She had the sound off and was busily coloring. Her little sister was so quiet these days, almost invisible. She'd probably heard her whole conversation with Peter.

"Whatcha doing there, Kerry-girl?"

Her little sister didn't look up. She had four white sheets of paper lined up, each one with a different jagged figure with checkmarks for eyes and an "X" for the lips, sealing the mouth.

Hannah changed the channel and plopped down next to her. Her sister's fingers were white, curled around the crayon from gripping so hard. Suddenly, the paper she was working on ripped.

"What's wrong?" Hannah laid a light hand on Kerry's back. "Tell me, what is it?"

Kerry squinted like she was about to get a shot at the doctor's; a wave of pain journeyed down her face and into her trembling lips. She sniffled and ran the back of her palm under her nose.

Hannah reached for the tissue box off the coffee table. "Here you go."

"Mommy forgot me today . . . she left me in the car at the grocery store," she spurted between hiccups.

"*What?* How?"

"I woke up and she was gone."

"For how long? Oh my God, Kerry, I'm so sorry." Hannah tried to pull Kerry into her arms but her little body stiffened against her touch. "Does Dad know?"

Kerry shook her head and blew into the tissue.

"Want me to talk to Mom? Where is she?"

"She's out. Said she had to go to another store."

"Why didn't you just go in and *find* her?"

"People were in the parking lot . . ." Kerry's eyes pooled before spilling down her cheeks. "I hid under the seat so no one would see me . . . it was so hot . . . me and Droge were so thirsty."

"Why did you *hide*?"

"If anyone saw me . . . they'd know I was *left*. I don't want people thinking bad things about Mommy or get her in trouble. They could take me from her . . . or put Mommy away again."

"It's not okay for her to leave you like that, you're too little to be left alone. Her job is to protect you. Something could have happened—" Hannah stopped, not wanting to scare her.

"I didn't want Mommy to get mad . . . like last time. She said if I unlock the door, strangers could steal me . . . I don't want to be *stolen*, Hannah!" She blubbered harder.

"She's done this *before*?"

Kerry didn't say anything. Hannah lifted her little sister's chin.

"Tell me. Has Mom *left* you . . . more than *once*?"

Kerry shifted nervously, her face now pink. She stared past Hannah's shoulder and sullenly nodded. Her chin dimpled before she collapsed into Hannah's lap, her tiny arms reaching around her sister's body.

Now she's ignoring Kerry, her little golden child?

A familiar ache stabbed at Hannah's chest and traveled down to her thumbs. Seeing Kerry crumble was like seeing herself at that age. She winced at the memories she'd buried —those times, too many to count, when she was little, her feet dangling off the car's bench seat, being strapped under a seatbelt, and told not to move . . . as she waited for her mother to come back for her.

She'd made up games to pass the time back then. Her favorite one had been playing a princess and deciding who could stay and who had to leave her kingdom. She'd sing herself a magical song, and then another one, burying her head over her lap so no one could steal her magic.

Mostly she remembered spending what felt like hours in that damn station wagon, tracing the ice formations on the windows, and praying that the next sound of footsteps coming from behind the car would be her mother.

I need to tell Dad. I need to tell him now.

CHAPTER 32

south beach, miami

WEEKS LATER, NO ONE HAD BOTHERED TO CLEAN UP Pedro's blood behind the stove at the pink safe house. Deacon eyed the sight each time he entered the kitchen, knowing it could have been his DNA splattered like a Jackson Pollock painting if Chalfont hadn't intervened. Now it served as a thorny reminder that he was the one the drug lord favored.

Deacon never thought he'd be back at that house again after the scare of being followed. It had turned out to be more cartel members, all of them angry over what had gone down that night at the docks. Chalfont's *familia* was coming undone.

The sight of guns and bloodstained walls contrasted sharply with the sane moments Deacon spent with Paul. He'd gladly take the old man and his wife, Ida, home with him back to Connecticut if he could.

Deacon nodded toward the armed men seated around the kitchen table counting large bags of uncut coke. They barely acknowledged him when he walked in, which he gratefully took as sign that none of them possessed the same fiery animosity toward him that Pedro had—or if they did, they at least weren't going to act on it.

This time, he didn't come alone. He wrapped his arm

around Claudia's shoulder and pulled her into his side, their signal that the show was about to start. He heard Chalfont's voice in the other room, and then Luis's. Deacon twirled Claudia around toward him. She laughed, playing her part. He waited until the drug lord was within a few feet of them before kissing her.

Chalfont stood in the doorway of the kitchen with a machine gun slung casually over his tank top and striped dolphin shorts. His obsidian eyes narrowed at the sight of Claudia's strapless pink lamé dress and white pumps. She flashed him her wide, flat smile, to little reaction. One of the men seated at the table took in an eyeful of her exquisite body, however, which she clearly enjoyed.

"Ah, Xavier . . . *bueno, bueno!*" Chalfont boomed enthusiastically. He ushered him into the dining room, where a map was spread across the large table.

Claudia continued flirting with the man in the kitchen.

Chalfont began pointing out drop points on the map in areas along the docks. "We'll have *hombres* here and here, should there be a *problema.*"

The drug lord leafed through a stack of papers, causing some of them to land on the floor. Deacon stooped to get them, as did Chalfont. Now at eye level, he had the pleasure of feeling the drug lord's heated, sour breath on his face.

The small man's eyes ricocheted in every direction as he whispered, "We think Thompson tipped off the cops that night when our group got ambushed. He's the one who began this whole *unpleasantness.* For that, he's no longer welcome in the *familia.*" He drew a finger across his throat.

"*Muerto?*" said Deacon. "When did *that* happen?"

"No, *you* have to *matarlo, esta noche. You* need to be the one; the men need to see your loyalty to them, *para la familia.* You and Luis head out together, before the meet time. I don't want another *problema.*"

They rose to their feet with Deacon staggering a bit, feeling lightheaded. Chalfont had never asked him to carry out a murder before. He wasn't a hitman. His role was to meet the shipments from the drop points and ride along with them to the safe houses.

"*Mi capitán,* I don't know—"

Deacon stopped talking when he saw what the drug lord held in his hand: a manila envelope with a crest comprised of primary-colored flags and ducklings. A wave of nausea struck him. He'd seen it before, but where?

"Is there already a *problema,* Xavier?"

Deacon swallowed. "No . . . *todo bien,* all good."

———

There was no time to contact the Feds about Chalfont's new plan that night, especially with Luis glued to his side. Claudia, too, was sent out with one of the henchmen's girlfriends to make a bank vault deposit. Deacon doubted that she'd be able to get to Kodak and Eastman in time for them to intervene. They both knew that the Feds wanted Thompson alive; his testimony was vital to helping bring down Chalfont and the cartel. But what could they do?

Climbing into Luis's car, Deacon hadn't a clue how the night would go. He hoped Luis would simply step in and be the hero.

"Radio?" Deacon asked with his hand over the dial.

"No," Luis sneered. He looked at Deacon and shook his head. He let out a short laugh.

"What's so funny?"

"That Chalfont thinks you're capable of shooting a man like Thompson."

"I'll do as he says," Deacon said with a shrug, sounding like the obedient soldier he was expected to be.

"I bet you will," Luis said salaciously.

Deacon ignored him. He couldn't wait for the ponytailed wonder to be out of his life.

———

Ten blocks from where they were to meet Thompson, Deacon noticed something out his window.

"Wait, slow down . . . what is that? Do you see it? There in the street?" He pointed over the dashboard toward the alley. "What's moving on the ground?"

Luis swerved off to the side, sprang from the car, and began running toward the objects in the middle of the road. Deacon followed behind him.

A young woman in a business suit was leaning over a man who was lying in the street. She was caressing his face.

Groceries were scattered around them like she'd thrown the bag up in the air, the makings of a dinner that would never happen. The man's body moved spastically on the asphalt, blood gushing from his neck, his face contorting while his eyes pleaded to the heavens.

Her head swiveled from the man to Luis and Deacon. She raised her hands as they approached and cried, "*No dispare, no dispare!* Don't shoot!"

Deacon's body jerked back as Luis fired two rounds into her chest.

"What are you doing? This doesn't concern us!" he yelled, covering his ears.

One more shot between the eyes and the man's jerky movements ceased.

"What the hell, Luis? It looks like a petty robbery . . . why did you have to *kill* them?"

Luis crouched next to the man's body, holding his wrist for a pulse. He dropped it off to the side and glared up at Deacon. "This is Thompson." He flicked his gaze toward the woman on the ground. "And his *esposa*. This is their *barrio*."

"His neighborhood? The meet point was at the docks. Was he even going to be there?"

Luis frowned pensively, surveying the alley.

"You should have let *her* go."

"No *testigos*, Xavier, ever!"

"We've got to get out of here, someone must have called the cops by now." Deacon rechecked the alley. "Whoever got to Thompson first is long gone."

"What's that damn sound?" Luis steamed.

"Feral cats, come on," he urged. But the cries rang in his ears too. It was strange. He'd never heard cats carry on so. The mewing grew louder. From the shadows, two little girls appeared, crawling over to the bodies. *Oh, my god.*

"*Silencio!*" Luis ordered.

The couple must have been their parents. They both tried in earnest to wake up their mother. The older girl was not more than eight, with large, soulful eyes and a delicate face. Her little sister, who could have been her twin, looked around five. Both wore pink smocked dresses and shiny black patent leather shoes with tiny gold hoop earrings and matching bracelets on each wrist that glittered in the moonlight.

"Hand me their *pulseras*," Luis barked.

Deacon didn't question his crazy request; all he wanted was to get out of there. Reluctantly, he slipped off the girls' bracelets and passed them. The girls howled more.

"Virgen de Guadalupe, 14 karat, nice." Luis kissed the medal on one of the gold bracelets between his thumb and forefinger and raised it to the sky before pocketing each of them. The gesture sent a sharp pain into Deacon's gut.

Luis yanked the girls up by their wrists and started to drag them toward the car.

Deacon blanched. "Wait, where are you taking them?"

"They're witnesses . . . they are going in the cold truck."

The older daughter screamed and bit Luis. Her eyes lit with fire, her little body quaking with rage. She wasn't giving up. She turned to Deacon, pleading in Spanish for him to do something, to save her and her little sister.

"Xavier, carry her!" Luis ordered.

I can't, I just can't. Deacon pretended not to hear him. He hoped she'd settle down and he wouldn't have to be a part of her demise.

"Xavier!" Luis yelled. "I'm speaking to you!"

"I can't kill them. How 'bout we let them run away . . . they'll be too scared to talk."

"We're not killing them, *estúpido*."

"Then why the cooler?" He'd seen Chalfont's people use refrigerated trucks before. They were a necessity in their line of work, mainly used to cart off the corpses, especially with the intolerably hot Miami temperatures. They acquired them from fast food chains like McDonald's and Wendy's. The cheery family-friendly logos on the outside concealed the human stench on the inside until they were able to dump them. Sometimes the bodies were packed in there with several others for weeks at a time. Deacon tried not to think about those trucks and their real cargo. He could no longer stomach the slogan, "Where's the beef?"

Luis pushed Deacon out of the way. He took cable ties from his jacket and began cow tying the older girl's hands and ankles together while the younger sister beat him with her tiny fists.

"Still so much to learn, Xavier. I don't understand why Chalfont puts up with you."

"What am I missing here? Where are they going?"

Luis stopped and faced him. "Their little *hearts* will fetch a *nice price*."

A wave of hot acid rose up Deacon's throat.

He ran.

He didn't stop running.

CHAPTER 33

darien, connecticut

HANNAH SPOTTED HIS BABY CHIPMUNK FACE AND MUSCULAR man-body from across the food court. Toby sat eating by himself, just like he had been the day Peter pounced on her for hanging with Bryan.

She collected the change from her fries and Diet Coke and stole another glance. She veered toward a table on the far side of the food court—then her footsteps slowed. *Don't even think about it.* She ignored her own advice, turned on her heel, and weaved herself back through the tables. She didn't know why she was doing it, nor could she restrain herself.

She idled at the side of his booth, realizing, to her horror, that her brain had wiped itself clean. Her ears burned; her feet suddenly stuck to the floor.

Toby's freckled chipmunk cheeks flushed upon seeing her. His Popeye arms flexed down to his knuckles, while his legs bounced under the table. She'd forgotten his annoying nervous energy.

His dark, heavy eyes sliced her to pieces, daring her to say something.

She clenched her jaw and dropped into the bench across from him. His brows pinched together, drawing his eyes into the center of his face. She held his stare for several seconds. They both looked away at the same time.

Toby exhaled and dropped his shoulders.

Hannah swallowed hard, wishing she hadn't begun this.

"You work here?" she mumbled, her voice sounding crackly and strange.

Toby glowered off to the side, causing her to follow his gaze. No one was there. His disdain was for her.

"What are you doing here?"

"It's a free country," he mumbled. His eyes shot off to the side again.

A prickly silence sprang up between them, sending sweat trickling down her sides under her T-shirt. Hannah knew this was a bad idea. But it was the closest thing to seeing Deacon's chocolate brown eyes again, even if they *were* on his killer's face. A part of her also wanted the opportunity to tell him off.

"Look at me. Bet you can't even do that," she snapped.

He obliged smugly, bestowing his go-to look of boredom. She'd seen it before.

"You f-ed up my life," she hissed, leaning over the table.

"And you, mine."

"How the hell do you figure that?"

"I lost my brother because of you!"

"Dude, really? You were the one who . . ." She mimicked pulling a trigger with her hand.

Toby's face drained of life. He crossed his arms, grabbing his broad shoulders, and sank lower in his seat. "Still . . ." he said quietly, breaking eye contact.

"Oh, that's right . . . I *made* you kill your half brother. My mistake."

"I didn't mean—never mind. You wouldn't understand."

"Try me."

The suspended air over the table thickened. Time all but stopped. Hannah swore to herself that he would have to be the one to leave; she wasn't going anywhere.

"I . . . I have no one now."

She looked up, unsure if the soft utterance had come from his mouth or her own thoughts. Toby's legs ceased moving. She no longer heard the busy sounds echoing through the food court. She just heard Deacon's. Brother's. Breathing.

Hannah sucked the air back into her lungs, containing the knife-wielding words she'd come to say. Their edges had suddenly dulled. She slouched low in her seat and stayed that way for a while.

Her weird exchange with Toby was still freaking her out when she woke up the next morning. She replayed the conversation in her head as she started getting ready for work. They'd said very little to one another. His face, however, had communicated a mini-series of pain. His eyes had mirrored back the same gut-wrenching emotions Hannah had experienced after losing Deacon, including those dark, faraway thoughts that found her when others weren't around.

Recognizing their shared sadness had brought her a strange sense of comfort even as it had upset her; she'd nearly broken down in front of him.

This unlikely commonality startled her. Before, she'd believed Toby to be a cold, soulless killer. Now she understood that Deacon had left the same crushing void inside of both of them.

Toby must have loved him too.

———

An hour later, she walked briskly through the mall's side entrance with sweat waterfalling down her back inside her T-shirt dress. She shifted the wide belt slung over her hips to the other side. It liked to move when she walked. The mall's AC felt wonderful today.

The stores' metal accordion gates were still blocking their entrances when she arrived, leaving just enough space for the first-shift employees to shimmy through. The Muzak on the sound system kicked on, accompanied by the rolling wheels of the cleaning carts and the occasional pair of high heels marching through. The early-morning sounds of a mall coming to life reminded Hannah of a high school orchestra tuning up before an assembly.

It was her morning to open. She braced herself for The Candy House's olfactory overload of chocolate, confectionaries, and salty nut mixes. She reached around for the latch on the employee door and began flipping on the overhead lights and illuminating the candy bays. She was entering her employee number into the register when she heard a familiar voice.

"Hey, Hannah."

Bryan. Her head popped up. "Oh, hey. So you got hired! Where are you working?"

He pointed to the nameplate on his red polo: "Chess King."

She nodded slowly, forging a straight face.

He read her thoughts anyway. "Yeah, I'm not *white* enough for Merry-Go-Round."

"That's bogus. It's their loss," she said. She hadn't considered the obstacles he faced applying for jobs compared to her. Bryan was so handsome and clean cut; how could they not hire him? The guy dressed better than she did and was far more polished.

Watching Bryan's face, she felt a stab of embarrassment, coupled with guilt. How could she work for someone like Howie who actively discriminated? By not saying more, wasn't she perpetuating the problem?

"I'm used to it," he said, resting his elbows on the candy bay in front of her. Hannah made a mental note to Windex the area before Howie arrived. He liked everything pristine, which was pretty annoying. Then again, maybe she'd blow off cleaning as a form of protest.

"Wanna hang out later?"

"Sure." Something jumped inside her chest when she answered.

"It's okay with your *boyfriend* this time?" he teased, pushing off from the counter.

"He's not my boyfriend."

"Later, then." He flashed her a grin before turning away.

"Later." Hannah blushed, enjoying the way his butt moved in his jeans when he walked. She pressed her lips together to conceal her smile. She was grateful that he didn't look back, though she was sure he knew she was watching.

"Is this table okay?" he asked as they were being seated later that afternoon.

So polite. "Sure. Looks great."

"I don't know about you, but I'm starving."

Hannah laughed. "Me too." She looked around the Irish pub–themed restaurant and saw a few families, a table of teenagers, and another young couple perhaps on a date. "Guess I didn't OD on the gummy bears at work as much as usual today."

A petite girl approached their table. "Welcome to Bennigan's! My name is Tammy. I'll be your server. How are you guys today?" She managed to show nearly every one of her teeth as she spoke. And they were big. Tammy was a cute, curly-haired blonde who looked like she'd just misplaced her pom-poms somewhere.

After she left, Hannah tilted her head in her direction. "See, that could have been *you.*"

"In my dreams. I'm not *that* perky."

"So you're going to let me use that sweet Chess King employee discount?"

"Funny . . . very funny."

Hannah laughed. "Just kidding. I'm sure their clothes are nice. Well. Some are . . . maybe."

"How's The Candy House for Diabetics?"

"We're bringing them in . . . giving people their sugar rush 24-7," she slung back.

"They let you eat candy *all day?*"

"We're supposed to be familiar with all the candies as far as ingredients and flavors so we can answer customer questions. If it's a dark chocolate with a more bitter cocoa taste, some people prefer that . . . or if it's on the mild side and maybe mixed with something salty . . . you get the idea. Our manager wants us to be able to make recommendations, especially when we're featuring new candy clusters. Sometimes customers will try something different . . . others just stick to what they know they like."

"Aren't you afraid of getting *fat* working there?"

"No, never. At first you want to try *everything*. After a while it gets old."

"Still," he said eyeing her like she had a weight problem.

Hannah's ears flushed. In that moment, she realized that Bryan reminded her of her dad.

"You two ready to order?" Miss Perky Big-Tooth twirled back around. She pulled a pen from behind her ear and tapped the tip against her pad. Hannah could almost hear her cheer: *Are you ready? Let's go!*

Bryan gestured for her to order first.

"I'll have a cheeseburger and fries," she said, raising an eyebrow, waiting for him to say something. *He probably wants me to order a salad.*

———

"Thanks for dinner," Hannah smiled. "Next time, I'll pay."

He waved her off like it was no big deal. "What do you want to do now?"

They strolled outside. It was a beautiful summer evening; the scorching temperatures had cooled some. He tilted his head in the direction of the benches in front of the restaurant. "Want to hang out for a bit?"

"Let's go somewhere else," she said. "I'm kind of sick of the mall. Been here all day."

They cut across the parking lot. She hesitated when she realized they were walking to his car. She didn't know him that well.

"Like my wheels?" he said after he closed her door and climbed into the driver's side. "Gotta love a VW Rabbit, circa '75."

"Hey, it's a car—more than I can say."

He smiled at her answer. His car smelled like Polo cologne. Compared to Peter's, Bryan kept his immaculate. The surfaces gleamed, the seats and floorboards looked freshly vacuumed.

"You take really good care of your car."

"Aesthetics are important to me."

"So where are we going?" she said sliding her hands under her thighs. The car's warm seats were a welcome change from the mall's chilly air conditioning.

His face looked thoughtful, as if he were going through a list of places in his head.

"First . . . I'd like to do this," he said, and leaned over to kiss her.

Hannah lifted her face to his, anticipating fireworks. All at once, his teeth clinked with hers and his lips felt altogether wrong. She jerked back, not sure what to do. He leaned in more and pushed his tongue into her mouth. Saliva streamed everywhere. She started to gag.

"What's wrong?"

"It's nothing," she said quickly, trying to figure out what was going on with her. She knew she liked him, especially the attention he gave her. *What's my problem?*

"What, you tell all of your *white* friends that you're stepping out with a *black* dude . . . and now you've changed your mind?"

Yeah, all of my friends. Right. "What? No, it's not like that. Why would you even say that?"

"I know how it goes."

"I didn't agree to go out with you because you were black. I thought you were funny and cute. And *nice*."

He didn't look at her.

"Guess I'm still getting over someone."

"That guy who broke up with *you*?"

"No, not him. Someone else." Hannah took a big breath and let it spill. "My boyfriend was killed. Shot at Gossamer Park just before Christmas."

Bryan's head jerked back. He sat up straighter. "Deacon Giroux was *your boyfriend*?" His mouth sprang open like an aluminum can.

Hannah's eyes widened. "Geez, you *knew* him?"

"Sure. Me and my friends scored some blow from him a few times. Had the guy's beeper on speed dial . . . he was *cold*. Real *cold*."

"*Cold?*"

"All business . . . never cracked a smile."

"Guess you didn't know him like I did." She sighed, her thoughts floating out over the front of the car.

"That's a *trip* . . . Giroux's girlfriend in *my* car. You deal?"

Hannah's eyes hardened. She shook her head.

"Why would you date a dealer, then?"

"I wasn't looking to . . . it's more complicated than that."

He didn't listen to her response. From the way his eyes were dancing, she could tell that all sorts of ideas were flashing through his brain.

"I'm not sure how I feel about this."

"About what, that I dated Deacon? Why does that matter?"

"It just does."

"You're all about aesthetics, so you don't like how this will look?"

He ignored her question and ran his fingertips up her leg. "Are you what they call a *little coke whore?*" He laughed sinisterly, his eyes bending into slits, his lips gleaming with more saliva.

"Hey!" She shoved his hand away and waited a beat to see if he was joking. He wasn't. "That's so uncool. What a *sick* thing to say."

He threw up his hands. "How should I know what you're into when you go with a guy like that?"

"I'm not a cokehead . . . and you're *really* full of yourself! So it's *cool* for you and your friends to *use* him to 'score some blow,' but God forbid someone else sees that he's more than that?"

"I have a pretty good sense of these things," he said, shifting in his seat, refusing to make eye contact with her.

"I think you're quick to judge someone . . . and you've got it all wrong. We weren't like that!"

She flung the car door open, leapt out of her seat, and took off through the parking lot toward her neighborhood. She looked back as she exited the lot, just in time to see his car speeding away in the opposite direction.

CHAPTER 34

south beach, miami

DEACON WAS LOSING IT. *I CAN'T, I CAN'T. I HAVE TO GET OUT. Those little girls! So small and innocent. What was their crime? Having a criminal for a father who messed with the wrong cartel?*

He couldn't shake the way the older girl had looked at him, her eyes begging for his help, so scared, or the way the younger one had kept patting her mother's cheek, trying to wake her up.

Luis would give them a warm drink to make them drowsy and fall asleep. Their little bodies would be wrapped tightly together in an icebox on wheels, until . . . *my God, my God.* He ran to the payphone. He had only minutes. *Come on, pick up, pick up, fucking pricks.*

"It's me. I need your help . . . someone shot Thompson. Luis killed his wife and finished Thompson off. His little girls appeared out of nowhere . . . no, he didn't . . . no, they didn't run. He's putting them in a Wendy's cold truck around the corner from Lummus Park near 11th. He may have already pulled away. Hurry. He's going to sell them . . . no, no . . . for their organs."

He'd just sealed his fate. Calling the Feds meant Eastman and Kodak's people would show up and Luis would connect the dots. He was a dead man.

CHAPTER 35

darien, connecticut

———

"WHERE HAVE YOU BEEN?" HANNAH'S DAD SCOWLED and stomped the floor in front of his recliner all the way to the front door when she arrived home. "It's nearly ten, *where were you?*"

Hannah shrugged. "You're never here when I come home. I didn't think I had to call you."

"Since when?"

"Since Mom's been back . . . since you guys aren't around anymore."

"That doesn't mean, young lady, that you can come and go as you please!"

"Okay, got it," she said not wanting to fight and still reeling from her whiplash of a date with Bryan.

"Where are Mom and Kerry?"

"In bed."

Hannah bit her lip. *It's now or never.* She lowered her voice. "Dad, you've got to listen to me. It's Mom. She's drinking and still taking those pills."

His face went blank. "What?" Then as her words sank in, his cheeks turned a bright shade of red.

Oh-oh. Here we go.

"That's not possible."

"Come here," she told him. He followed her to the kitchen. She glanced back at him before yanking the top freezer open.

"You'll break the handle doing that," he scolded.

"Dad, I found this the other day—" She reached behind the frozen dinners into the ice trays and came up empty. She unloaded all of the boxes onto the counter.

"What are you doing?"

"Mom stashed a large peanut butter jar back here the other day filled with yellow and blue pills." Hannah sighed exasperated. "She must have moved it."

He studied the contents of the freezer, his face unreadable.

"I'm not making this up. She's taking pills again. And worse, she's been leaving Kerry alone in the car when she's out shopping. It was over 90 degrees yesterday, the poor kid could have *died*."

"Your mom's been distracted. She must have forgotten she had Kerry with her."

"No, this was on purpose. She told her if she unlocked the door and got out, someone could steal her. That's playing with her head. Not an accident. Kerry says she hid because she was afraid they'd put Mom away again or they'd take *her*."

Her father pressed his lips together. No matter what she said, would he ever believe her? She spun back toward the sink and yanked on the dishwasher handle.

"Again, Hannah, you're going to break the appliances!"

Steam rose up and swarmed her face. "Someone ran this

. . . I wanted to show you what's really in her mugs . . . listen, Dad, she's worse now than before. You've got to see that . . . do you? It's like she's not even here. She barely speaks to me or Kerry."

"Your mom's been under a lot of stress. We both are."

"What stress? She doesn't do anything except sleep."

"Now I know you're exaggerating. She takes care of Kerry."

"Dad, the TV takes care of Kerry. Mom's never around or she's upstairs in her bedroom."

"You shouldn't talk about your mother like this."

"If I don't, who will? It's time we stop pretending everything's okay, because it's *so not*. Dad, you have to do something. If you won't do it for me, do it for Kerry."

CHAPTER 36

south beach, miami

DEACON'S EYES FLEW OPEN AT THE SOUND OF THE morning's first cars driving past his latest lodgings—behind the dumpster of a local chicken shack on Miami's west side. Paul once told him it was Ida's favorite place because of their famous cornbread. They met their friends there once a week. He hoped Paul would show up soon. He could really use his help after he came clean about everything—starting with his real name.

He rolled out from under his blanket of newspapers, noticing for the first time traces of yellow paint that speckled the stained cement around him, along with a purple spray-painted pledge of love: SUSIE + GIAN 4-EVER!

The amenities were a crude departure from the Leslie, let alone his parents' mansion in Darien. Though Deacon was not a stranger to hiding behind dumpsters, things had escalated considerably from his days of running from park bullies.

He was certain that Chalfont and his henchmen had been watching every hotel, street, and inch of Miami since he took off that night. He was delaying contacting the Feds again, not trusting that they wouldn't return him to the drug lord to resume the mission. He needed time to figure his escape from this hellish place before either side got to him first.

He rubbed the city's grime from his face, feeling wrecked after a restless night on the street and his recurring nightmare of Thompson's daughters pleading for him to save them. Their desperate sobs infiltrated his psyche. He shut his eyes and pressed his fingers against his eyelids, trying to erase the girls' watery doe eyes and trembling lips.

Stop crying, he ordered the voice in his head. He was becoming delusional. Then he heard it again. He stuck his head out, trying to locate the source of the noise, and saw an elderly man pitifully wailing alone in his car.

A strange feeling tightened in his chest, turning to a sharpness that grabbed at his sides. He propped himself onto his elbows, waiting for the old man to stop. He didn't.

Man up. Deacon heard the words his father told him as a little boy. *Men don't cry*. The private moment was none of his business, and yet he found himself unable to ignore the man's pain.

Anger rose inside of him like a flash flood. He didn't have the energy for this; his own problems were wringing his gut out like a wet rag.

Still, something pushed Deacon to his feet. He marched up to the car. The old man looked up and then away, signaling with his hand that it was nothing, move along.

Deacon stood his ground. "You okay?" he shouted into the man's window. The guy nodded and waved him away again. Deacon stepped back. He paced in a small circle and came back again. "I can help."

The man rolled down his window an inch and tilted his mouth toward the opening. "I don't want any. Go away."

"I'm not selling. Can I call anybody? Do you need help or something?"

The old man shook his head and cried harder, folding his arms over the steering wheel.

Deacon waited. He leaned against the guy's car, knowing he was probably pissing him off in doing so. He needed the man to stop, to suck it up, whatever "it" was. He didn't know why he cared so much.

"Were you robbed? Do you need the police?"

The man shook his head and relented. "I'm going to die. Die alone."

"Aren't we all, buddy?" Deacon said bitterly. He'd seen too many heads blown off to count. The next one would surely be his.

"No, not like this. They're going to *kill* me . . . it's only a matter of time."

"Who are *they*? Tell me what happened."

"My best friend was stabbed yesterday. These streets have gotten so bad. They prey on the elderly. We come here to retire and they rob and kill us. We fought wars for these kids, preserved their freedom, and still they aim their knives and guns at us."

Halfheartedly, Deacon said, "Man, sorry about your friend . . . how did he die?"

"He'd gotten a young man's car detailed as a thank you for helping him with some gang members who were trying to rob him . . . you know, in that drug store up there on the corner." The man pointed over his dashboard.

A coldness spread up Deacon's spine. His mouth went dry.

"It was a black Camaro with custom rims, a gorgeous car. The kid never locked it. And Paul . . . oh Paul, he just wanted . . . he wanted to do something for him . . . to thank him . . . for *everything*."

The blood rushed to Deacon's feet.

"The hooligan even etched his name in the side of the car . . . proud of what he'd done . . . murdering my best friend!"

Shaking Deacon asked, "W-what did it say?"

"*Larga vida a Pedro.*"

CHAPTER 37

darien, connecticut

STILL IN HER PAJAMAS, HANNAH HEADED TO THE KITCHEN for some water when she saw her mother sitting on the corduroy couch alone in the living room sipping from one of her mugs. The end of her mother's nose was red, like she'd recently been crying.

This is early even for you, Mom.

Hannah crossed her arms and held on to her shoulders as she leaned against the doorway. "Um, see Kerry anywhere?"

"Your father drove her up to Gamma Mimi's. There's more for her to do there, living near that Girl Scout camp in Manchester."

"You sent her *away?*"

"She was bored here. I thought your dad's idea was a terrific solution."

"For whom, *you?* Finally get that *nuisance* out of your way?"

"*Watch it.*"

Watch what, So-Called Mom? Stop lying to yourself . . . and *us.*

"What?"

"Nothing," Hannah answered, her eyes flicking away.

"Say it."

"When are you going to start acting like a mother for once?"

"I will. I . . . I am." Her mother sighed. "Just need to rest, that's all. You and your sister are a lot of work."

"Mom, I told Dad about the peanut butter jar in the freezer . . ."

Her mom's face fell rigid. Her lips stretched into a tight line silencing her for several seconds. "He didn't say a thing to me. That was probably one I had before I went to the hospital."

"No, it was last week."

"Guess I forgot about it."

"Why was it in the freezer?"

"Keeps the pills fresher . . . these doctors give you so many at one time."

"Why are you still taking them if they weren't good for you *before*?"

"I'm not."

"Mom, the *jar*."

"Oh that, I threw it out. That was one from before."

Hannah rolled her eyes. "Don't you *want* to get better?"

"I told you, *I am*," she said and took a swig from her cup.

Hannah glared at her.

"What now?" her mom said like she was being inconvenienced.

Hannah's eyes dropped to the floor. "The day I found you . . . when you overdosed . . . I thought you were *dead*."

"I think I've repented enough for that . . . I don't need to apologize to you or to anyone, for that matter . . . it was an *accident*, Hannah."

"Was it? Or did you want to leave us for *good*?" Hannah choked on the last word.

"What a thing to say! It's not about *you*. Or your father, or Kerry."

"Who, then? Baby Michael? The one you lost?"

"Are you *trying* to hurt me?"

The sight of her mom's beaten expression made Hannah's eyes well up, but it wasn't enough to stop her. "No, Mom. I'm trying to understand . . . what can I do? I want to help. You're disappearing. It's like you're not even here. I can't talk to you. I want so badly to tell you what's going on in my life. I have no one to talk to. I need a *mother!*"

"I can't . . ." Her mother flew off the couch and was already on the stairs before Hannah realized what was happening, her coffee cup leading the way.

When? When will be the right time, Mom? When you don't wake up the next time?

"I don't get why I still love you," Hannah whispered to the empty couch before her mother's bedroom door slammed shut.

CHAPTER 38

July 15, 1985

Dear Kerry-Girl,

I hope you're having fun at camp and staying at Gamma Mimi's house. I miss you although it was only yesterday that Daddy took you up there. I saw that you forgot Droge bear on your bed and he misses you terribly. I wrapped him in one of your blankets and extra bubble wrap (the kind that you like to pop!) so he stays comfortable on his trip and I put a small bottle of honey in the box in case he gets hungry.

I've asked Gamma Mimi to read this to you and I hope she does. If not. I know you know these words:

I love you,

Hannah

Hannah kissed Kerry's Droge bear and tucked him in the box, along with the letter and the honey. She smiled as she taped the package closed, and noticed her father watching her from his recliner.

He cleared his throat. "What do you have there?"

"A package for Kerry." She completed Gamma Mimi's address, then took the cap from between her lips and replaced it on the marker. "Would have been nice, Dad, if you'd told me you were taking her there. I would have liked to have seen her before she left."

Her father looked at her blankly, like she wasn't speaking English. She didn't wait for a response.

"You and Mom keep doing that . . . not including me in family stuff."

"We didn't think it mattered to you."

"Well, it does. What happened to Mom and Kerry . . . " Hannah swallowed the lump in her throat. "I found them, Dad . . . *remember?*" She pushed away the package to avoid smearing the marker. She didn't care if he saw her cry.

"What's going on?" her mother asked, cautiously descending the stairs. Her far hand was hidden behind her body; from her disheveled hair, Hannah guessed that she'd just been napping.

Hannah knew she'd heard the conversation. Her mother's coy act irked her. As she stepped into the living room, Hannah eyed the coffee cup laced between her fingers.

"Nothing," she said, wiping her face.

"What's in the box?"

"Droge bear, for Kerry."

"Don't send her that, Hannah. I told her not to bring it."

"Why? She's all by herself there. She may get scared in an unfamiliar place, especially at night."

"She shouldn't use him as a crutch anymore. Besides, he's practically threadbare . . . what would Gamma think of us?"

Hannah's eyebrows knitted together as she nodded toward the cup in her mom's hand. "Talk about *crutches*. You don't seem to care what people think . . . especially your own family."

Her mother's face colored like she'd been slapped. From

the corner of her eye, Hannah spied her father's pinkish complexion already darkening to rhubarb. She ducked her head and gathered the package from the table, trying to escape before the yelling began. She didn't care. She'd ask Peter to take her to the post office.

Her mother's pitchfork stare stopped her. Hannah froze, then released the package. The unacknowledged mountain between them accumulated another frosty inch. Hannah readied herself for the landslide.

"I'm trying, dammit . . . I'm try . . ." Her mother's voice trailed off. She blinked rapidly, squeezing her wrist and pulling it into her stomach, as tears released down her face.

"Hannah! What the hell!" Her dad darted from his recliner toward her mother like she was about to fall.

"Stop. I'm fine," her mother said, holding up her hand. She stepped back awkwardly, looking unsure of the floor underneath her.

Hannah's voice softened, her tears matching her mother's. "I'm trying *too*. Trying to hold everything together . . . pretend that our family's okay . . . but we're *not . . . are we?*"

"That doesn't give you the right to speak to us this way," her father admonished, his face on the verge of boiling.

Hannah's temples started to pulse. She pulled on the ends of her hair and looked up at the ceiling as if summoning someone up there for help. "Stop this holier-than-thou stuff, Dad. You're not helping Mom by treating her like she's made of *glass*."

"She's *still* recovering."

Hannah shot him a look, pointing at her mother. "She's *still using*, Dad, and drinking too . . ."

"Stop it! Stop it. This isn't easy!" her mom cried, lowering the cup in her hand and tucking it behind her leg like a small child.

They didn't move.

Her mother's eyes slid to the floor. She grasped her opposite shoulder just as her upper body folded like an accordion. She backed into the hanging picture frames on the wall behind her, and released the cup from her fingers. As it clattered on the floor, she rode the wall down to the ground, her hands clasped in prayer over her nose and mouth.

The air felt suspended in the room. The burnt-orange starburst clock clicked loudly from the kitchen, poking holes in the pockets between them.

Hannah crouched down to help her. "I'm sorry, M-Mom, I'm sorry—"

"I'm a terrible mother," she said weakly. She let her head fall back against the wall with a smack. Then she did it again. And again.

"Stop, Mom!"

"I failed all *three* of you . . ."

Hannah glanced briefly at her father. She had a feeling her mother wasn't including him in that number.

"I can't stop. I try, every morning I tell myself, this is it, no more . . . don't look at me that way, Hannah. You have no *idea*!" Her voice revved up an octave, then cut out.

Hannah's eyes grew wide. Her mother's face reminded her of Kerry's when she cried. She'd never noticed the resemblance before. Pieces of her mother lay scattered on the floor. She saw herself in her, and all at once her heart began to fill.

"No . . . I don't. I can't honestly say I understand what it feels like. I don't know what this *thing* inside is . . . this urge to take those pills and drink all of the time. What do I know? I overdose on ice cream and can't stop sometimes, especially after a bad day. It's hardly the same, I know. But Mom, if Dr. Shapiro isn't helping . . . don't try and fix it alone. It's too big . . . it's destroying whatever trace of a family we have left."

Her mom bent her head into her knees, her forehead wrinkling into the center of her face. It was the same face she made whenever Hannah or Kerry made a mess in the kitchen.

"My father told me all I was good for was to get married and have children . . . then look what happened . . . I couldn't even do *that* right. Complete failure."

Hannah reached out, intending to touch her mother's forearm, but stopped herself, fearing her mother would jerk her arm away. Instead, she tried to think of the right words.

Her brows lifted. "You're sort of like Betty Ford, Mom, and no one calls her a failure."

Her father, who was standing over them, coughed. "That's a good point, Donna."

"If a former First Lady can get addicted to pills and alcohol, it can happen to anyone," Hannah added.

Her mom braced her lips and dispatched another tear down her cheek.

"Your dad sounds like a jerk by the way," Hannah said.

"He was." Her father's head bobbed.

My mother married someone like her own father.

Hannah rose and looked her father in the face. A rare, slight smile formed there—and then dropped. He peered over his glasses at her. Her cheeks reddened as she watched his eyes travel from her T-shirt to her frayed jean shorts.

"What now?" she said, throwing her hands on her hips.

The lines around his eyes tightened. "It's nothing."

"No, you don't. Don't even start on my face or my clothes. That's not okay."

He let out a sigh. "I don't like the strings hanging from the bottom of your shorts. I think a young lady should—"

"Are you going to call me a *prostitute* again?"

Her father squinted like he'd been asked a hard question. She could see his brain searching for the reference and it infuriated her.

"You don't even remember when you kicked me out of the car on the way to church, do you? Well, I do. I'll never forget it. I'm human, Dad. I have feelings, you know. Cut me a break already. Mom and Kerry can screw up pretty majorly, but with me even the littlest stuff gets you mad. And it's always about my appearance. Why is how I look *so* important?"

Her dad frowned. "Thought I was helping."

"Helping would be accepting me for who I *am*."

"I think this summer your skin looks better," a small voice uttered from the floor. Her mother tilted her head up toward them. "The sun helps some?"

Hannah's jaw dropped. *Who is this woman?*

"Yeah, I guess . . ."

Her father removed his reading glasses and began cleaning them with a napkin he picked up from the table, as if this rare moment of honesty between the three of them was a regular occurrence.

"Just lay off of my looks for once," Hannah said. "I'm never going to be perfect."

Her father raised his lenses toward the ceiling and inspected them without responding. When he seemed satisfied, he returned them to his face and helped her mother to her feet.

"There you go, dear," he said as she rested her head on his shoulder.

They're so dysfunctional, Hannah thought, watching them together. *And they always will be.*

CHAPTER 39

HANNAH AND PETER JUMPED TO THEIR FEET IN UNISON with the rest of the crowd as Robert Smith's voice cut into the first song of the evening. Jewels of color and flashing lights ricocheted across the theater, illuminating the people nearest the stage. A euphoric frenzy spread everywhere. Everything came alive in that moment, and Hannah's insides soared.

She grinned as she and the crowd around her were sucked into the magic of The Cure, together, in the same space and time. She wanted to bottle the extraordinary sensation of all her senses being set on fire. Mostly, she wanted her uncontained happiness to never end.

She swayed to the music and found herself tearing up at the overwhelming magic and beauty, song after song. Then someone laughed.

She turned to see Peter pointing at her face.

Hannah cupped her hands over her nose and wondered why he'd try and ruin her first concert for her.

I shouldn't be here with you, she thought, just as she had so many times before.

Peter smiled, took her hand, and draped it around his waist like he had when they were dating. Glued to the side of him like a conjoined twin, Hannah found it hard to breathe.

I don't want this. I don't want to get back together. You're not the one.

"Amazing, right?" Peter screamed into her ear.

Hannah nodded. She blotted her cheeks and ran the middle finger of her free hand along her lower lash lines to corral her mascara and eyeliner.

A dull pain rose from her right thumb and passed up her arm and into her chest. It sank in deeper until it reached her back.

"Everything okay?" Peter asked.

She nodded and pressed her lips together to stop them from giving her away. *Calm down,* she told herself.

"Here, have a beer," he offered, opening his jacket. Its lining held several cans. She took a sip of the Bud Light, and then a longer one, welcoming the grainy, sweet bubbles storming her throat.

"Whoa! Go easy. We need to make those last," he chided.

She glanced up to see if he was kidding. He wasn't.

"We should get some weed," she burst out. She didn't know where the idea had sparked from, but at that moment, standing among the explosive Technicolor crowd and at this theatrical stage show, it seemed like the most amazing thing they could do.

Don't think. Just party to forget.

Peter's face calcified. His gaze traveled back to the band. Without looking at her, he leaned over and said, "Why, is that what you used to do with *him*?"

"F you, Peter," she said, pushing him away, her face stinging from his comment. She wished she had another way home. She started to walk away from him.

He grabbed her hand. "Stop. I don't want to fight."

"I'm going to the bathroom," she yelled, yanking her

hand away, and left without waiting for a response. He didn't try to stop her.

She joined the long, winding line for the women's bathroom alongside other sweaty females, many of them with their hair teased and sprayed so it stood high above their faces, resembling The Cure's front man; their black-shadowed eyes and the stark red lipstick bleeding into the corners of their mouths made them look more clownish than Robert Smith, though.

Hannah ran cold water on her wrists and splashed some on the back of her neck to cool off, then blotted herself with a paper towel. She peered into the mirror and gasped at the sight of the girl behind her—the one with the long, jet-black hair and olive skin sporting tight jean shorts and a denim vest with concert pins.

"Jade!"

"Oh . . . hi." Jade grimaced.

"I haven't seen you in a while." Hannah figured she was probably there dealing. She wasn't ready to let her go; she stuck by her side as she walked out of the bathroom. She had a tired, run-over appearance that made Hannah wonder how much she was still using.

She knew it was the beer talking when her mouth unexpectedly spewed out, "So how's Gillian?" *Not like I care.*

Jade shrugged, her face indifferent. "We broke up last December. After I came by your house."

"Why? Never mind." *God, that was stupid*, Hannah thought. Then she leaned in and whispered, "So can I buy a joint?"

Jade wrinkled her face. "Since when do *you* smoke?"

"Just feel like it tonight . . ."

"Deacon wouldn't like it, you know."

Really, you're going to go there? Hannah knew it was a snarky thing to do, but corrected her anyway. "Yeah . . . he *would not have liked it* . . . but I'm tired of people telling me what I should and shouldn't do. Do you have one or not?"

Jade unfastened the metal button on the front of her vest. She slid her first two fingers into her front breast pocket and pulled out a partially smoked joint.

"Here," she said looking over her shoulder and concealing it in her hand as she passed it to Hannah.

"How much?"

"Just take it."

"Thanks. Got a light?"

"Let's go in there." Jade motioned toward a back stairwell. They walked around the bathroom, away from the snake-line of girls. She heard the beginning of "Let's Go to Bed" and felt the urge to run back to her seat. Her feet, however, kept following Jade.

Hannah lit the joint on her second attempt and inhaled like she'd seen people do. It immediately burned her throat. Her eyes watered while she held her breath, trying to hold in the smoke. Jade then took a hit. Her eyes flitted off in different directions. A couple of guys passed and she daintily held the joint behind her leg like an expert.

Hannah exhaled, unable to hold it in any longer, and coughed a few times. She gently swallowed; her throat felt thoroughly singed.

"Seeing you reminds me of him. I still miss him."

Jade ignored her and kicked the tip of her white Tretorns into the railing in front of her.

"Do you . . . still miss him?" Hannah asked. She didn't care if she sounded like a moron. She needed to talk to someone, someone who knew him like she did.

Jade took another hit and offered the joint back to her. She declined.

"Everything has changed. I don't remember him much," Jade answered, still not looking at her.

"What do you mean, 'don't remember'? It's only been a few months."

"Eight," Jade said emphatically.

"So you don't remember him much . . . but you can correct *me* on when he *died*?" Hannah said, getting annoyed.

"*God*, you're clueless," Jade said, rolling her green eyes.

"Clue me in, then . . . I'd love to know what you know."

"I can't . . . I gotta go. Do you want this?" She extended the joint to her.

Hannah shook her head. She felt a little fuzzy around the edges. "What are you saying, Jade?"

A boy flung open the door to the stairwell, startling them. "Jade, Jade! Been looking all over for you!"

Jade started walking away with the guy. Before she exited the stairwell, she glanced back at Hannah like she wanted to tell her something.

"Jade, *please*. Help me understand."

She just shook her head and slipped out the door.

———

"You smell like pot," Peter announced when they got back in the car after the concert. The corners of his mouth created a condescending smirk.

Hannah's ears rang. She relished the reverberation; it made her feel like she was taking home some of the night's exhilaration with her. She wasn't going to let Peter ruin her high from seeing The Cure for the first time and from seeing Jade again.

He reached over and patted her leg like she was a child. She didn't bother to listen to anything else he said. She tilted her seat back a bit and closed her eyes. She'd be home in an hour or so.

When she woke, they were driving into one of the parking lots in Gossamer Park. Peter knew not to bring her anywhere near the lot where Deacon had been shot. She was unfamiliar with this spot. It looked deserted; not a car or person was in sight.

Peter put the car in park and turned down the radio.

"What time is it?" Hannah asked, squinting at the dashboard. She blinked a few times to lubricate her cloudy contacts. Her mouth tasted cottony and stale.

"Not too late . . . here," he hiccupped and reached for her face. "Come here, you."

Hannah leaned away from him, sniffing the air. "Did you finish off the rest of the beer?"

Peter laughed and yanked her toward him.

She dropped her eyes and lowered her chin to her chest. She wished she were already home. Her mind raced through the excuses she could give but knew it would be easier if she stayed just a little bit longer. Maybe he'd sober up if she got him talking.

He tilted her chin up. "I'm sorry I teased you about crying. I wanted things to be good between us tonight, like they were before."

"Yeah . . . well, it was fun anyway. They sounded great."

"I'm glad we went. Happy early birthday."

"Thanks," she said, flashing a quick smile and stuffing her hands under her legs.

"I've missed being with you." He grinned, his sea-glass eyes shining. "I never stopped . . . *wait* . . . here's our song . . ." He turned up the radio excitedly and belted out the lines to "Every Time You Go Away."

She laughed at his attempt to sing. "Our song?"

"Yeah, love Paul Young, don't you?"

"Sure, though I think it's originally a Hall & Oats song—"

"The *words*, Hannah, they're how I *feel*."

Oh, shit. She had no words before he grasped the back of her neck, pulling her toward him.

She twisted her head and moved away from him. "I'd like to go home now."

"Oh come on, don't be like that. I've missed you. It's okay. Just one kiss . . . I swear."

He kissed her gently and she had to admit, it felt nice. Familiar. She relaxed. Old Peter was back. They could make out a little, no big deal.

He pulled back searching her eyes. His lips tentatively touched hers again, then he began running his hand up her thigh and around the side of her waist. He softly moaned as his fingers traveled under her shirt and over her bra. Her body tensed at his touch. She knew what he wanted and her brain sputtered for the right words.

"Stop, Peter." *Say it louder.* "I don't—"

"God, I love your body. I can't get enough of it."

With her eyes half open, she envisioned herself as a robot; she wanted to be home. She got the feeling that she could sit there numbly and he wouldn't care as long as he got what he wanted.

He started to unbutton her shorts.

"Peter, I don't—"

"Shh, I got something," he said retrieving a thin package from his back pocket.

"That's not—"

He kissed her harder, his tongue entering her mouth like an unwanted intruder. He tasted like sour Bud Light and eggs. In one motion, he released the lever on the side of her seat, leaning her back horizontally, and climbed on top of her. He pulled off his T-shirt and lowered his board shorts from his hips.

"Oh, baby . . . I can't wait to be with you . . . been dreaming of this . . . I love you . . . love *me*, Hannah."

He ripped the corner of the Trojan wrapper with his teeth. She saw him slip on the condom. She closed her eyes and told herself to just go with it; he'd be done soon. She would figure everything out in the morning. He kissed her neck and she cracked her eyelids watching him move his hips. In her peripheral vision, something shimmered on the driver's side seat under the streetlamp. Her lids fluttered until they peeled back wide.

"What's that? What the *hell* is on the seat next to me?"

"Shhhh, baby. Just relax. You feel *so* good."

"Oh my god, is that the *rubber*? You slipped it off when my eyes were shut?"

"Shhh, I've got it, I've got it . . ." he said as his breath quickened and he started to groan.

She grabbed the base of him and squeezed hard. She punched and kicked him off of her like a wild animal, surprising herself—and him, too, judging by his bewildered face.

"Get the hell off of me!" she cried.

"God dammit!" he yelled slamming his hand on the dashboard. He held his crotch and began swearing, bringing his fist between his eyes. He pulled up his shorts and leaned out the car window. With his hands between his legs, he groaned like an injured animal.

She dressed madly and threw his shirt at him. "You're an asshole! What the hell were you thinking? Trying to 'spread your seed' or something?"

"Relax! You wouldn't have gotten pregnant . . . and I don't have an STD. Or AIDS."

"Oh, so then it's okay?"

He didn't look at her.

"Damn it, I should have stopped you. What's my problem?" She clawed at her bare legs. "I'm not this. I don't want to be *this*!"

"I've been so patient . . . I just got carried away," he said in a low voice, his chin in his chest. "I just figured—"

"You figured *what*?"

"That deep down, I was the one you wanted. *Not him.* Hannah, you slept with a low-life drug dealer, but you won't sleep with *me . . . what the hell*?"

"You're obsessed with him. Deacon has nothing to do with me not wanting you. Get it through your thick skull!"

Peter hid his face from her, his shoulders shaking.

"How could you put me at *risk* like that?"

"I used to watch you guys at school last year. He'd meet

our bus every morning. I'd get a few minutes alone with you, but once you saw him, you forgot I was even there. It *killed* me the way you looked at him . . . and how you kissed him. I could tell you were sleeping together. I f-figured that you didn't use protection with *him* . . . b-because you loved each other . . . and I wanted it to be like that with *us*."

"You are so fucked up, you know that, Peter? Take me home, take me home *now*!"

CHAPTER 40

south beach, miami

———

2:19 A.M. DEACON COULDN'T KEEP HIS EYES CLOSED OR calm his brain. The new guy in the top bunk snored like a wild boar, and the man on the other wall had been repeating "damn, girl . . . that's it, girl," all night.

Deacon rubbed his eyes and attempted to rub off his entire face. *Stay put*, he told himself. Chalfont and his henchmen were crawling all over Miami looking for him. By now they knew he was no Xavier Coyne.

For a week, he'd been hiding North in Miami Beach at a men's shelter. He'd convinced the director with the carefully placed comb-over that he was an addict in need of treatment after finding the shelter's address in a Yellow Pages chained to a payphone. The shelter was a four-story pink building with a Spanish façade and an *Alive with Pride in '85* banner hung across its entrance.

His dirty clothes and ripe body odor—courtesy of sleeping on the street for days—had worked in his favor. He'd also acted the part during his interview by clawing at his skin and acting jumpy like he remembered his customers back in Connecticut doing.

The director eyed him skeptically. "We don't house criminals," he told him.

Deacon knew his face had never appeared in the newspapers. "I whole-heartedly agree with that decision, sir. I just need a few days to get clean and I'll be out of your *hair*."

He'd given the director his Rolex and gold jewelry to end his hesitation. Those things had also been enough of a bribe for him to not turn Deacon away when he voluntarily relinquished the gun Chalfont had given him.

"Sell this too," Deacon told him, as he placed the gun on the director's desk. "I want nothing to do with it."

Even with that, Deacon knew he wouldn't be able to stay long. The place was overcrowded and swarming with desperate men.

He'd waited several hours in the lobby for a room to open that first night. All walks of life came through the shelter's doors, from slick executive types to an elderly man wearing just his soiled underwear.

He thought about Paul and how much he missed him. He'd still be alive if it weren't for him. *Dammit, Paul. You and your stupid cars.*

A handsome, preppy kid around his age started rambling to him in the waiting room. The boy's body shivered as if it were the middle of winter. He clutched his stomach and cried in between asking the empty chair beside him nonsensical questions, asking about a callback and where Rachel had gone.

When the boy began dry heaving, Deacon retrieved a garbage bag from the admissions desk and offered it to him. The young man continued to throw up into the red rain slicker he'd bunched up in his lap, ignoring the proffered bag, until nothing more came up. Then his body heaved some more.

A middle-aged gentleman walked through the doors with a much younger man whom he lowered gently into the open seat next to Deacon. They were accompanied by a couple of women who began whispering impatiently to the staff and to one another.

The men's shirts hung on their bony shoulders like clothes on hangers. Their shrunken bodies appeared too narrow and small for their heads. The younger one kept yanking his long-sleeve striped shirt over the sore on his arm. The older man gently kissed his lover's sunken cheek before brushing his own tear away.

Talk of quarantine and a "special floor" floated from the employees behind the admissions desk. One lady with a clipboard and glasses balancing on the end of her nose announced repeatedly to whomever was in earshot, *We're full. We can't possibly take them. There's just too many coming through our doors.*

Deacon stayed in his spot and watched, transfixed by the couple, even when the young man expectorated blood onto his striped sleeve. He knew he was one of them: alone and forgotten, riddled with his own sores and disease.

2:26 a.m. He couldn't settle down. His lack of sleep was making him crazy. His ulcer burned, and the fried food at the shelter wasn't helping. Something told him Hannah needed him. Or maybe it was *he* who needed her—more than ever.

The one payphone in the place was conveniently out of order, sending him onto the street to find another. He wandered toward Flamingo Park, south on Washington and across Lincoln. He turned down Drexel Avenue and found one on the corner. The stagnant evening air had transformed the phone booth into a hothouse. He cradled the receiver on his shoulder and scrounged up some change.

He longed to hear her voice and to know that in this ugly world, where children were kidnapped, sliced up, and sold for parts on the black market, someone like her could still exist, someone far away from the evil and greed of men like Chalfont and Luis. That somewhere, good people like Paul could still be kissing their wives goodnight. That damn dirty car. *Thank you for everything.*

Maybe, just maybe, Hannah could forgive him for his part in all of this: for the innocent people who died, those girls, Paul's life. Could she forgive him and still want to lie at night in the crook of his arm? Would she still love him, the *old* him, Deacon Giroux? Whoever *he* was.

He held his breath as Hannah's phone rang. *Talk. Say something, you coward. Just do it already.*

She picked up. "Hello?" She sounded strange and it threw him off.

His mouth opened. He forgot how to speak. He stepped out of the phone booth, pulling its armored cord taunt. His blood pulsed in his ears like he'd just sprinted.

"I-I . . ."

"Fuck you! I can't take this," she cried. "I'm not *yours*, I never was . . . what you did was unforgivable! Don't. Call. Me. AGAIN!"

From behind, Deacon felt a warm breath engulf his ear. A voice yelled next to his face, "Xavier . . . Xavier Coyne!" He jumped and quickly cupped his hand over the receiver.

Claudia stood behind him, laughing.

"Shit, what the fuck?" he whispered tersely. He put his finger over his lips to silence her. He jammed the phone back up to his ear. Hannah was gone.

Claudia smacked her lips against his. "Been looking all over for you, cowboy."

CHAPTER 41

darien, connecticut

———

HANNAH CALLED OUT SICK THAT MORNING. HER RED, swollen eyes resembled two puffed balls stuck to her face. She'd barely slept. She was supposed to open and probably would be fired for giving her manager such short notice. *Screw Howie and his all-white staff mandate. Prick.*

She lay in bed, scratching at the bumps on the back of her arms. Soon she would move on to her face. Thoughts of last night kept thundering through her head. What Peter had done was unforgiveable; what she'd done was almost worse. She was disgusted with herself. Her nagging inner voice chimed in: *What were you thinking, letting him have sex with you because it would be easier than saying "no"?*

Her guilt poured through every cell. All summer she'd toyed with his feelings, knowing it was wrong. *Did I somehow cause this? Is it my fault?*

She'd consented to having sex with a condom. But by Peter removing it without her knowledge, it crossed the line; she'd been violated. *What kind of person does that?*

Guys could casually fool around with girls who were in love with them. But when girls did it, it was akin to playing with matches. It still didn't exonerate Peter's actions.

Hannah vowed to never be that girl again. *Stupid, stupid.*

And then Peter had the nerve to call her. At least, she thought it was him. What she'd heard on the line hadn't made sense.

Jade's face last night at the concert and her unspoken words as she walked away kept nagging at Hannah. What was she keeping from her?

Hannah pulled up the phone from the floor by its cord and dialed Deacon's private line, hoping Toby was awake.

"Yo!"

"Hi, it's Hannah. I know this is a really strange request. But can we meet?"

She took the long way around the mall to avoid seeing anyone from work. When she got to the food court, she made a beeline for his table.

"What did you hear exactly?" Toby asked as soon as she sat down. His right knee was bouncing like a sewing machine needle at warp speed.

Does this kid ever stop moving? she wondered.

"Something like 'flavor coins or savior something . . . maybe braver coins?'"

"Braver coins, braver coins . . . hmmm, not sure . . . could it have been a wrong number?"

"Someone has been calling my house in the middle of the night and hanging up after several seconds ever since Deacon died. About once a week, sometimes more."

"That's creepy. Think it's Gillian?"

"Not anymore. For a while I thought maybe someone blamed me for his death and was harassing me."

"You never thought it was *me*, did you?" Toby cocked his head to the side.

Hannah rolled her eyes. "Just thought is was kids, mostly . . . or maybe one of Deacon's former customers?"

"Savior of coin, huh?"

Her eyes lit up. "I think more like that Catholic high school up north, Xavier something?"

"That's weird, I just read about some kid from Xavier." He reached for the newspaper from the table across from them. He pulled out the local section and started flipping through. His constant amped energy made Hannah dizzy. "Nope. I got my stories mixed up. This is about Xavier Catholic getting a new headmaster."

Hannah exhaled and leaned back against the booth, folding her arms over her chest. "I saw Jade last night at The Cure concert. She acted funny when I brought up Deacon. Maybe she knows what happened the night of his death."

"Don't we already know? We were both there," he said flatly, slumping back into his seat.

She touched his arm lightly. "I know . . . but what if we don't know *everything*?"

He gazed down at her fingertips and looked as if he wanted to say something but thought better of it.

"Truth?" He stared soberly at her, resting his head on his hand. "I've blocked out most of that night. I don't even remember the gun going off. Only that he was suddenly lying on the ground."

Hannah nodded knowingly. "My brain has jumbled up a lot of that night, too."

He sighed deeply. "Okay, let's ask her what she knows."

Hannah shook her head. "I've tried. But *you* could."

"Jade never gave me the time of day. She was only interested in Deacon and his drugs . . ." Toby's brows shot up. "Wait, I have an idea."

They walked to the payphone by the mall exit. He deposited a quarter and turned back to her. "Deacon's pager, right?"

He entered the phone's seven-digit number and hung up. Less than a minute later, the phone rang.

She grabbed his arm before he picked up. "Wait, what are you going to tell her?"

He smiled mischievously. "Is Deacon there?" he said in a deep voice.

Hannah nodded her approval.

"That's not going to work, I only deal with *him* . . . what do you mean he's no longer at this number . . . where the hell is he?" His voice grew sterner. "I'm not going to repeat myself. Tell me where I can find him . . ." His voice took on an ominous tone. "No, we both know that's not true . . . right, Jade? Yeah, I know who you are and I know *exactly* where to find you . . . why don't you start again and tell me where he is . . . *or* . . ."

Toby hung up with a stunned look on his face, his hand still glued to the receiver.

"Oh my God, what just happened, what did she say?" Hannah demanded.

He gaped at her, unable to speak.

"What, *tell me!*"

"She said . . . 'He wouldn't tell me where he was going.'"

Hannah moved numbly back to their table. She didn't hear anything Toby said after that. Everything swirled around her, spinning faster by the second.

"It's not possible," she kept uttering softly.

"I know. But why would she say that? Just as easy to stick to her story that he was dead than to say *that*." His dark eyes fastened on hers. "Holy crap!"

"She's lying, I know it."

"He *fucked* with us?" he said, squinting and tilting his head to the side as he fell into the booth. "So I'm *not* a murderer?"

"No, no!" Hannah shook her head furiously.

He placed a hand on her shoulder. "Calm down . . . let's think. If it's true, why would he do this?"

"He hated his life so much . . . he didn't want to stay . . ."

"Then those prank calls started and never stopped."

"Why bother . . . he wanted us to believe he was *dead*, Toby!"

"Savior of coin, Xavier of coin . . ."

He grabbed the same newspaper from the nearby table, this time leafing through all of the sections.

"God, I'm stupid. I knew I read something. 'Xavier Coyne' . . . is that it?"

Hannah shrugged, looking away.

"Says here, Xavier Coyne, a young kingpin in Miami . . . has managed to elude authorities . . . described as charismatic and street smart . . . few have seen him . . . over the last six months there's been a slew of arrests connected to multi-kilo cocaine shipments coming in from Colombia."

"So?"

"You don't think that's strange? How many Xavier Coynes could there be? Who does he sound like, Hannah? And why would this guy call *you*?" He paused and his auburn eyebrows knitted themselves together in the middle of his freckled forehead.

She bit her upper lip and let his words swim around her head. *Why would a drug dealer from Miami call me and hang up?*

Deacon's face flashed before her. *I just called to hear your voice.*

"Oh, my, God." The hairs on the back of her neck stood up straight. "Wait, wait do you have a pen?"

She scribbled "Xavier Coyne" above the headline. Then she began scrambling the letters: "Vixen . . . convex . . . coaxer . . ."

"Try using all of the letters," Toby suggested.

"Wait, coaxer veiny?"

Toby snorted. "Is that what happens when you give blood?"

"Very funny . . . how about . . . anorexy vice?"

"Skinny police?" He snickered exposing his deep dimples.

"Cervix ya one?"

"Yeah . . . I'm not going to touch that one."

Hannah smiled despite how mad and confused she felt. She knew he was trying to make her feel better.

"This guy's got a lame name, whoever he is," she said dropping her shoulders and leaning back against the booth.

"Now *that* rhymes."

"Funny." She pressed her lips together. "I've got nothing here."

"It's not code for anything?"

"No, just a stupid name."

His leg ceased moving under the table. "He didn't exactly call *me* . . . he called *you*."

"If it's even him."

"Wouldn't you want to know?"

"Hell yeah." Hannah spread her hands on the table and began smoothing out a tablecloth that wasn't there. She stopped when she realized she was mimicking her father.

"Could you help me find out . . . if it really is him?"

Toby tipped his chin up, then deadpanned, "It's the least I can do after shooting him."

Hannah guffawed, her hand flying over her mouth. "I don't mean to . . . it just sounds funny when you say it like that. But it's sooo not."

———

They walked outside, both of them still in a daze, and stopped by a bench under a tree. The late-morning July sun felt good at first coming out of the mall's air conditioning. After several minutes, sweat began traveling down Hannah's back. She lifted her hair off her neck and leaned her forearms on her knees. It was already too hot in the shade.

"I'm not sure what I feel right now. Relief, I guess? Hope that it's true? I want to believe what she said." She turned to Toby. "Are you sure you heard her right?"

"Yeah, I'm sure. Jade's a crack-smoking junkie, it doesn't take much to break her."

"You scared *me* with that menacing voice of yours. Where did that come from?"

"Babette. She's not exactly warm and fuzzy mother material."

"No, definitely not." Hannah grimaced.

"My mom and I may not have had much, but I know she loved me. Deacon didn't even have that."

"I don't get it. Why aren't you still living with your mom? Why stay at the Girouxs' when they treat you like crap?"

"It's part of the *deal*."

"What deal?" Her head swung back to him. "Wait . . . no fricking way, his parents made a deal with you?"

He shook his head, making his sweat fly. "I wouldn't have to do any time for accidentally shooting Deacon. And in exchange, I'd move in with them."

"Why in the world would they do that?"

"I think Kingsley thought he owed it to my mom after all these years. She sort of had a breakdown after their relationship ended."

"Your mom too? Pills?"

"More like refusing to eat."

"Geez."

"Anyway, she's in treatment, sort of . . . and I'm trying to not add to her stress."

"That's screwed up."

Toby stared pensively at the pavement between his feet. He pulled his shirt from his chest airing it out. Then he stretched out his legs and placed his hands behind his head. Sweat marks circled his armpits. He didn't seem to care.

"My parents are screwed up too." Hannah said softly. "My mom's addicted to pills and booze, and my dad has been in denial for a while. She overdosed back in December—

along with my little sister, who downed my mom's prescription with a bottle of Yoohoo."

"Geez."

"Wait, it gets worse. They both spent a month and a half in rehab. After they came back my mom relapsed, and she hasn't been able to stop. We sort of had a 'come to Jesus' meeting about it the other day where I said a few things . . . and she cried. My dad was pissed at me at first. But now she's attending an outpatient treatment center and is trying again . . . trying to stay off of it." Hannah's face stilled, hearing herself confessing all these personal things. To Toby, of all people.

"That's rough. Your sister, too? Yikes." Toby shook his head.

"Yeah, it's kinda f-ed up."

"My story's not much better. In addition to my mom's problems, my girlfriend got pregnant last fall. She demanded that I pay for the abortion, then I found out it wasn't even *mine*."

"I . . . heard about that." Hannah ducked her head. "I'm sorry, Taylor's a bitch."

"They all are."

A car drove toward them through the parking lot. Hannah swiftly turned and shielded her face in case it was Howie —the last person she wanted to see. She pressed her lips together and brought her fingertips to her mouth. *I have to know.*

"Tell me why you covered for Gillian. How come you never told the cops that she put you up to bringing a gun to the park that night?"

Toby wheeled around to face her. "Her name was never brought up. Kingsley handled the cops."

"Wasn't he pissed that you'd taken his gun?"

He pulled a face. "Huh? I didn't take it."

"But the newspaper said—"

"He gave it to me on my birthday . . . promised we'd go to the shooting range, learn to handle a gun properly."

"Weren't you underage? That's illegal."

"Kingsley's from the South, the *deep* South; they teach their boys early, or so he says. Never happened, though; we never went. He says things and doesn't follow through. None of it matters now. I'm never touching a gun again."

"Me neither."

"You know, Deacon could be cruel—a dick, usually—but *they* were the ones who screwed him up. Did you know that our father didn't have a clue that he was sending me to the *same prep school* that Deacon's *grandfather* had sent *him* to?"

She heard Deacon's words in her head: *I once told my parents I made the high school swim team. And needed to go to practice at school, early in the morning . . . I know . . . the school doesn't have a pool. Now you know how involved my parents are.*

"How did you figure it out . . . you know, that you were *brothers?*"

"Not until the kids at boarding school talked about Deacon leaving with his mother and moving back home. I never knew his last name before that. When I found out, I kept badgering my mom to take me out of there and let me go to the public school near her house. Eventually she did, my senior year."

"What was that like, being the new kid and in the same grade as your half brother, who was also the most well-known and probably feared kid in school?"

"Deacon blew me off most of the time. I knew I bugged him. I let the whole thing get under my skin. He was pretty screwed up, too, I think. Now that I see the Girouxs for who they are, I'm sure they didn't pay him much attention. They're consumed by their own lives . . . with wealth, their appearance and status . . . nothing else matters. I see that now. There's no *family* living in that house . . . at least, not the one I wanted."

"I think we loved each other, once," Hannah said wistfully, pulling strands of hair across her lips. "I'm probably romanticizing the short time we had together, you know, only remembering the good stuff. But I know I loved him."

"It looked to me that he felt the same way. Guess that bothered me, too, at the time."

Hannah punched his shoulder playfully. "I noticed."

"I was pretty fucked up after that night. I swear, I never meant to shoot him. I didn't know what I was doing . . . I'm sorry I scared you. Gillian got into my head and I was caught up in all the stuff about Taylor's pregnancy, especially since I was raised by a single mother—her wanting an abortion and all—that . . . that . . . I went crazy, I guess."

"People can make you do some crazy things . . . like take LSD by yourself. That's how Deacon and I met."

"Now *that's* fucked up."

Hannah punched his shoulder harder this time. "Ow!" she exclaimed, realizing she hurt her hand more than she hurt him, and laughed at herself.

CHAPTER 42

south beach, miami

––––––

CLAUDIA GRITTED HER TEETH. "YOU CAN'T DISAPPEAR LIKE that, X. What the hell were you thinking? Eastman and Kodak are trolling all over Miami—the airports, everywhere—looking for you."

Deacon braced himself. "Were they able to save those two little girls?"

Claudia looked away. "They never found the Wendy's truck."

"Fuck!" He brought his fist to his lips and closed his eyes, clenching his jaw.

"I know that's a hard one to swallow. You have to let stuff like that go. It'll drive you crazy."

"Christ!" Deacon began walking around in circles, his hands on either side of his head. "I hate this!" he screamed. "I hate this *life*!"

He lowered himself onto the curb and jammed the edge of his palms into his forehead. "What about Chalfont . . . Luis?"

"They have the whole cartel combing the streets for you."

He looked up at her. "What did you tell them?"

"The truth. I didn't know where you were. You should have found me. I'd have gotten Eastman and Kodak to put you in witness protection."

"More like jail."

"So you think it's only street life or jail for you?"

"There's no official record of me working for you guys. It's not like I signed something. I'm only *one* of the DEA's many secrets, and not its first informant. It would be easy to dispose of me."

"We're not killers, Xavier."

"Sure feels like it. Eastman and Kodak coerced me into working for them. They cuffed and shackled me and took away my identity, then fed me to the cartel. I didn't even graduate high school. Everyone thinks I'm dead. I'm in hell down here."

Claudia swung her long, wavy tresses over to one side, lowered her ample chest toward him, and stroked his face. "We're safe, cowboy," she said sweetly. "Our cover is secure. We're getting so close to taking Chalfont down. We can spin this . . . convince them that you just got scared. We can figure this out and still make 'Xavier Coyne' work."

"All of Chalfont's men are out looking for me because I didn't do what Luis asked . . . I abandoned them. They see me as a traitor now. I've seen what Chalfont does to people like me."

"You want *out* from all of this?" Her sudden sharp tone sliced the air, making Deacon flinch. She straightened her spine and punched her fists into her hips. "You can't use this slip-up to weasel out of our mission. I won't allow it. We will see this to the end. For my little boy, and for all of the other innocents that bastard has destroyed. You're going back to Chalfont, and you're gong to plead for his forgiveness." She crossed her arms and lowered her eyelids midway over her icy eyes. "And if he wants *more* from you . . . you'll do *that*, too."

His mouth fell open. "You mean sleep with him?"

"You think the Feds recruited you for your *brains*?"

His face stiffened. "That was the plan this whole time? Not to *just* get into Chalfont's business, but get in bed with him? You're smoking something. No one can make me do that, especially not *you*."

The sound of fireworks caused them to turn. Deacon searched the sky and quickly realized his mistake. He dove behind Claudia's white Ferrari as the automatic weapon fired again. He stayed low, covering his head, his heart thudding against the asphalt. In seconds, the street resumed its silence.

His fear overpowered him, pushing him into the ground and paralyzing him to the point that he thought he might have actually been hit.

He had to move.

He crawled on his elbows and peered around the car's tires. A yellow Corvette with tinted windows pulled away— with Chalfont's long, hairy arm resting outside the driver's side window.

Deacon popped up his head, looking for Claudia. She was no longer near him. Then he saw her—her body twitching in the middle of the street, her eyes splayed open, her legs pretzeled underneath her. Claudia's throat emitted a gurgling sound, and then nothing.

He scrambled across the sidewalk, staying low to the ground, and fell into a shadowed doorway, trying to contain his exploding chest. *What the hell just happened?* His brain stormed with twisted thoughts, including how little time he had left.

You think the Feds recruited you for your brains?

CHAPTER 43

darien, connecticut

HANNAH HESITATED IN THE DOORWAY BEFORE LEAVING her room. She filled her lungs and followed the sound of sighs, clearing of throats, and turning newspaper pages coming from the living room. The returning chorus of her parents' habits and mannerisms were a welcome change—as was her mother's newfound sobriety.

Her mom was spending more time on the main floor and less in her bedroom these days. Hannah and her father tiptoed around her to avoid stressing her out, and she still seemed to be wound tight. Seeing more of her felt like progress, at least.

"Mom, remember I told you that I got accepted to a summer writing workshop?" She knew she hadn't. It's not like her mother would remember anyway.

Her mom swallowed slowly and laid her paperback romance facedown on her lap. It was good seeing her reading again, and without a coffee cup nearby. Her eyes shot over to Hannah's father in his recliner; his face was partially hidden by his *Connecticut Post*. "I do not," she announced, still looking over at him.

"Well, it's next week and I thought—"

"She got accepted into a writing workshop?" her father said, lowering his paper and glancing at her mother.

"What's it about?" her mother asked, still looking at him.

"They invited me. I guess . . . I-I show promise . . . as a writer."

"Sounds like a scam," her father said, burying his nose back into his pages.

"I agree," her mother said primly.

"Well, it's not. Look, here's the letter." She held it out to him.

He skimmed it briefly and frowned. "Young lady, we don't have this kind of money," he said, waving his hand like he was brushing crumbs off a table. "How are you going to pay for this?"

"I worked all summer and saved my paychecks."

"Why would they invite *you*?" her mother said, like Hannah's initial explanation wasn't sufficient.

"Gee, thanks, Mom."

"Donna," her dad said, "they'll take anybody these days as long as they cough up the cash. It's like those Draw Winky ads in the *Pennysaver*. 'Draw Winky and test your talent to win a commercial art scholarship or cash prize.' No one ever wins. Their 'free professional evaluation' is merely a *form letter* they send out to *everyone* telling them that they have 'potential' so they fork over the dough for some shady home-study art course." He swirled his right thumb along the tops of his fingers to illustrate his point. "They prey on people's egos. Just another scam."

Hannah pulled a face. "It's not some ad in the *Pennysaver*. It was through my school. My English teacher, Mrs. Myers, helped—"

"Isn't that teacher the one who's . . . you know . . ." her mother said, shifting in her seat.

"You mean *gay?*" Hannah sighed, rolling her eyes. "Mrs. Myers is the best teacher in the school, and she was the *first* person to believe in me."

"It's a waste of money, anyway," her dad huffed.

Her mother's head bobbed in agreement.

"I'll pay for the whole thing, including my bus fare. *Please.*"

Her mother coughed lightly and straightened her back against the couch. "Charles, I'd like to get away, maybe somewhere up the coast, before the rat race of school starts."

Her father's face softened. He studied his wife for a moment. "Where would you like to go, dear?"

"I know money's tight with the hospital and rehabilitation bills and now the new outpatient center—"

"No, no, it's fine. We *should* go. We'll let them know at the center and get you some time away."

"So can *I* go then?" Hannah held her breath. She was afraid to believe it.

"No, you should stay here while we're gone," her dad said firmly. "And watch the house."

"*Watch* the house?" she asked incredulously. "No one wants what we have here. Trust me."

"Oh, Charles, remember last time . . ." her mother whispered this last part as if her daughter had a fatal disease. Hannah watched her father's face pucker with disapproval. Her eyes flicked back to her mother.

Well played, Mother. You mean the weekend I nearly died?

"We'll give you one last chance. Don't disappoint us," her dad said like he was on the set of *Father Knows Best.*

How the hell did asking to attend my writing workshop turn into your *vacation, Mom?*

She closed her bedroom door behind her and leaned her head against it. *I should be grateful,* she told herself. Her mom was becoming herself again, no matter how dysfunctional that person was. Maybe this time her recovery would work.

Seeing her father cow to her mother, though, only solidified the permanency of his role with her. Her parents would never change.

She could, though. Maybe she could be braver than she'd ever thought possible.

CHAPTER 44

south beach, miami

DEACON MOVED QUICKLY, TRYING TO BEAT THE SUNRISE as he took the long way back to the men's shelter. His body, buoyed by adrenaline, kept him alert for Chalfont's car as he darted down alleyways and crossed over streets.

He'd closed his eyes when Claudia died—not from grief but from shame combined with a sense of relief. He felt nothing; just another day in Miami and another dead body of a girl he never really knew. At least she'd be with her son now.

Why her and not me?

None of it made sense.

Hannah's final words did, however, along with the foolish hope that once sustained him.

She hates me. She's known all this time and doesn't care. F-ing Jade. She must have told her.

He cringed at his stupidity in thinking his time in Miami would one day be worth it, in believing he'd see her again and gather her up in his arms and never let go. *She doesn't want you, asshole.*

How many more dead bodies was it going take for him to get the balls to disappear from this world? He should just let Kodak and Eastman shoot him in the back with one of their shiny guns as he runs away. *Not another day*, he swore. *I won't spend another day here.*

Deacon stopped.

His shiny gun . . .

The manila envelope with the flags and the tiny ducks had been on the table at the diner with Kodak and Eastman, just before he met Claudia. The envelope had contained his new IDs as Xavier Coyne. Why would Chalfont have in his possession the same envelope as the Feds? Had he been sending him a message that he knew his real identity? If that were true, he'd be dead already; Deacon was sure of it.

His shiny gun . . .

His heart sank.

He traveled another block, then stopped on the corner to make a call.

"Yeah, it's me . . . yeah, stop yelling and listen. Chalfont took Claudia out and he's headed for me next. My cover has been compromised. I have to get out of here. Yeah, I'll talk. Tell you whatever I know, which isn't much at the moment . . . Calm the fuck down! I'm the one living on the streets, not you!"

He pulled the handset away from his ear and let Kodak go off. The guy was headed for a heart attack, and now would not be a good time for it. Deacon was reluctant to contact him at all, but he knew he needed the Feds with Chalfont still out there.

"Are you done? Chill, 'Kodak Camera' . . . I can get you someone else that will be of great interest to you, with connections to the cartel. No, I alone have to do it. This one is personal and needs to be carried out on *my* terms. I know . . . I realize that. I'll be in touch."

Deacon held onto the handset like it was a lifeline. He thought of another person who would be up this early. He sucked his lips into his mouth and fished up the faded, ripped phonebook from where it dangled. He flipped through it until he found what he was looking for, then fed the phone another quarter and dialed.

"Miss Ida? Yes, hello. I'm . . . I'm a . . . well, I was a friend of Paul's . . . Xavier . . . that's right. Paul always said you were an early riser. I'm *real* sorry for your loss . . . I miss him, too . . . yes, Paul and I talked cars . . . that's right, I re-member him telling me that." He released a cordial laugh, even though he wasn't following what she was saying. "Miss Ida, I was wondering if you could use some help with all the crime happening in the city . . . yeah, it's been terrible . . . maybe some protection now would be good? Yes, I'd be happy to. Uh-huh. I understand. Well, I'm sort of in be-tween places right now . . ."

Deacon looked around. The only two places he was in between was remaining the Feds' indentured servant and be-ing Miami's most dangerous drug lord's next boy toy.

"That would be great . . . thank you. See you soon."

August 1985

CHAPTER 45

darien, connecticut

HANNAH'S ALARM RATTLED ACROSS HER NIGHTSTAND BEFORE the sun had a chance to crack the earth's horizon. Her heart started pounding as soon as her feet touched the carpet. She packed her clothes and a small bag of toiletries and makeup, along with a separate cooler she found in the attic, and filled it with soft drinks and whatever snacks she could scrounge up. With Kerry away, there wasn't much in the cabinets.

Just get something at the mall, her mother had told her when she asked about groceries before her parents left for Maine.

She wrote a note to her parents explaining why the writing workshop at Simon's Rock was important to her. She made up another bit for good measure—that she'd already paid her tuition for the workshop and it was nonrefundable. She added that she'd be home in a couple of weeks (in case they returned earlier than planned). She signed it just as a pair of headlights traveled across the windows in the front of the house.

She heaved one bag over each shoulder and let herself out through the garage.

"Whose car is *this*?" she asked as she climbed into the

passenger seat. Toby was already drinking a Coke. He passed her a cold one.

"Ole man Kingsley's." He smiled and patted the steering wheel. "A '63 Corvette Stingray Coupe."

"It's so pretty!" she exclaimed. She had never ridden in a car this beautiful. "Is it gray?"

"Baby blue . . . cream interior."

"And tinted windows to boot. Very nice. Got some balls there, Toby. I feel like we're in the Batmobile with the split window in the back. Where's *your* car?"

"Parked in town. I figured our search mission needed a cool getaway car."

"That's assuming we've got this right. We may be way off."

Toby tilted his head to one side. "Worst case, I'm getting to see a few states. I've never been to Florida before. You?"

"Never. This is another pretty reckless thing I'm doing. What's with these Giroux boys . . . always making you do stuff and take chances."

Toby chuckled. "Yeah, we're a dangerous bunch."

She leaned back and immediately missed having a head-rest. They had a sixteen-hour drive ahead of them, and sleeping was definitely going to be difficult in this car.

By the time they turned onto the highway, Toby's left leg was already bouncing like crazy.

"What is it?" Hannah gestured to his leg.

He glanced down. "Nervous, I guess. It's a bad habit of mine . . . I never stop moving. Used to drive my mom and especially my teachers nuts. I was a pretty rambunctious kid."

Can't imagine that. "Everyone's got something," Hannah said, shaking her head.

"I feel good about what we're doing. We deserve some answers. Making us believe he was dead . . . that's bull."

"You know, we're putting a lot of trust in Jade. She's not exactly reliable."

"Yeah, but she sounded scared, and you've said she's been acting funny about him. It sort of makes sense that there's more we don't know."

"If he's really the one making those calls, why couldn't he tell me what was going on?"

"I dunno. Maybe he thought your phone line was tapped. You said Peter told you—"

"*Don't* . . . don't say that name, ever again!" she screeched, covering her ears. Her outburst surprised even her. "Sorry . . . I . . ." She grabbed her forearms and pressed them tight to her chest.

Toby shrugged. "Okay, the tall skinny guy who pounced on me that . . . err, night . . . told you that two cops showed up and took Deacon away before the ambulance got there. Maybe they weren't who they said they were."

"I think you've watched too much TV," she said, arching her brow like a pirate.

"Then again, I may be spot on."

———

Hannah stretched her arms over her head, yawning. "How long have I been asleep?"

Toby was busy squinting at the map he'd folded over the steering wheel.

"I'll read the map. You drive," she offered.

"I want to get us at least to South Carolina; then we'll pull over so I can sleep a little."

"I have a driver's license, too, you know."

"No can do. I'm a terrible passenger."

"Jumpy?"

"The worst. Hey, I ate a bunch of your snacks, now I need something more like a sandwich. I should have warned you, I eat all the time."

They stopped at the next rest stop and ordered. Hannah took a big bite of her burger, surprised by how hungry she was. She saw Toby eyeing her as she ate and tried to slow down.

"Don't take this wrong, but—"

"What? I'm starving," she said, grabbing a napkin to catch the juices flowing down her chin.

"No, not that. After everything that's happened, why do you even trust me? I wasn't exactly nice to you when we met."

"No kidding. You were a stuck-up prick."

"Geez. Don't hold back now." He grinned.

"It's true. I thought you were one of those popular kids, some jock who's full of himself. You were dating Taylor, for God's sake." She rolled her eyes.

"I wasn't popular. Deacon was the only one I knew at Darien."

"Why do popular people always say they aren't popular, when you guys know that you are."

"I never felt that way. If anything, I never felt like I fit in at Darien."

"Join the club."

Toby laughed.

"After summer ends, what are you going to do? Are you going to college?"

Toby wrinkled his forehead and looked down at his food. "I still need my GED. Then I don't know what I'll do. Can't exactly waste time at the mall for the rest of my life."

"Deacon didn't know either. Hmmm, you two really *are* related."

"You're quick."

Hannah smiled. "It's weird that we're sort of friends now."

"And going on a mission together to find my asshole brother!"

"The soap opera never ends."

"I've been thinking. We haven't a clue where to start looking. For all we know, Xavier Coyne, aka Deacon, could be long gone."

"I thought of that."

"We need to come up with a plan . . . like how to narrow down all the places he could be."

"I'm more worried what happens if we find him."

CHAPTER 46

———

"THANK YOU *MIAMI HERALD*!"

"What is it?" Hannah asked, looking over Toby's shoulder. She was carrying a cold six-pack of Diet Coke, along with a large bag of chips, up to the man behind the counter at the small bodega. The steady diet of junk food they'd consumed over the last few days was wreaking havoc on her stomach. Between the scorching temperatures of Miami in August and the endless queasiness she'd been experiencing since they'd arrived, she would need a real meal soon—one with some vegetables.

"This says that our boy, Xavier Coyne, was believed to be in the vicinity when a shooting occurred on Monday. A woman was fatally shot. It doesn't mention her name. It happened in South Beach near the Ocean Drive Promenade . . . not far from here. How big could it be?"

He grinned at her, but Hannah couldn't bring herself to smile back; her stomach had just dropped at the mention of him being with another woman. Then her brain filled with dread, imagining what kind of trouble Deacon had gotten himself into. Assuming this Xavier guy was even him.

The store clerk eyed them suspiciously and placed Hannah's change on the counter instead of in her outstretched hand. "You're looking for *Coyne*?" he asked quietly, leaning over the counter.

"I see the change, thanks," Hannah replied, waving her hand.

"No," said Toby, "he means *Coyne* as in Xavier Coyne." He looked excited. "Have you seen him?"

The man's eyes darted to the entrance and the aisles behind them before answering. "No one *sees* him. You just know when he's been around. People talk in this neighborhood." The clerk pushed off the counter and stepped back.

Toby glanced at Hannah, then back to the store clerk. "I don't follow you."

The man leaned in again. "He comes in here late at night . . . I know it's him from what others have said. He doesn't say much. But I can tell. Keeps a low profile. Young, cocky . . . movie star looks."

That sounds like him, Hannah thought. "Do you have a picture?"

The man gave a subtle headshake and gestured for them to move along; another customer was waiting. He didn't look at Toby and Hannah again, acting like the conversation hadn't happened. Their chance to ask him more questions was over.

"What do you think?" she asked Toby as they stepped outside the bodega. She tied up her wild, humidity-loving tresses in a loose bun and wiped the back of her neck. "Sounds like we're looking for a reclusive rock star."

"My brother's always been a charmer," Toby said, lifting his face to the bright orb in the sky. "Geez, it's hot, the sidewalk is frying my feet. Let's jump back in the car and drive around."

"Deacon hates the heat."

"Guess we can skip the beach, then."

"He likes the water, though my gut tells me he wouldn't be hanging out there," Hannah said. "We should keep going store to store, see if he's made any recent visits. Maybe someone knows where he's staying."

———

"We never said how long we were going to give this witch hunt. Guess this was a dumb idea," Hannah said, yawning into her oatmeal. It was Friday morning, and they were eating breakfast at a diner near their motel. They'd arrived the Friday before, late in the evening. After six days of searching, they were both tiring of Miami—especially the tourists and the unbearable heat.

At first it was weird spending stretches of time with Deacon's brother. Hannah noticed that the more Toby joked around with her, the more relaxed he got, and his nervous energy stilled a bit. He wasn't so bad to hang with then.

The first night he'd slept in the car, giving her the bed. She'd offered to switch the next night and he wouldn't have it, though he'd finally agreed to sleep on the floor. Hannah found it surprisingly gallant of him, and sort of sweet. She got the feeling he was doing it out of respect for Deacon, and that made her like him even more.

"Let's go to the beach today, take the day off," Toby said before shoveling another forkful of eggs with ketchup into his mouth. Between bites, he flipped through the newspaper. Every day he scoured it, hoping for another news story that would give them a clue to Xavier Coyne's whereabouts.

"Or head back home?" Hannah asked tentatively.

He threw the newspaper off to the side, looking discouraged. "Yeah, you're probably right. No one wants to talk to us. You can tell they've all heard of this Coyne guy. He's like a celebrity around here, but at the same time they're scared of him. How about that club owner who wanted to know if we were cops?"

"We should place a personal ad in the paper like in that Madonna movie, *Desperately Seeking Susan*," Hannah said. "DESPERATELY SEEKING XAVIER COYNE: meet your former girlfriend and the stepbrother who shot you at the corner of blah, blah, and blah."

"That'd be good . . . if my brother ever read a newspaper in his life."

"Yeah. Not his thing."

Toby and Hannah spent half the day at the beach without saying much. She could tell Toby was feeling as deflated as she was that their search had come up empty. Part of her didn't want to give up hope in finding out what had happened to Deacon that night, while the other part prayed that Xavier Coyne would call her house again. This time, she'd know what to say.

"These *old fogies* move so slow, how do people live here and get used to *this*?" Toby said, tapping the steering wheel, as they waited for a crowd of senior citizens to cross the intersection.

"Some of them are cute. I love seeing the couples still holding hands," Hannah said, resting her elbow against the window.

"More like racing their walkers at a snail's pace. But the streets by the Promenade were really nice with those colorful buildings."

"The Art Deco district," Hannah said, nodding. "I like that area too."

"This part is so poor," Toby said. "Crawling with beggars and homeless people. It's sad."

"Totally."

Toby laughed and pointed at the last stragglers crossing in front of them. "See that skinny guy wearing the floppy hat and sunglasses? He's going to lose those plaid pants any minute."

"Aww, he's pushing his grandmother. Don't make fun—" Hannah gasped.

"What?" Toby's eyes flew to her.

"Look at him. He can't stop staring at the Corvette."

"Yeah, so? I'm sure one doesn't see too many baby blue '63 Stingrays around here," he said smugly.

"No one can see us through these tinted windows, right?"

"No, but—"

"*Look* at him . . . his height, the way he walks . . . Toby!" she whispered.

"I don't know . . . maybe? Shit. He won't stop staring."

"You said this was Kingsley's car!" Hannah's heart thudded hard against her chest wall. She lowered herself in the seat, suddenly scared.

"What are you doing? He can't see us! And we're looking for *him*, remember?"

"I'm freaking out!"

"Roll down your window or I'll do it!"

"Shoot, he's staring again." Her voice fluttered up an octave.

The car behind them laid on the horn, forcing them to pull through the intersection.

"Keep your eyes on him, Hannah, I'll pull over as soon as I can." Toby swung his head back over his shoulder as they passed. "He just looked back. Connecticut plates, baby. He knows the car!"

She sank lower in the seat, tears springing to her eyes. "I can't, I won't . . . I'm going to be sick."

Toby laughed. "Calm down, he couldn't see us. There's no way he'd assume the two of us were inside. Not in a million years."

"Oh my God, I'm freaking out. Do you think it's him?"

He turned onto the next block. "We're following him, I can tell you that much."

"I can't believe this. Oh my God, oh my God!" she said, pulling at her hair.

"He's not exactly dressed like himself," Toby said.

"Think he's in trouble?" She gulped.

"Who cares—he's fucking alive. I'm not a murderer!"

Toby's elation set Hannah's tears in motion. He reached over and put his arm around her, squeezing her shoulder. "Bingo, brother, we found you," he whistled through his teeth.

CHAPTER 47

———

"ARE YOU SURE THIS IS THE RIGHT HOUSE?" HANNAH asked, eyeing the quaint shaker-style home with its long row of steps leading up to the front door. Dark drapes were drawn on all of the windows, which added to her uneasiness. She was focusing on taking long, deep breaths, but it wasn't doing much to calm her down.

"Positive," Toby said. "It's the house he wheeled her into, see the ramp? You should go in first. Then break it to him that I'm outside and not here to take him out again. I'm not sure what he'll do when he sees me. Kind of ended badly back there in Connecticut."

"You think?"

Toby laughed, giving her shoulder a light shove. "Go, you're stalling."

Hannah avoided the front steps and used the wheelchair ramp off the side of the house to access the front door. She carefully turned the handle to the screen door, pushed on the inside door—which was already ajar—with her fingertips, and stepped through with little sound. She held her breath as her heart clocked in at a mile a minute.

The overwhelming mustiness of the air hit her first. The house's temperature matched the boiling weather outside.

She squinted, adjusting to the low lamplight in the room. There were framed photographs everywhere. A small black-and-white wedding picture featured a man in a military uniform and a bride wearing a dress with a sweetheart neckline and her hair set in victory rolls like they did in the 1940s.

It appeared that an English garden had sprouted from every corner of the room, from the Laura Ashley wallpaper to the floral upholstered furniture circling the Victorian rug. A walker stood next to two winged chairs with a half-finished needlepoint on one of the ottomans.

She picked up the men's suit jacket draped across the back of the couch, wondering if its owner was in the next room. She brought it to her nose and it reminded her of her parents' mothball-laden couch in the basement.

She jumped at the sound of voices coming from what she assumed to be a bedroom. Footsteps sounded in the hallway, moving in her direction. Hannah froze.

All at once, the bright overhead light in the adjacent kitchen flooded the space where she stood. She was caught.

He stopped at the sight of her.

Panic rose up her throat, thinking she was in the wrong house. Then he lowered his sunglasses, revealing those chocolate-brown eyes she thought she'd never see again. Something that had lain dormant since that ill-fated night in Gossamer Park now yanked at her chest.

Under his floppy hat was a shock of white-blond hair that gave him a strange punk-rocker vibe. His eyes steadied on hers as he began unbuttoning his oversized shirt. It slipped off his shoulders and fell to the floor.

Hannah swallowed nervously.

He unbuckled his belt. The plaid trousers fell, too, without trouble. His black T-shirt fit snug across his chest and shoulders. His tanned biceps poked out from his sleeves. Hannah lowered her eyes to his hips, where his shorts hugged him perfectly. Her cheeks grew warm. She blinked several times and bit her lower lip.

She needed air. *I'm not seeing this. It's not real.*

He had grown taller since she last saw him. All that time, when he was supposedly six feet under, he'd been *here*, his body looking better than it had a right to.

The light scruff on his face made him appear older and cursedly sexier. He was leaner than before, his cheekbones more pronounced; new creases circled his eyes. She gaped at the apparition before her. *It's not possible.*

This blond doppelganger wasn't moving, therefore he couldn't be real, her brain rationalized. She was bound to wake up, any minute now.

He took a step toward her. Hannah's hammering heart accelerated its pace, cutting off her breath. She leaned toward the wall with her arm extended, intending to steady herself, and missed; she stumbled and smacked her head into it first. *What am I seeing exactly?*

"I thought you were going to be my father. How are you *here?*" he whispered, stepping toward her.

The sound of his voice fired the gun that she hadn't known was cocked in her head until that moment. The reverb shot down her face and neck and into her arms. Her vision blurred with tears. She was flooded with an overwhelming sense of relief that he was still breathing.

She knew it then to be true.

She really had been waiting for him to come back to her.

He took another step toward her. Her hands flew up, signaling for him to stay back. She stumbled backward, and he darted forward and reached out to catch her.

"Oh my God, oh my God . . ." she said, swatting him away.

He brought a finger to his lips and motioned with his head for her to follow him.

The anger welled up from her stomach and stampeded her throat, catching her by surprise. *Don't you dare tell me to be quiet*, she thought, *I'll kill you myself.*

"This way." He ushered her outside, holding open the kitchen's side door for her. They walked out to a modest patio with grass and weeds popping up around its brick pavers. A couple of rusted-out chairs and a small hibachi grill that had seen better days stood off to the side.

She couldn't look at him, though she could feel his eyes never leaving her. She read his silence for cockiness, which infuriated her more.

"You've been pretending to be dead . . . why in the world . . . you couldn't just break things off like a normal person? You opted for a charade instead? *You asshole!*"

Deacon ran his hands through his hair, pulling on the back of his head.

She wondered what story she'd hear now.

"You just screamed at me saying to never call you again, and somehow you're here?" He began walking around in a circle. "Wait . . . wait a minute, I never broke up with you." He squeezed his eyes. "*You* ended it, remember?"

"I didn't know it was *you* who was calling. I thought—never mind . . ."

"What happened? Did someone hurt you?"

She gathered her elbows and pulled them into her ribcage. "Yeah . . . *you*. You left. Were you like, 'Let's make her into the gullible fool'? Was that the plan?"

"The gun, Toby . . . all of it was real, Hannah."

"I saw you *die*," she said, her eyes blazing into his.

"It takes more than that to take *me* out," he said lamely.

She wasn't playing.

He exhaled and dropped his shoulders. His eyes were shadowed with exhaustion.

"I never told you. One night after we were together, these undercover cops pulled me over and tried to arrest me. The scumbags threw a bag of coke in my trunk and acted like they'd found it on me. Then everything turned. They didn't go through with the arrest . . . instead, they wanted to cut a deal."

Hannah grew quiet, her breathing slowed.

"They threatened to bring you up on charges as an accomplice, paint you as the queen of operations." Deacon's voice cracked; his eyes flitted away.

"But I never—"

"Didn't matter. They said they'd pardon Jade, and put her charges *on you*. They'd been watching me for months. I couldn't . . . I wouldn't let that happen."

"When I went unconscious that night, they jumped to put their plan in motion. They confirmed me dead and sent me to this weird facility outside of town that was part hospital, part rehab, I think."

A chill ascended the back of Hannah's neck.

I forgot to tell you I saw one of your friends here, her mother had said when she went to see her in rehab back in December. *A tall, striking boy. I think he was visiting someone down the hall.*

She'd blown off her mother's remark, thinking she was just being delusional. Her mom had only met Deacon one time, and she'd clearly been high that day. Apparently, he'd made an impression. If only Hannah had listened to her.

"I woke up two days later with those cops at the foot of my bed. Turns out they were federal agents, DEA."

"This is too crazy," Hannah mumbled, more to herself than him. She pressed a hand to her forehead. "Wait, what about your parents? They buried you, I thought. I couldn't bring myself to go to the cemetery. But Jade told me. What did they *bury*, then?"

"No clue. The Feds probably threw something into the ground. After working with these guys down here, I feel confident saying an extra corpse probably wasn't too hard to find."

Hannah's cheek twitched.

"They faked my death, forced me to leave everything and everyone I knew, just so I would work for them. They said they'd take my life away . . . and yours . . . if I didn't cooperate."

"You left . . . to *protect* me?"

"I'd rather have died that night than live knowing I dragged you down into my world and helped end yours."

She stared at him for several seconds, then turned to hide her face. It was too much seeing him before her. She pinched the top of her hand to stop her emotions from charging forward.

"When were you planning to *resurrect*?" she snapped, looking back at him. Her eyes filled, giving her away.

"When it was safe," Deacon said carefully, his defenseless eyes reeling her in. "Hannah, I never stopped thinking about you, wondering what you were doing, who you were with. I'd call in the middle of the night just to hear your voice. I was always going to come back for you . . . *for us*."

She tried gathering up his ocean of words before they had a chance to penetrate her parched heart, containing them. *It's too late.*

"So now you're the son of some Miami drug lord, like the papers say?" Her voice came out panicked, not cool and collected like she hoped.

"Hannah . . ." He started to walk closer, then jerked back at the sight of Toby emerging from around the side of the house. He threw himself in front of Hannah. "Are you back to finish the job, prick?"

Hannah stepped around Deacon and faced him. "We drove down together."

His head whipped back toward her, then toward Toby. "What, are you two a thing now? *You dick*," he sneered at his brother, balling his fist up and lunging toward him.

Hannah latched on to his arm and pulled back forcefully. "More like a couple of detectives. We came here for you, idiot . . . for *you*."

Deacon stopped.

Toby didn't take another step as they sized one another up. "Hey, good to see you're alive. Big relief."

Deacon clenched his hands. "If you hadn't shot me, they would never have taken me away. You helped put this whole nightmare in motion."

"It was an accident," Hannah said with a sigh.

Deacon's mouth dropped open. "You're on *his* side?"

"Don't twist this. You don't get to do that. Toby and I started talking this summer and realized that we were both still trying to deal with what happened that night. We became suspicious after I got that last call. We took a gamble and came down here to find you."

Toby thrust his hands in his pockets and glanced down at his feet. "I owed you that after what I'd done . . . I had no idea what your life was like, man. No wonder you didn't want a brother," he said in a low voice, shaking his head. "After . . . that night, Kingsley got my sentence reduced, he made a deal with the officers. I moved into the house, into your room. Judge ordered me to see a therapist every week in exchange for doing time. Then everything changed. Under their roof, I became invisible. I wanted your life for so long, wanted desperately to be a part of a real family. The joke was on me. I've never been lonelier."

CHAPTER 48

DEACON PULLED BACK, LETTING TOBY'S WORDS SINK IN. As they did, a realization reared up—one he did not want to face.

His shiny gun . . .

"My father cut a deal with you? The guy who *shot* me?"

Toby nodded. "Kingsley's an asshole. They both are. I was incredibly jealous of you, but I never wanted you dead . . . I just wanted the pain to stop. I hated my life; I was so lonely. That night in the park, I was really messed up. I would have killed myself if Hannah hadn't been there."

Toby's eyes shifted to Hannah's. Hers were wide and full of sadness.

Deacon had never heard Toby speak so honestly before. He knew it had to be Hannah's influence. She had that no-BS, truth-serum effect on people.

For eight months, Deacon burned with hate for his stepbrother and what had happened that night. In one swift moment, the face of his enemy had shifted.

"The pain," he murmured, staring into the brown, overgrown garden behind Hannah. "I know it well. I was such a dick because . . . *I* was jealous of *you*. The way Kingsley was with you. I saw him visit you at boarding school. That handshake you guys had, all of it. You were a constant reminder of how little he cared for me. I know that I egged you on that night. You know what my first thought was after you shot me? I'll never forget it."

Toby's eyes grew big.

"Relief. Relief that all of my pain would finally be over . . . but then *you* were there," he said, turning to Hannah, "and all I wanted to do was put the whole night in reverse."

Toby stepped forward. "I never meant to . . . the gun just went off. I didn't know—"

"You stole his revolver from the desk in his study."

Toby shook his head. "No. He *gave* it to me on my last birthday."

"Of course he did," Deacon said under his breath. "That's fucked up. *Jesus Christ.* And he gave you the Stingray, too? You know what? I'm not surprised Kingsley had you move into the house. You replaced me, put the family picture back together. Funny thing is, what you're saying makes me feel somewhat better. All this time, it wasn't about me; *I* wasn't the one who was unworthy of their attention. They're just so screwed up. They didn't know how to raise a kid."

"Big time." Toby nodded.

God, it was never about me.

Deacon rocked his head to either side, running his hands through his hair. "I needed to hear that," he said, watching Hannah. She still wouldn't look at him. God, he'd missed her. He wanted to inhale whatever breath she had inside and kiss her for a long time. But something in her eyes told him to take it slow. She wasn't going to take him back so easily.

Toby stepped closer. "Helping find you this week was the first time I did something for someone else. Seriously, br—"

He cleared his throat. "It felt good, that's all. Now that it's over . . . I don't want to go back to them. Guess I'll go back to my mom's . . . I don't know."

Deacon picked up a piece of broken paver and threw it into the garden. "Good thing you're a bad shot . . . *bro.*"

Toby's head bounced up, as did Hannah's, hearing Deacon acknowledge him as his brother—a fact he'd adamantly denied the night at the park before the gun went off.

Deacon could feel Hannah smiling next to him. Her eyes were on Toby and his crimson face, which wore a grin that kept growing. She was happy for him.

"You and him?" he asked her again, motioning toward Toby.

She rolled her eyes and turned away.

"Relax, it's nothing like that," said Toby.

Deacon's eyes didn't leave Hannah. He wanted to hear it from her.

"Pretty messed up, those Girouxs," Toby said, stepping closer and playfully punching Deacon in the shoulder.

"Fucking bad shoulder, dick," he bellowed, wheeling around and rubbing his upper arm. He waited a beat before grabbing Toby in a headlock. Toby's inflated muscle arms started slapping at him as they began pivoting in a circle. Their wrestling evolved into a full-blown slap fight, until Toby finally fought Deacon off of him. As soon as he freed himself, Toby immediately began fixing his hair.

"Not the hair," Deacon said, laughing. "Can't mess the hair, douche."

"Dick," Toby grumbled before curling up the corners of his mouth.

Deacon glanced over at Hannah, who was now standing with one hand on her hip, her other one pulling loose strands from her bun across her lips. He'd missed seeing her do that. *God, she's beautiful.*

"Just come here, already," he said, pleading with his eyes.

"No," she said coolly, folding her arms over her chest and shifting her weight to the other foot. Her attitude confused him more.

"I know I screwed up, but I never stopped thinking about you. I must have called your house a hundred times, just to hear—"

"I know. That's what led us here." She pressed her forearms into her stomach. "Before . . . when we were together . . . your dealing scared me. Your beeper going off all the time, your customers, selling . . . it all came first. You even stashed drugs in my bedroom. What the hell, Deacon? You used me!"

"That's not how it was . . . not for me," he said, dropping his head. "I made a bunch of mistakes, especially that first weekend . . . I fucked up. Dealing is what I did to piss off my asshole parents. I never wanted you involved in any of it. Not you, not ever. You were the only good thing in my life. I was better . . . when I was with you."

"Better? Deacon Giroux, the king of high school?" She shook her head. "The drugs were always first. I don't want to be around that life and those kinds of people . . . no matter what I may still feel." Her voice caught on the last word.

"I'll take the 'may,'" Deacon said quietly, almost to himself, hope flooding his body. *That damn hope.*

"I'm lost. What's going on?" Toby said, scratching his head.

Deacon moved closer to Hannah. "I've already promised myself . . . after everything I've been through down here . . . the people who have died because of me . . . that if I ever survive this, I'll give up dealing for good. I don't want this kind of life anymore . . . not *ever*."

Hannah studied his face. Her lips began to tremble; she covered her nose and mouth with her hands.

He cautiously touched her shoulders, turning her toward him. "I'd rather push a broom . . . fix a street light . . . anything but this. I want to build things, not break people apart. *Please*, Hannah."

He reached down for her hand. She followed his touch and met his fingertips with hers, ever so lightly. The electricity from her body traveled into his forearm and elbow, and throughout his body. She lit him up from within; he could hardly contain his exquisite joy.

Neither of them moved.

She tilted her head up, revealing those unguarded eyes of hers, emerald pools on the verge of breaking. The depth of her sadness struck something inside of him.

"I'm sorry for what I did. I don't deserve you." He dropped her hand.

CHAPTER 49

———

"WHO'D YOU CALL JUST THEN?" TOBY ASKED AS HE WALKED into the kitchen from the patio, leaving Hannah outside. She hadn't said anything to either of them since she and Deacon touched hands.

"Just my ever-present camera crew. Eastman Kodak, heard of them?"

Toby crinkled his nose and began opening kitchen cabinets. "Your Miss Ida got any food around here?"

"And *who* are *you*?"

Both boys' heads whipped toward the tiny woman in the oversized cardigan and bright orange hair. She spoke with a clipped tone, though her eyes were gentle and kind.

"Sorry, Miss Ida," Deacon said. "My brother stopped by for a visit. Your sister and your lady friends called and are on their way over for sewing group."

"Good, put some more chairs out in the living room."

Holding on to the counter, she shuffled over to Toby. She wrinkled up her face as she gazed at him. "You're a big boy! I see the family resemblance. So where's your lady friend?"

"Outside still," Deacon said, watching Hannah through the kitchen window.

"You're going, then?" She squinted at Deacon. "I sure enjoyed hearing the soap opera going on outside my window. It was better than my stories on television, I tell you!"

"I should have said something to you before . . ."

She waved him off. "Paul always knew it was some convoluted story that brought you here." She smiled through soft, wet eyes. "I miss my Paulie, that big galoot . . . every day." She sealed her lips together when Deacon placed a hand on her shoulder. "Fix our martini pitcher before you go, will you? Chill the glasses first. Olives . . . here, use this jar. Don't be chintzy like last time!"

She then turned to Toby. "What are *you* staring at? The ladies are going to need chairs . . . *go!*"

———

Hannah sat in the front with Toby on the drive back to Connecticut. It bothered Deacon big time the way they interacted, his brother teasing about her map reading skills and her joking about Toby's constant need for another drive-thru or bathroom break. He watched them through gritted teeth.

He may not deserve Hannah, but he'd be damned if he was going to let Toby have her.

He closed his eyes, not wanting to witness her grinning at his brother yet again. These two had clearly formed a sort of bond while he'd been in Miami. Hannah also seemed to quell the nervous energy right out of his brother. Maybe Toby was more normal than he thought. Or, worse, maybe he was secretly in love with her.

Deacon longed for sleep, but found himself wanting to hear her voice.

If it hadn't been for her coolness toward him, combined

with his nagging guilt and self hatred, he would have pulled her into the Stingray's back compartment with him and never let her go.

He told himself that he needed to wait. The danger was far from over. Chalfont's henchmen could be in any passing car. He lay low in the cramped space, not wanting to risk anything. He hadn't come this far, made all these sacrifices to protect her, just to lose her again.

———

He woke with a start as the Stingray entered the exit ramp. The sun was well up in the sky. Toby had driven through the night.

He untwisted his aching neck from the ledge he'd used as a pillow. It had been a long time since he'd been in the back of that car. He'd hidden there sometimes as a child, curled up under a blanket behind the driver's seat when his father commuted to work, so he could surprise Brenda, Toby's mother, who was also his father's campaign secretary. His fingers trailed over the initials he'd etched in the back of the driver's side seat, D+B. Brenda had been his first crush.

"Again?" Hannah yawned toward Toby, stretching her arms overhead like she'd dozed off too. She glanced back at Deacon. Their eyes locked for a millisecond before she turned away.

"Yep, that Coke went right through me. Want anything?" Toby asked her, then peered into the rearview mirror, "D?"

"Fine," Deacon replied curtly. He hated this.

Hannah got out and released her seat forward. She leaned against the car with her arms slung across her chest.

Deacon stood slowly, unfolding each of his long limbs and ducking his head as he rose out of the car.

"Are you even going to look at me?"

"Why? Thought you'd died again back there," she said motioning to the trunk.

"Ouch." He rested his body over the hood stretching his back.

"A lot has happened in eight months, you haven't a clue."

"Tell me," he said facing her. "I want to know."

"My family . . . my mom . . . I dated a couple of guys," she said without looking at him.

"I knew you would."

"Some messed up things happened."

"Do I need to take anyone out?"

"I don't need you to *protect* me."

"I know, I can see that."

"I don't need a boyfriend to save me. I can handle things on my own. I can see through my parents' shit and figure out what *I* need."

Toby strolled up the path looking rather pleased with himself, his shirt half out of his shorts, his hands holding a large to-go bag and a drink the size of a Big Gulp. He slowed his pace when he saw them talking and watched while he took long sips of soda.

"I'm trying really hard not to pull you into my arms. It's killing me."

"Don't," she said, her eyes cold.

"Hannah, I don't want to waste another minute. I don't know how much time I have. It's too long of a story. I'm re-lieved to finally be out of that hellhole . . . seeing you gave me the courage to finally get out of there. Thank you for that."

She nodded, unable to meet his gaze.

"I thought I was going to die in Miami before you and Toby showed up. And now I don't know what I'm going to do. Once the cartel knows my story, where I'm from, it's only a matter of time. You won't want to be with me when that happens. I'm never going to be at peace. The people I ratted out, their families, and the other cartels will be coming for my head forever. I'll always be watching over my shoulder."

"Xavier Coyne will be hunted, not Deacon Giroux," Hannah said, lifting her curls off her neck. She dropped them back onto her shoulders and sighed.

"I don't know who that is anymore," he said quietly, eyeing a rogue ringlet.

Hannah and Toby exchanged a look.

"We'll figure it out," Toby said to him. "Wanna sip?"

CHAPTER 50

THE THREE OF THEM GOT BACK INTO TOWN AFTER midnight. They rented a motel room outside of Darien and fell asleep as soon as their heads hit the pillow.

Deacon was the first one up in the morning. He'd spent most of the night watching Hannah sleep in the bed next to him. She hadn't invited him to join her. He didn't know what he was going to do or if he would be able to leave her again.

At the first crack of sunlight, he stealthily grabbed the car keys on the table next to Toby's head and slipped out of the room. *Time to resurrect.*

He drove along the familiar streets to his parents' neighborhood, all the while feeling like he'd aged a couple of years. He entered the garage code. The electronic screen on the keypad flashed another error message after his third attempt. *Shit, they changed it.*

The humid August morning pricked the little hairs at the back of his neck. Each released breath felt warmer than the next. His hands itched with moisture punching in the numbers again. The screen locked up, refusing further entries. He'd become an outsider. The thought unnerved him.

I'm a Giroux, dammit.

He moved to try another door on the side of the house; then, out of nowhere, the garage door electronically opened.

Deacon glanced back at Toby's red Camaro coming up the long drive. *Where was that car hiding?*

He stepped inside the garage without wasting another minute. It smelled of car polish and leather conditioner. Its black-and-white floor tiles were pristine as ever under Kingsley's assortment of colorful vintage cars. A few more had joined the collection. However, there was only one he wanted to see.

As a kid, he'd admired his father's buttercream '56 Cadillac Fleetwood Coupe De Ville—especially its hood ornament with the flags and tiny ducklings—three legless martlets on either side of the family crest of Antoine de la Mothe Cadillac, the founder of the city of Detroit.

His fingertips brushed over the tiny ducklings, just like they had years earlier. *Geez, I'm an idiot,* he thought, *for not recognizing that damn emblem sooner.*

He stared at the door that led into the house. An immovable weight sat upon his chest at the idea of coming back from the dead and seeing his parents after all this time. *It's game time.*

He opened the door and stepped inside. *What the . . . ?* The house had been utterly transformed. The once dark walls and moldings had been repainted in shades of cream. The mahogany wood floors now sported a whitewash finish, making the grand foyer appear more spacious. The huge pedestal table with the clawed feet groped a beige oriental rug instead of the blood-red one. The most dramatic change was the mirrored ceiling, which lent itself to more of a *Studio 54* than a country club vibe. Everywhere the air felt lighter and more modern.

I die and she redecorates?

The sensation of sharp claws swiping his back stopped him cold in front of the table of family pictures. Each one featured his parents and Toby's clueless, hopeful face. The same press pictures he'd once taken with them.

You think you can erase me?

He choked back the golf ball growing in his throat and turned down the hallway with renewed vengeance. The smell of his mother's floral perfume floating through the corridor nearly destroyed his nerve.

A couple of steps from the parlor, his chest fell to a buried pain he hadn't succumbed to in a long time. He turned and locked eyes with his mother, who was seated on the settee with one of her paperback romances on her lap. Several seconds volleyed between them, the silence strangling every molecule in the room.

"Shit!" Babette finally exclaimed, slamming the book closed in her lap. Her eyes filled with fire as she stomped her pumps on the floor like an angry child.

"Hello, Mother, good to see you, too. From your reaction, I guess you've known all this time," he said hoarsely, his emotions taking him by surprise. He leaned against the doorframe, not trusting his wobbly legs.

"Of course I did. You think I'm *stupid?*"

"Geez, missed you too."

"Why are you here . . . and what's with that *hair?*" she snarled.

"Blond and back from the dead," he said, crossing his arms. The hollows of his cheeks caved in from clenching his teeth.

"You shouldn't be here. We buried you in the family plot. If people in this town find out you're alive, we'll look like fools! You'll create a scandal, one your father—*we*—cannot afford!"

He rolled his eyes. "Oh, Babs, I'd be glad to tell them everything. You'll probably lose your membership at the country club, the yacht club, *and* at the Four Seasons. *Really* like what you've done with the house . . . especially the new family pictures. That worked out for you, huh? Adding a *murderer* to the family unit."

"That damn kid couldn't hit the side of a barn! You being here is only going to complicate things. We don't need *two* of you."

"There's a quota, nice. What exactly did you bury, Mother?"

"At least this bastard doesn't want anything from me . . . he's not *needy* like you."

"That's because he already has a mother . . . a wonderful one at that."

"That *whore*? Oh, please."

"Hell, if I were married to you, I'm sure I'd find a number of women I'd rather sleep with than—"

Babette sprang from the couch, her taloned hand spread like a lion's paw, and struck him hard across the face. His head jerked back. Then he grabbed her wrist, making her wince.

"Ungrateful son of a bitch," she spat.

He tightened his grasp, and she grimaced more. "Got that right, *bitch*." He dropped her arm and took several steps backward, his eyes daring her to do it again. He sensed the presence of someone in the hallway and ignored it. He'd come this far and couldn't stop now.

"What, you can't figure out a way to make money off of me, too? Two sons have to be worth more . . . get all the sympathy you want. Poor Babs."

"You had a *very expensive* burial. I paid *big* to keep things private."

"What did you have them bury?"

She folded her arms and lifted her chest. "I just made sure the family name looked good."

"What . . . across my tombstone? Didn't you wonder where I went? Worry I'd been kidnapped?"

"Nope. You weren't my problem anymore . . . still aren't."

"Like when you left me at six years old to live with that sadistic, sick asshole? Good ole Pierre. When I wouldn't play his dirty games, he'd hold me down and burn me with his cigar."

Babette's face went white. Her hands pressed to her sides.

Chills climbed up Deacon's shoulders. He grabbed her wrist again, this time jerking her palm open. "Just like he did to *you*, didn't he?"

"Shut your mouth, you're *disgusting*." Babette pulled back her hand, covering it protectively.

"God, who *haven't* you slept with, Mother? Who's really the whore?"

"What the hell is going on?" Kingsley strode into the room with a teacup and saucer in his hands. His outstretched pinky dropped at the sight of Deacon. "My God . . . it's not possible."

Deacon cocked his head, his eyes narrowing. His father, dressed in a khaki-colored silk Armani suit with matching monochromatic pocket square and tie, had never appeared more dapper or self-assured, his leading-man features more handsome. He was nothing like the "father in mourning" Deacon had expected to find.

"You knew, as well," Deacon said softly, the familiar pain spreading through him. "Both of you did. Do you even know what *happened to me* down in Miami?"

His father rested his teacup on the large ivory credenza next to him. He casually stuffed his hands into his trouser pockets like a spectator at a polo match and stared up at him with a practiced blank expression.

Babette lowered herself onto the settee, her book falling to the ground. "Kingsley, you knew all this time?" she said tentatively, her fingers finding her pearls as her lips commenced their silent mantra.

They both knew I was alive and didn't tell one another?

His father licked his lips. He shifted his weight forward in an attempt to meet his son's full height. "Yes . . . yes, I did. I signed the papers," he said, leaving his southern drawl out on the table.

"What papers . . . his *death* certificate?" Babette laughed snootily like she was holding court at Bridge Club.

Kingsley slipped his long fingers into his breast pocket and pulled out a key. He unlocked one of the sideboard's drawers and withdrew what Deacon had feared.

His father's face held the hint of a smile as he waved a manila envelope with the crest of his Cadillac Car Club—legless martlets and all. He cleared his throat like he was giving a speech. "Here's my copy . . . agreeing for you to be an informant for the U.S. Drug Enforcement Administration."

"When did you do this? When I was still seventeen?" Deacon said in disbelief.

"Meet Xavier Coyne," announced Toby, appearing in the doorway.

All three spun around and stared at him. Deacon couldn't decipher his brother's tone. Had Toby switched his loyalty back to his parents? He couldn't think about that now.

He stepped toward Kingsley, lacing his fingers together and bringing his thumbs to his lips in a last-ditch prayer. "You helped them *take me away*?" he asked, the stinging tears unavoidable now. "But *why*?"

"They needed your help to catch a few people . . . it was the right thing to do." His father meandered to the bar and began pouring himself a bourbon. It was still morning. He didn't seem to care.

Deacon studied his father's stance. Cocky. *But of course.* "Because they had something on *you*. Something that could upset your career. You're up for re-election next year, and whatever you were hiding would have affected that. It's all about you, *Dad*. Always has been."

Kingsley sniffed. "What do you know about it? It's politics, kid. Plus, I figured it would get you off our town's streets, away from that abomination of a career you'd chosen, and force you to finally fulfill your civic duty. Remember, I suffered too . . . the embarrassment and disgrace of being forced to step down from lieutenant governor after the 'accident.'" He tilted his head in Toby's direction.

Deacon guffawed. "Civic duty? You mean be a snitch for the Feds, spend every day knowing I was always one step away from being sliced, diced, and thrown away?"

Babette released a guttural laugh under her breath.

Deacon spun in her direction. "Fuck you!" he screamed.

Babette's malicious, smiling eyes squeezed back into her face and downgraded to a venomous stare.

"Like you weren't living the high life down there in Miami. I heard about your escapades, *Xavier Coyne*. Dressing like a gigolo, living large, partying all night . . ." Kingsley puffed out his chest and pulled down the sides of his suit jacket.

"You hated me this much? Enough to sign away my life? My *life*! Even for you, that's *cold*. I don't understand. What exactly did you get out of the arrangement? What did you do that was *that* bad?"

Kingsley pulled a loose thread from his suit. "The Feds promised to look the other way . . . preserve my political ties. Keep Chalfont and his goons off my ass."

"Tell me more," Deacon coaxed.

"Come on, D, let's get out of here," Toby urged, walking further into the room.

"No . . . I want to hear it. Come on, Dad. I'm sure it was the deal of the century. You, the southern boy with the ever-present chip on his shoulder, finally getting to run with the big boys—dangerous ones, at that."

His mother cackled haughtily. This time Deacon ignored her childish antics.

"I agreed to help the cartels with transportation routes so they could conduct their business and I could carry out mine." Kingsley smiled. "It was genius, actually."

"And then you double-crossed them." Deacon cocked his head. "Pretty cunning . . . *you* should have been the informant."

"Oh lord, Kingsley. You're going to sink us both," Babette warned, her fingers flying to her choker. Her lips moved like she was reciting the rosary on speed.

"Let me get this straight," Deacon said. "The cartel is bankrolling your campaign and you gifted your son to the Feds for *insurance?*"

"Of course." Kingsley straightened his stance. "I'm a shoo-in this time."

"I saw the same manila envelope on Chalfont's desk sporting that damn Cadillac Club emblem," Deacon said, disgust creeping into his voice. "You didn't even try to hide your involvement. If anything, you flaunted it."

"It was *worth it*! After all this time, look at all the good I've pulled off in this town and in Washington. I've made a name for myself . . . finally out from Pierre's grasp after all these years being married to *this.*" He motioned to Babette like she was a failed show horse. "His selfish, spoiled daughter whose only contribution to this marriage was . . . a *loser* of a son."

"Like *you* were some prize!" Babette growled.

"Come on, D, you got what you needed," said Toby, coming up behind Deacon and pulling on his shoulders.

"What the *hell* does that mean?" Babette demanded, staring at them.

"You leave with *him* and you can forget coming back!" Kingsley shouted at Toby. "You're no longer welcome here. You're no longer a Giroux!"

"Fine by me . . . *Pops.*"

The boys walked briskly out the front door to the driveway. Deacon opened the mailbox and tilted his chin toward the parked car tucked behind the trees, farther down the drive.

"And this *misión* is *terminada*," he announced, closing the mailbox. He hustled over to Toby and stopped him before he could reach his annoying candy-red Camaro. "Oh, and I'm driving," he said, putting a hand to Toby's chest. A smile crawled across his lips. "Bro."

Toby groaned and dropped the keys in his brother's spread fingers. "This one time . . . little brother." He grinned and got into the car.

Deacon jolted the engine to life, spun the vehicle around, and gunned it down the driveway.

Eastman pulled the electronic bug from his ear and clapped his hands like a toy monkey with cymbals. He slammed the car door and hurried to the mailbox, keeping his cigarette lit in his mouth. His toothpick legs moved at warp speed compared to his partner's stumpy ones.

"The kid came through," he announced to Kodak when he eventually caught up to him, all red-faced and ragged.

Eastman wound the wire around his hand before slipping the device into his pocket. He squinted while taking a drag, holding in the smoke for a few seconds. "Bet you didn't expect Giroux to confess!" he crowed on the exhale.

Kodak's eyes popped like corn kernels as he gazed up at the mansion and all its grandeur. He used a hanky to wipe the sweat from his upper lip and brow. "I always liked that kid." He said with a leer, patting Eastman's back.

"Yeah, right."

Eastman grabbed the lion doorknocker and rapped loudly. They waited. He thwacked it against the door again, and they heard a pair of high heels trotting toward them from inside.

Eastman glanced back at his winded partner on the steps. "Hey buddy, here's your *Kodak moment* . . . smile!"

"Shut up, Virgil."

CHAPTER 51

CRAMMED BETWEEN BOTH GIROUX BROTHERS IN THE front seat of Toby's red two-seater Camaro convertible, her lower body sharing the passenger seat with Toby, while her upper body leaned toward Deacon, Hannah tried not to think about the heat radiating between her shoulder and Deacon's. She'd meant what she'd said to him. She *had* changed.

Just how the three of them had managed to find their way back together after that ill-fated December night in the park was too bizarre to comprehend. But here they were, driving through the streets of Darien like the three of them in one car was nothing short of normal.

No one said a word as they passed Gossamer Park.

She pushed her thoughts aside and held her breath as they turned onto her street.

"Shoot, they're back already." She grimaced at the sight of her parents' station wagon in the driveway. "That was quick."

Deacon pulled up to the curb and shifted into park. "Want me to come in with you?" he asked, his intense eyes lingering on hers.

"I've got this," she said firmly, her lips returning a small smile. "Now I have to rescue *me*."

Toby stepped out and retrieved her bag from the trunk. "Good luck in there," he said, giving her one of his chipmunk-cheek grins.

She walked up the path to her house. Everything about it seemed different—smaller, older, she didn't know what. Then again, maybe it wasn't the house that was different.

"Hello?" she called out.

Her parents were waiting for her in the living room. A blur out of the corner of her eye rushed toward her.

"Kerry! Oh, I'm so glad to see you. How are you, honey?"

Her little sister's face beamed before she threw her arms around her big sister. "Good now," she said with a giggle, her sweet, melodic voice warming the air and everything in sight.

Hearing Kerry's little voice and seeing her face light up renewed Hannah's strength.

"You're really okay, aren't you? I can't believe you're finally home!" Every part of her had missed this little person.

Her eyes drifted over to her parents. Her mother sat perched on the gold corduroy couch, her father in his recliner.

"Glad to see everyone's finally together again," she said tentatively.

"How was the workshop?" her father started from behind his newspaper.

"I wasn't at the workshop. It was last month."

"We know," he said, folding the paper across his lap and glaring at her. "I spoke to Mrs. Myers."

The butterflies Hannah had carried into the house suddenly stopped fluttering and fell into a clump in the pit of her stomach. She took a deep inhale and another stab at the truth.

"I went to help a friend. Um . . . y-you've sort of met him before. Anyway, he was in a bad place. I'm back now." Her eyes volleyed between them. "I guess I'm grounded."

Her father cleared his throat. "We're very disappointed in you, young lady. We go out of town and *again* you—"

"Where did I *work* all summer?" Hannah interjected. "Do either of you know?"

"What?" her father said, unmistakable annoyance at having been interrupted in his tone.

"Do you know where I worked this summer?" Hannah repeated.

His eyes darted to her mother, who moved her head slightly.

"Just what I thought. That's because neither of you ever asked or cared."

Her parents' eyes flitted around the room as if the perfect parental comeback hung somewhere on the wall.

"I had a lot of time to think about things this week. Don't get me wrong, I'm grateful, Mom, that you're doing better. I kept praying"—her voice caught as she glanced down at her little sister, who was still clutching her tightly—"for you and for Kerry . . . but Dad, Mom, you've left me on my own for so long. You can't get lost again, forgetting about us . . . we *need* you."

Her eyes filled at the sight of their blank expressions. Would anything she said get through to them? She looked down, feeling the warmth emanating from Kerry. She tapped her little sister's nose lightly and got a smile.

"All right . . . where *did* you work this summer?" her father said.

"The Candy House." Hannah grinned. "We got to try everything."

"*Humph*," her mother grunted, swatting at the air. "All that sugar . . . not good for your sk—"

"Stop," Hannah commanded, holding up her hand. "My skin, my hair, my clothes . . . you know what, guys? It's hard enough to feel like I don't belong with the kids at school. No matter what I do, I'll never fit in there," she said, trying to stave off the lump forming in her throat. Her vision blurred as she pulled Kerry closer. "It's worse, though, when you don't fit in at *home*."

Her heart sank as she watched her father press his lips together, her mother cover hers with her first two fingers. Feeling like all of her clothes had fallen to the floor, Hannah lowered her head and crossed an arm over her chest. Her shoulders trembled. Still, Kerry didn't let go of her.

"You're our daughter," her father said slowly, "and, apparently, the glue around here." He cleared his throat. "You're smart . . . and beautiful . . . and you make us proud. Well, *most* days," he added as her mother nodded toward him.

A startled laugh escaped Hannah's lips. This was not the response she'd expected.

"I love you, Hannah," Kerry piped up.

She rubbed the top of her little sister's head. "I love you too, Kerry."

CHAPTER 52

TOBY OPENED THE BATHROOM DOOR, SENDING HIS shower steam billowing into the room. Dressed in just a towel, he wiped the hotel mirror and peered at his face briefly. He glanced back at Deacon, stretched out on the bed.

"You haven't moved since we got back here. What's up?"

"No beeper, no problems. I'm still dead around here, remember?" Deacon said flatly, his eyes half closed.

"Dude?"

Deacon pushed in his temples with his fingers. "Our fucking father . . . Babette. I keep replaying it in my head what they did. Like an ass, I thought they would care that I was alive. That things would be different, you know? Most normal parents would. But they used me, then just wanted me out of the way."

"Don't, man. They're not worth it. Besides, you're finally free!"

"Yeah, free. Whatever that means."

"Hannah call?"

Deacon shook his head.

Toby threw on clothes and combed his hair with his fingers. He stood in front of the TV and started flipping through the channels.

"You're hogging the set again," Deacon said.

Toby fell onto the club chair next to the bed and clasped his hands behind his head. "It's not like I'm used to sharing."

"Me neither. Anyway, we should go." Deacon lifted himself to his elbows.

"Where?"

"I have a bunch of cash stashed all over this town. We're going to need it."

"I thought you weren't going back to dealing."

"Hell no. But what are we going to live on?"

Toby smiled and grabbed his keys and wallet from the bureau. He lifted his chin and threaded the arm of his Ray Bans through his collar. "I can't wait to see people's faces when they realize you're alive."

Deacon cocked his head back. "Who cares? The important people already know." He flipped down his Carrera glasses from his head to the bridge of his nose and started ticking off a list with his fingers. "Here's the order: get food, fix the hair, figure out what to do with the rest of our lives . . ."

"I've kind of gotten used to your ridiculous blond hair." Toby said laughing—then winced when Deacon punched him in the shoulder. "Dude, that hurt!"

CHAPTER 53

"YOU'RE MY MARY," KERRY ANNOUNCED, LAYING HER head on her sister. Sharing a bowl of popcorn between them, the Zandana sisters sat cross-legged on the couch watching another episode of *Little House on the Prairie*.

"Okay, Half Pint." Hannah smirked as she used the nickname of the younger sister on the show. She grabbed a handful of popcorn and nudged Kerry. "How was camp and staying at Gamma Mimi's? That *had* to be fun."

"Ugh, her house smells like pee," Kerry said, pushing up the tip of her nose so it resembled a pig's.

Hannah laughed. "It sure does. I always hated going there. She's always judging people, that woman. I don't think she ever approved of me, giving me the stink eye all of the time. Poor Dad. Guess that's where he gets it."

Kerry sighed and leaned her head again. After a moment she asked, "Do you think Mommy is going to get better?"

"I think so . . . I can tell that she's really trying this time. It's got to be hard for her. Like they said in our last family counseling session, recovery is a one-day-at-a-time process. In Mom's case, she could be trying to just get through the next hour."

Kerry's shoulders sank a little. Hannah reached around and squeezed her into her side.

"But don't worry. We, Zandana sisters, we'll stick together. Now that I'm not working, we should have more time to hang out."

"You're going to be home more? What about your boyfriend . . . not Peter, the one before?"

"What? How do you know about *him*?"

"Mom and Dad used to talk about him . . . they worried about you dating him."

"They did? Hmm, I didn't know they knew—"

"He got hurt in the park, right? Dad said something to Mom when we were in the hospital."

"He did?" *Maybe they do care*, she thought.

Kerry hopped up and raised the volume on the TV.

Hannah yawned and stretched her arms overhead, flexing her socked feet over the coffee table. "I don't know what's going to happen there."

"Wait, this is the good part," Kerry interrupted. "Laura tells her fiancé, Manley, that she loves him, but she will never obey him. She tells him that she doesn't want their marriage vows to include the word 'obey.'"

"Atta girl, Half Pint."

CHAPTER 54

DEACON CRADLED THE PHONE NEXT TO HIS EAR, LISTENING to the Feds shout at him on speakerphone from one of their undisclosed locations. He imagined Kodak eating a hot dog or two as Eastman chain-smoked. A few minutes in and their disgusting noises gave them away; that was exactly what they were doing.

He leaned back on the couch in the second-floor apartment he shared with Toby, peering at the water outside his living room. Two TVs sat side by side across from him, facing two identical couches. Neither only child had mastered the art of sharing yet.

They'd picked the place because of the view. For Deacon, it was just what he needed. The serenity of the lake calmed him, just as the water used to when he swam competitively. No longer did he want it to swallow him up. If anything, he longed to float on it for a while and see where it carried him.

Contemplating the lake's calm surface had become his therapy, his way of making sense of his life's dangerous detours while also dreaming of a new road ahead. Some days he fared better than others.

On late-night walks around the lake, he found himself talking to Paul a lot. It comforted him to have someone up there like him on his side.

He heard Kodak cough up a wad of hot dog. Deacon jumped at his chance to interject. "Got it. I won't speak of it again. Never met the dream team of Eastman and Kodak before in my life. Trust me. I won't be reliving those days anytime soon. Yeah. And the news story you planted about the Miami police taking out Xavier Coyne was appreciated. I hope it works. But what about the cartel, any signs of Chalfont?"

Outside a blue heron with a long beak and curved wings took off from the lake. He watched it soar over the treetops and disappear into the clouds.

"Yeah, I know. I was hoping you were going to tell me you had him and the *familia* in custody. I guess 'on the run' will have to do." Deacon switched the phone to his other ear. "One more thing . . . and it's my only request in exchange for my guaranteed silence. Yeah. I want Thomas's record cleared of any wrongdoing. What was recorded in Massachusetts . . . erased. It never happened. Good. Also tell him,"—his throat tightened, catching him off guard—"tell him *redo*. He'll know."

September 1985

CHAPTER 55

THE LIBRARY'S ARCTIC AIR HIT THE FRONT OF HANNAH'S body as she stepped through its double glass doors. It was the Sunday before Labor Day—school was starting that week—and the placed was deserted.

She hadn't been back since last December. It held too many memories of when she and Deacon were dating and would meet there to throw off her parents. Back then, they'd always ended up somewhere else, usually at his house. She swore to herself that today she wasn't going anywhere with him.

She spotted him at the back table in the corner nearest the windows and smiled.

His serious face tugged at her chest. He was probably leaving town again.

"Thanks for meeting me," he said.

"Sure." She lowered herself in the chair across from him and slung her LeSportsac on the seat next to her.

"You look back to normal. I kind of liked the Billy Idol hair," she joked, feeling a little nervous. They hadn't spoken in a couple of weeks.

"It was pretty awful. How are you?" His hand reached for hers, then stopped inches away.

"Getting ready for school—you know, the usual stuff. Junior year, *wahoo*."

"That's good," he said quietly. "Um . . . I've had a lot of time to think about things—especially what happened between us before the night in the park—and I wanted you to know that I'm sorry."

"Which part?" she asked, folding her arms on the table.

"Good point. I guess I deserve that."

"I'm not mad, Deacon. I've realized that I'm pretty okay being on my own."

He pushed up his brow with his fingertips and leaned his elbow on the table. "This is harder than I thought . . . um . . . I'm not used to admitting stuff . . .wait . . . okay, here goes." He scanned the surrounding tables and the columns of book stacks that fenced them. They were alone. He took a breath. "You know that cocky bullshit act of mine . . . it's not real."

"I know."

"Babette took me away from home when I was six because she discovered Kingsley had fathered another child, months before me . . ."

"Toby."

"My parents were pretty shitty to one another as far back as I can remember. My father let her drive off with me, and then she dumped me at my grandfather's, and he . . ." Deacon looked like he was choking on his words. "He m-molested . . . me."

"Oh my God." She reached for his hand.

His expression clouded. He gently plucked her hand from his and slowly rotated his palm.

"What is that . . . oh my God . . . he burned you!" Her

eyes stung at seeing the circular scar in the center of his hand. "I never noticed it before."

"I never let you see it. My hand was not his only target."

"There are more?"

Deacon lowered his head, his eyelashes glistening.

Hannah collapsed over her arms, terrible images of his childhood storming her head. "I—"

"Shhh," he said softly, lifting her face and wiping the corner of her eye. "Let me get this out."

She nodded, blinking back tears.

"Because of my own demons, I know that there were moments where I made you feel *unsafe*."

Hannah's jaw sprung open, unsure of where he was going with this.

"It's okay, you can tell me."

"Um . . . the pictures I found in your room . . . oh . . . the time you held me down in your father's study, I felt this anger come over you, like you were possessed . . . it scared me." She gasped. "Wait—what did *they* do to you? Did something happen in that *house*?"

"My parents were indifferent toward me and it basically screwed with my head . . . I never felt like they wanted me. I've been angry with them for a long time . . . for not protecting me from that monster and his dirty games. He'd molested my mother, too, and she *still* left me to live with him."

"I'm so sorry . . ." she whispered.

Deacon took a breath. "Hannah, I'm not proud of the asshole I was back then. I want to be a better man, not like the monsters my family creates."

His hands found hers and squeezed them into his.

"I was on my way to becoming that . . . a monster . . . before I met you. You were the only good in my life and I couldn't let what I'd done destroy that. Miami kicked me in the ass. I saw how low I'd become and the amount of pain I'd caused in this town with dealing and creating addicts. I messed up people's lives, broke up families. I was no better than some kid in a gang." He winced. His chocolate eyes lifted to hers. "I especially wish I could reverse the pain I brought into the life of the only person who ever showed me . . . that I was worthy . . . of love."

Hannah swallowed hard. She had not seen any of this coming. Her head kept bobbing, but no words would come out. It was all too much.

The minutes crept by. His eyes never left her face. She realized he was waiting for an answer.

"I didn't come here to get back with you," she said slowly.

"I know."

"For once, I'm finally figuring things out."

"Me too."

"I don't want to be that girl again . . . like I was last fall."

"I know."

"I'm afraid I'll lose myself if I let you sweep me off my feet again." She smiled weakly, her eyes damp.

"Then don't," he said softly, dropping his eyes away. He released her hands.

"I'll try not to."

EPILOGUE

darien, connecticut

DEACON LOWERED HIS WINDOWS TO THE CHIME OF the final bell. Driving over to his former high school, everything seemed different and yet the same, as if he was seeing his hometown with new eyes.

He'd never noticed before how vibrant the New England landscape and its fall colors were, the way the apricot- and cherry-colored leaves sugared the tree branches and lawns and linked its storybook houses and sidewalks together like one endless park.

It was a far cry from his life in the cartel.

He never wanted to see another palm tree again.

He pulled up to the front of the school. The warm sun rested on his forearm. He lifted his face to the sky and inhaled deeply, vowing to never take any of it—or *anyone*—for granted again.

He turned to look at the students streaming from the building and caught the redheaded terror gaping at him amidst a cluster of girls. They were dressed alike in their Forenza V-neck shaker sweaters and acid washed ankle-zipper jeans, their hair short and spiky like their queen's. Her minions turned in unison and stared.

Deacon couldn't resist a sarcastic wave and a little taunting, though she couldn't hear him. "Hey there, Gilly girl, bet you can't believe I'm alive. Uh-huh, that's right."

Hannah's face lit up as she made her way to the other side of the Camaro. She acknowledged Gillian with a tilt of her chin before opening her door. "Aww, leave her alone," she said as she slid into the car. "She seems happy. Found her new coven for the year. All is right in girl world."

"She mess with you anymore?"

"I don't notice. How's work?"

"Giroux Brothers Construction is a go. We signed today."

"Hey, that's great!"

He kissed her hand and pulled away from the curb without letting go.

"Yeah, instead of breaking families apart, maybe I can start building some good."

"Proud of you. And Toby. Look how far you two have come."

"I know, it's crazy. We've become a real family. Guess we both got what we wanted."

"You're in a good mood. What's up?" She nudged him, smiling.

"I've got two pieces of news."

"Surprise me."

"Did you know we met this week a year ago?" he said, squeezing her hand.

"Maybe I did, maybe I didn't. You never finished your story last night before Toby needed the phone."

"Damn call waiting. That butthead, ever since he started seeing that bubble-headed waitress at Bennigan's . . ."

Hannah snickered. "You mean pom-pom Tammy?"

"We've *got* to get two phone lines. How's your mom's new job?"

"She likes it. The other day she asked me to help her pick out an outfit."

"That's good. She could use some help in that department," he teased.

She swatted his arm. "And here she thinks you're so polite!"

"I've got her snowed. See? I still got it."

"Where are we going today?" she said, still laughing.

"Not yet. That's your second surprise."

Minutes later, he pulled up next to the lake near his apartment.

"There's something I want to show you . . . a pretty spot on the other side of the water. I think you'll like it."

He walked around the car and opened her door. He reached out his hand and she took it. Together, they headed toward the open space.

"I like this, getting to know one another again," he said. "A lot happened to you when I was gone."

"Yes and no. Dating sucks, by the way. Some guys can be jerks. But I did learn a few things about myself. I used to think that I needed a guy's attention to feel, I don't know, worthy or something. Those weeks on my own, I realized that I like who I am. I have a lot to offer."

"That you do." Deacon smiled.

"My dad was going off last night about something that broke in the house. He was getting mean and I just ignored him . . . I'm not afraid of him or my mom anymore. Whatever they do or say, or their hang-ups about how I should look and dress, I realized that their words can no longer crush me."

Deacon squeezed her hand nodding.

She glanced over at him, watching his face as she spoke. "Parents are human, I guess. They're flawed and imperfect with issues that have nothing to do with us, you know? I think they come with baggage that is not meant to be ours. We can't change them. But we can control how we let them affect us."

"You taught me that, Hannah. I was on a bad path . . . blaming my parents for everything. I knew what I was doing to people when I was dealing and I *still* did it. You saved me from myself and from continuing to hurt others."

"I'd do it again," she smiled, wrinkling up her nose.

"So more about these jerky guys . . ."

"My lips are sealed."

"Have I not been a gentleman . . . not rushing our courtship?"

"Our *courtship*? You're kidding, right?" Hannah side-eyed him.

"I'm serious. I told myself if I ever got the chance to be in your life again, I would do things the right way. I'm not messing this one up again."

"Oh really." She grinned, a glint in her eye. They walked a bit more—then she suddenly dropped his hand, spun around behind him, and climbed onto his back. "Now, mush!" she commanded, cracking an air whip with one hand like he was a sled dog.

"This is not helping the no-contact rule, having your legs wrapped around me."

"I didn't make that rule," she said, snuggling up to his ear.

He came to an abrupt halt, tilting his head to one side. He swiveled her body around like she weighed nothing. His hands clasped under her backside.

His eyes widened as he scanned her face. It was like he was seeing her features for the first time. He slowly touched his lips to hers, once, and then again, without leaving much room for words. He pulled away, catching his breath. "If I start . . . I may not . . ."

Hannah smiled. "I've created an addict, I see."

"Quite," he said huskily.

She lowered her feet to the ground, lightly resting her palms on his waist. He ran his hands through her hair. She closed her eyes at his touch, kissing him more and inching herself closer until no light shined between their bodies.

She pulled back and caressed the side of his face. "I like you like this."

His forehead touched hers. He sighed at her imitation of him, the first time he saw her without makeup. He'd meant those words then, and he knew he felt them now too.

"You like me . . . like *what*?" he asked, his eyes searching hers as he joined his hands at the small of her back.

"*All. Mine.*" She beamed. Her kaleidoscope eyes reflected a love he'd thought he'd never see again.

The warm fall breeze blew between them like running scarves. He hugged her tighter.

Hannah stepped back. He waited for her to say something. Instead, gently, she unbuttoned the top of his shirt, moving it off his bare shoulder. She ran her fingertips lightly over his chest. Little bumps rose across his skin. He shivered at her touch.

She raised herself up on her toes, holding on to his shoulders, and kissed the area where the bullet had entered. Then she reached for his hand and touched her lips to the inside of his palm.

Deacon closed his eyes, feeling himself fall deeper. She knew his secrets, and he hers. His eyes filled and her beautiful face sharpened.

"I *love* you like that, Hannah. You're the one person who knows everything . . . and still kisses my scars."

He cocked his head to one side, smiling at her. *I'm one lucky son-of-a-bitch.*

"First time . . ." she said, her face aglow. "Say it again. I don't believe I heard you. You love me like *how?*"

She wiped the lone tear rolling down his face before it dropped.

"Like . . . *this.*" His mouth found hers, sending currents through them both, all the way down to their toes. His shaking hands gently cupped her face like it was a precious chalice, summoning her soul with the promise of a brilliantly colored road ahead.

He spoke softly, gazing into her sparkling blue-green eyes. "We're going to make it. I can *feel* it."

"Let's go."

acknowledgments

There are so many friends, family members, book bloggers, and kind readers who reached out and supported me throughout this journey. Your encouragement to complete Hannah and Deacon's story kept me going on numerous occasions. For that, I'm utterly grateful.

I'd like to personally thank my early readers—Caitlin McCarthy, Kristen McManus, Morgan Rath, and Alane Adams—for your invaluable insight. A special thanks to Pilar Corcuera Botana and Alisa M. Delgado for your guidance editing the Spanish.

Many thanks to Beth Pulaski Photography for the wonderful author photo, and to Samantha and Sydney de Lannoy for being my go-to team for all things Connecticut, and for not minding that I often veered from the facts.

One of the many themes in this duology is about finding people in your life who celebrate you, just as you are. I'm blessed to say that I have that in my dear friends, near and far. You weirdos mean the world to me. And you know who you are.

Much gratitude to my amazing publisher, Brooke Warner at She Writes Press; my patient project manager, Cait Levin; and to Julie Metz and her creative team for the striking cover. A warm shout-out to all my She Writes Press and Spark-Press sisters, who remind me every day that we're in this together.

I'm forever indebted to my fearless editor, Krissa Lagos,

who helped shape the story of Hannah and Deacon into an even better one.

This duology would not have found its wings if it weren't for Crystal Patriarche, Madison Ostrander, and the rest of my rock star publicity team at BookSparks. Thanks also to Maggie Ruf at SparkPoint Studio for continuing to make HeatherCumiskey.com beautiful and fun.

I'm blessed to be a part of the Cumiskey-Pulaski-Al-Ferranto clan. You guys had me at hello.

Forever love to my mom, dad, brothers, and all the de Lannoys. You will always be my home.

Lastly, to the men in my life—Mac, Finn, and Fletcher, and my rock and soul mate, Mark: this two-part love letter is for you.

about the author

Photo credit: Beth Pulaski Photography

Heather Cumiskey was born and raised in Garden City, New York. Her essays have appeared in *Kids' BookBuzz* and *Germ Magazine*. She lives in Maryland with her husband and three sons. Catch up with her at HeatherCumiskey.com.

SELECTED TITLES FROM SHE WRITES PRESS

She Writes Press is an independent publishing company founded to serve women writers everywhere. Visit us at www.shewritespress.com.

I Like You Like This by Heather Cumiskey. $16.95, 978-1631522925. When social outcast Hannah captures the attention of a handsome and mysterious boy who also happens to be her school's resident drug dealer, her life takes an unexpected detour into a dangerous and seductive world—and she is forced to reexamine what she believes about herself and the people she trusts the most.

How to Grow an Addict by J.A. Wright. $16.95, 978-1-63152-991-7. Raised by an abusive father, a detached mother, and a loving aunt and uncle, Randall Grange is built for addiction. By twenty-three, she knows that together, pills and booze have the power to cure just about any problem she could possibly have . . . right

Beautiful Garbage by Jill DiDonato. $16.95, 978-1-938314-01-8. Talented but troubled young artist Jodi Plum leaves suburbia for the excitement of the city—and is soon swept up in the sexual politics and downtown art scene of 1980s New York.

Cleans Up Nicely by Linda Dahl. $16.95, 978-1-938314-38-4. The story of one gifted young woman's path from self-destruction to self-knowledge, set in mid-1970s Manhattan.

Keep Her by Leora Krygier. $16.95, 978-1-63152-143-0. When a water main bursts in rain-starved Los Angeles, seventeen-year-old artist Maddie and filmmaker Aiden's worlds collide in a whirlpool of love and loss. Is it meant to be?

The Rooms Are Filled by Jessica Null Vealitzek. $16.95, 978-1-938314-58-2. The coming-of-age story of two outcasts—a nine-year-old boy who just lost his father, and a closeted young woman—brought together by circumstance.